we are THE SMURFS

BRIGHT NEW DAYS!

BY FALZAR AND THIERRY CULLIFORD

ILLUSTRATED BY ANTONELLO DALENA
AND PAOLO MADDALENI

AMULET BOOKS • NEW YORK

Library of Congress Control Number 2022940921

ISBN 978-1-4197-5541-5

SMURF™

© *Peyo* - 2023 - Licensed through Lafig Belgium - www.smurf.com

Original lettering by Michael Brun
Book design by Brann Garvey

Represented by:
I.M.P.S. s.a.
Rue du Cerf 85
1332 Genval
Belgique

Printed and bound in China
10 9 8 7 6 5 4 3 2 1

Amulet Books are available at special discounts when purchased in quantity for premiums and
promotions as well as fundraising or educational use. Special editions can also be created to
specification. For details, contact specialsales@abramsbooks.com or the address below.

Amulet Books® is a registered trademark of Harry N. Abrams, Inc.

ABRAMS The Art of Books
195 Broadway, New York, NY 10007
abramsbooks.com

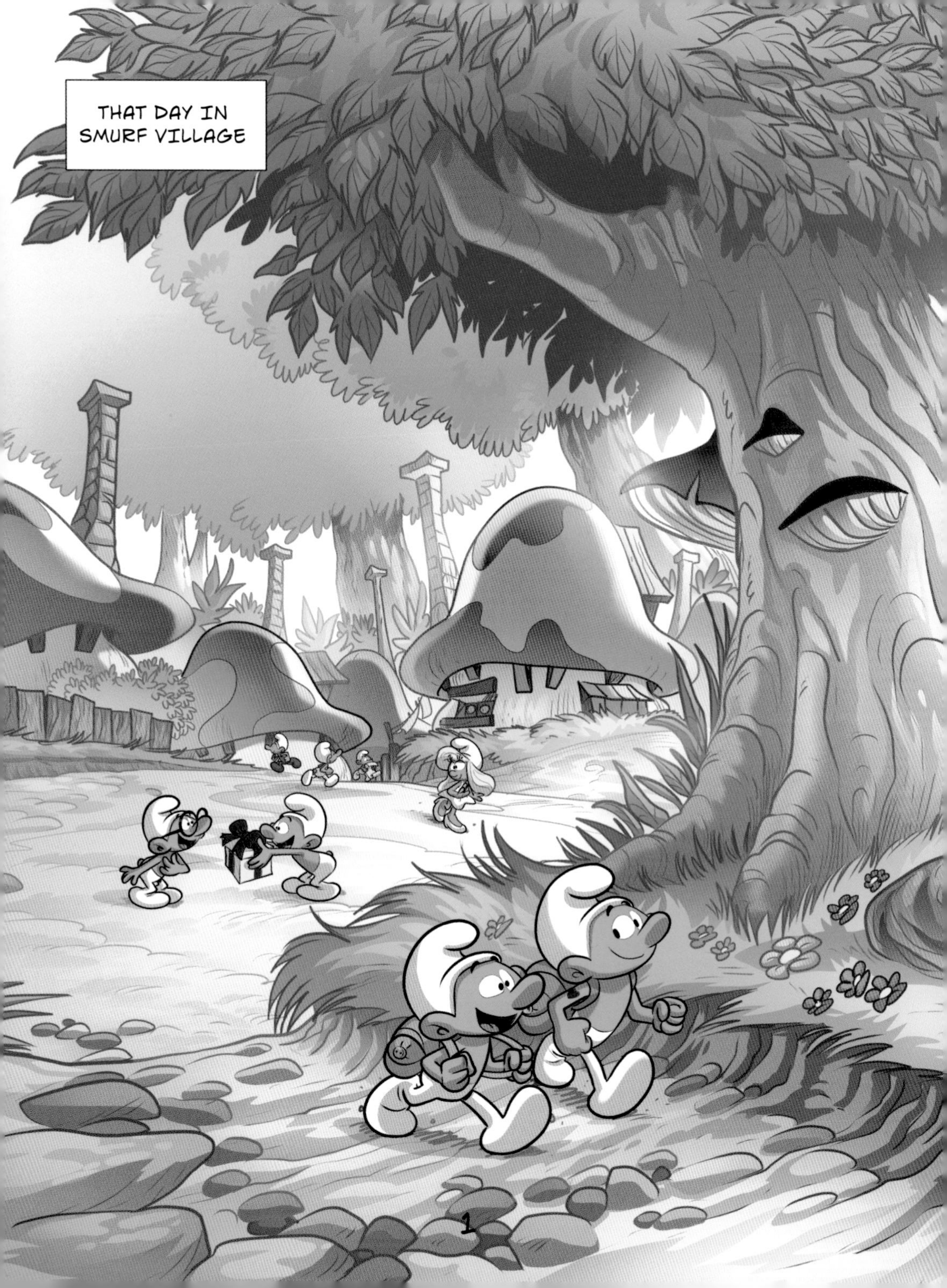
THAT DAY IN
SMURF VILLAGE

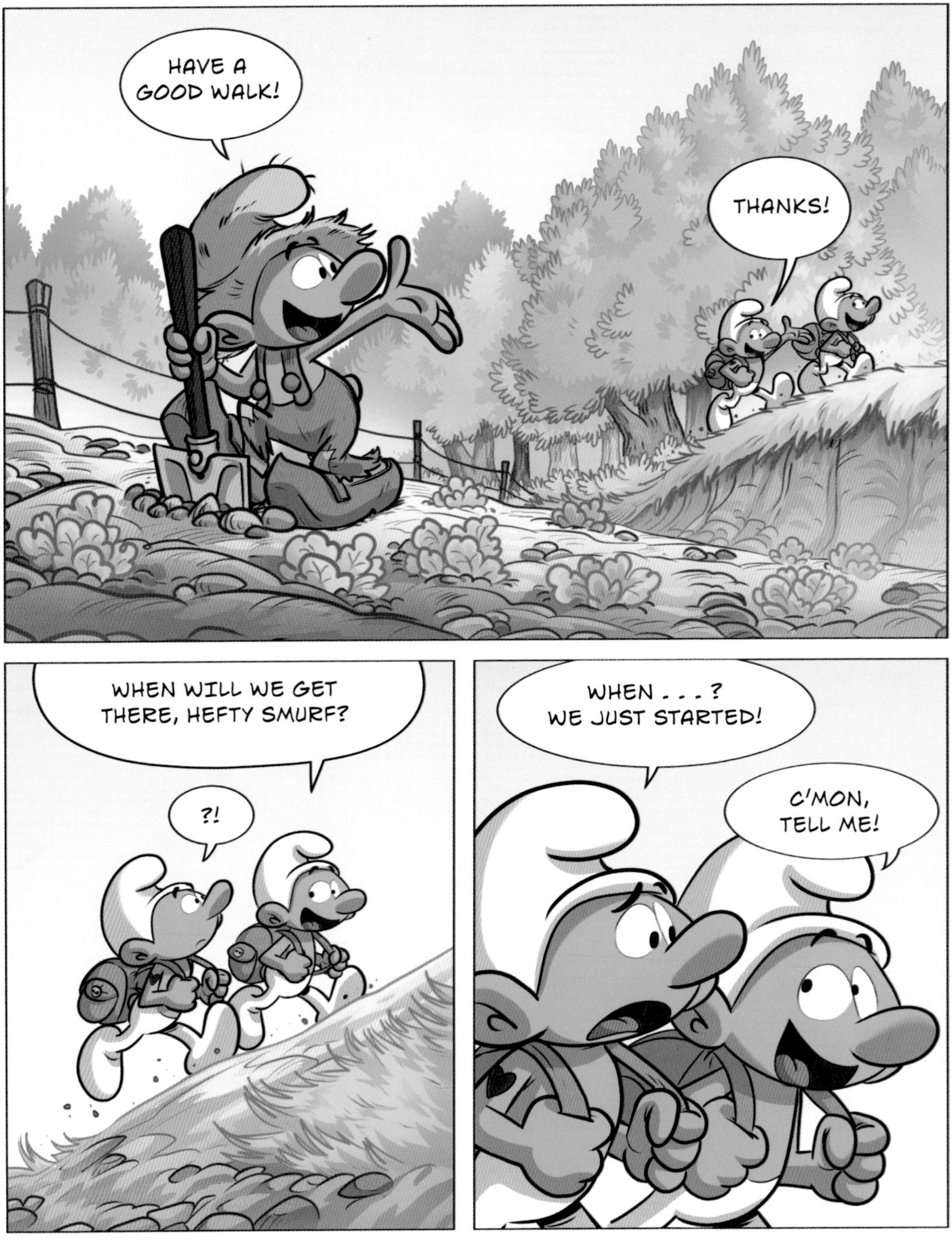
HAVE A GOOD WALK!
THANKS!
WHEN WILL WE GET THERE, HEFTY SMURF?
?!
WHEN . . . ? WE JUST STARTED!
C'MON, TELL ME!

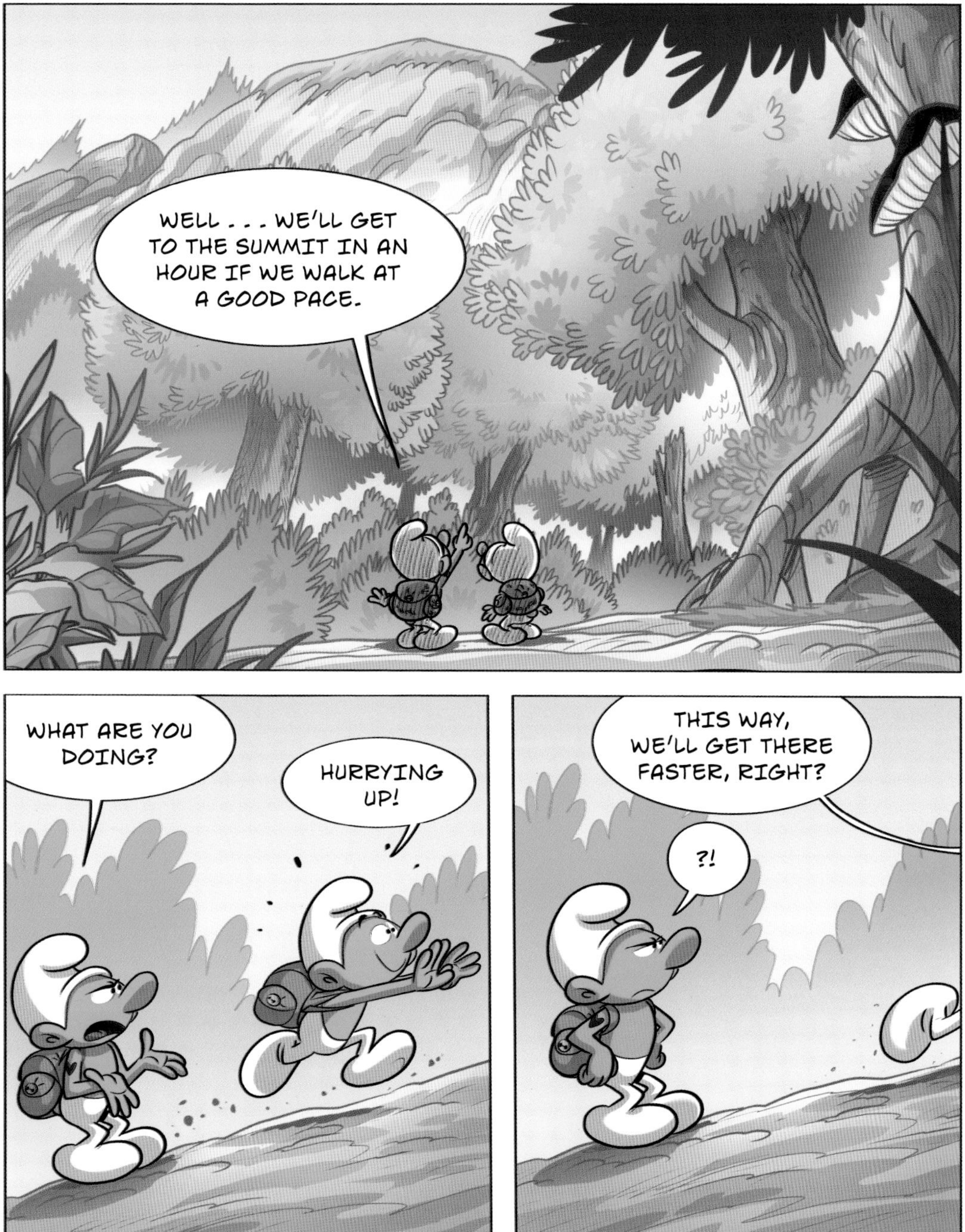
WELL . . . WE'LL GET TO THE SUMMIT IN AN HOUR IF WE WALK AT A GOOD PACE.
WHAT ARE YOU DOING?
HURRYING UP!
THIS WAY, WE'LL GET THERE FASTER, RIGHT?
?!

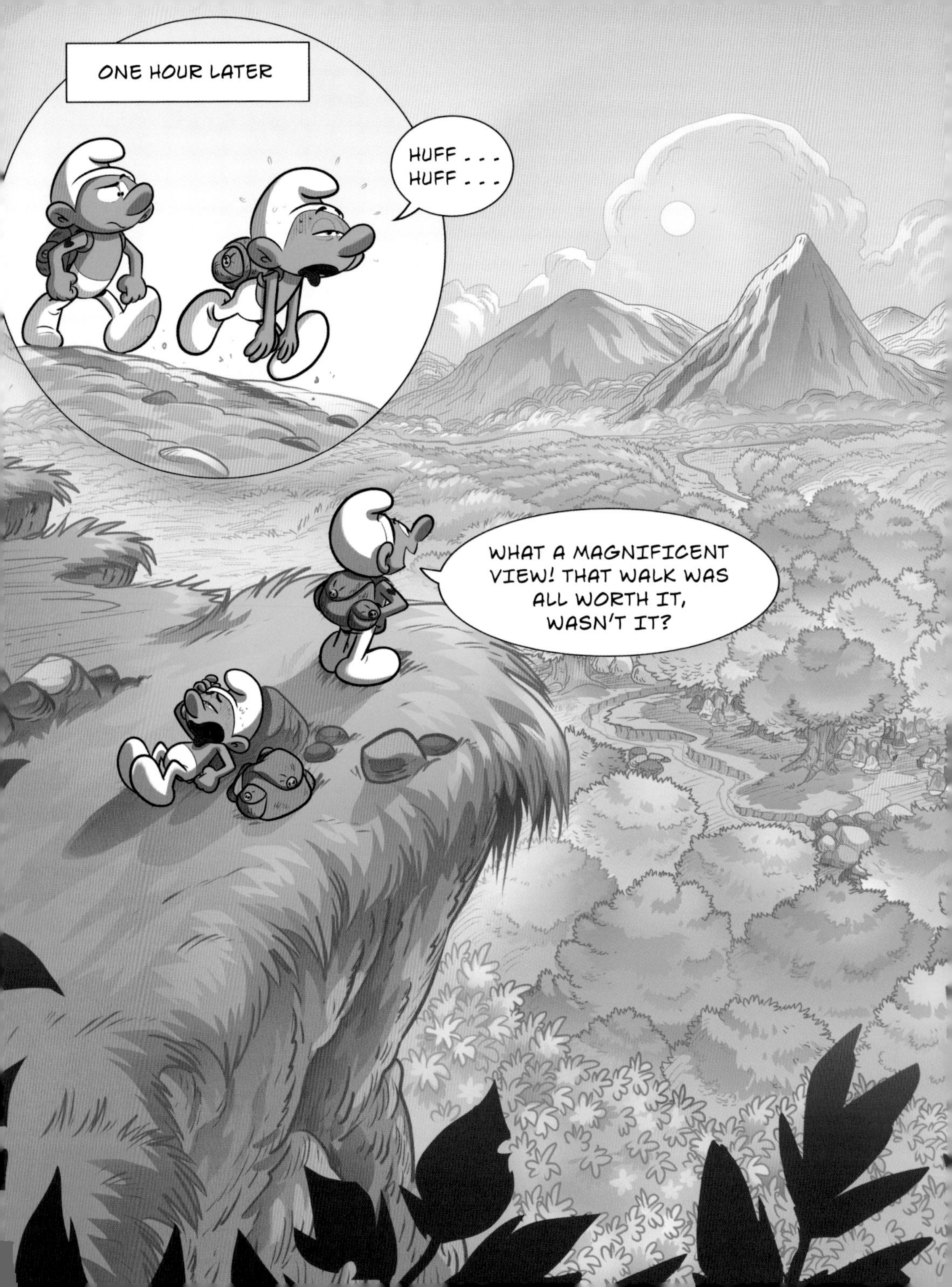
ONE HOUR LATER
HUFF . . . HUFF . . .
WHAT A MAGNIFICENT VIEW! THAT WALK WAS ALL WORTH IT, WASN'T IT?

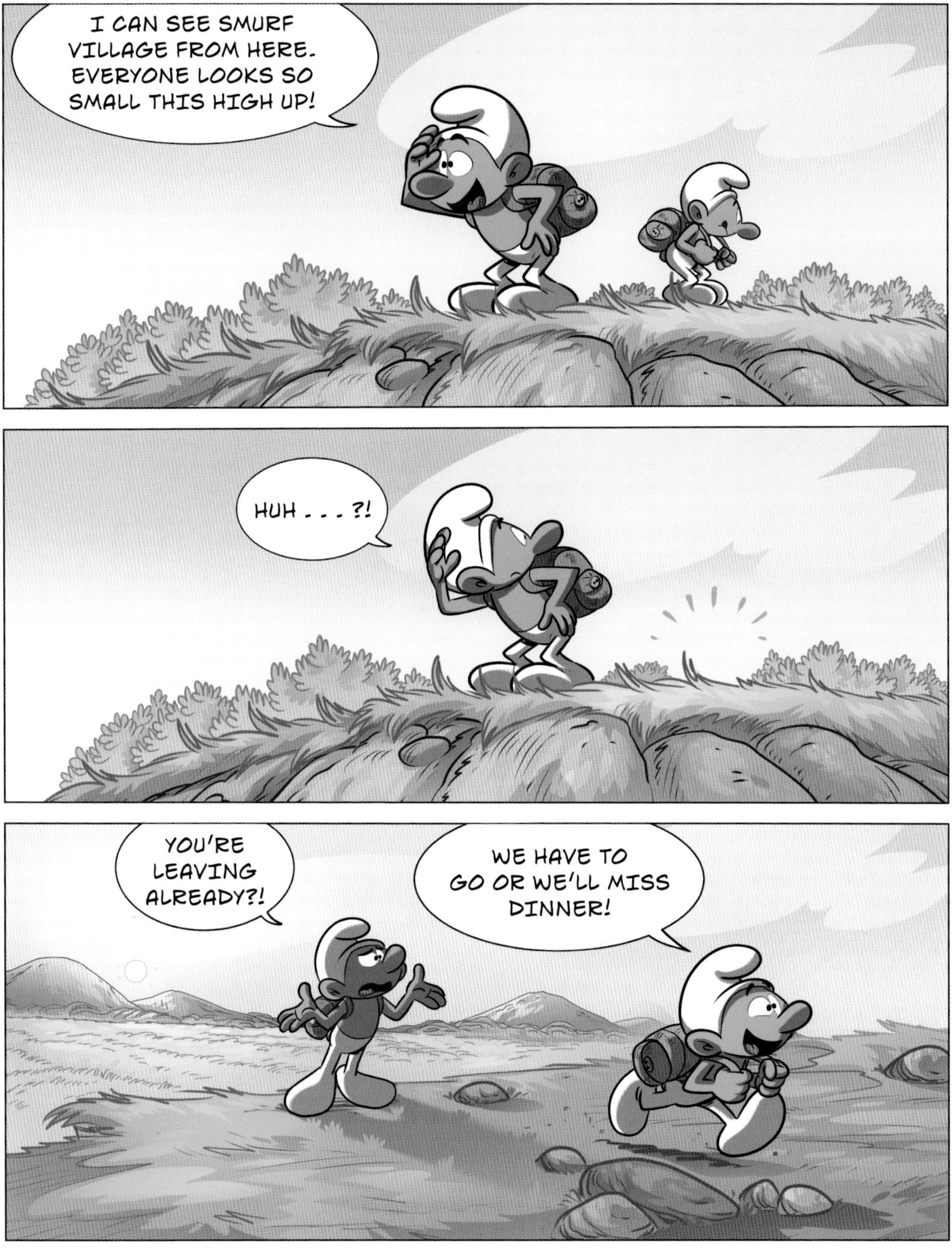
I CAN SEE SMURF VILLAGE FROM HERE. EVERYONE LOOKS SO SMALL THIS HIGH UP!
HUH . . . ?!
YOU'RE LEAVING ALREADY?!
WE HAVE TO GO OR WE'LL MISS DINNER!

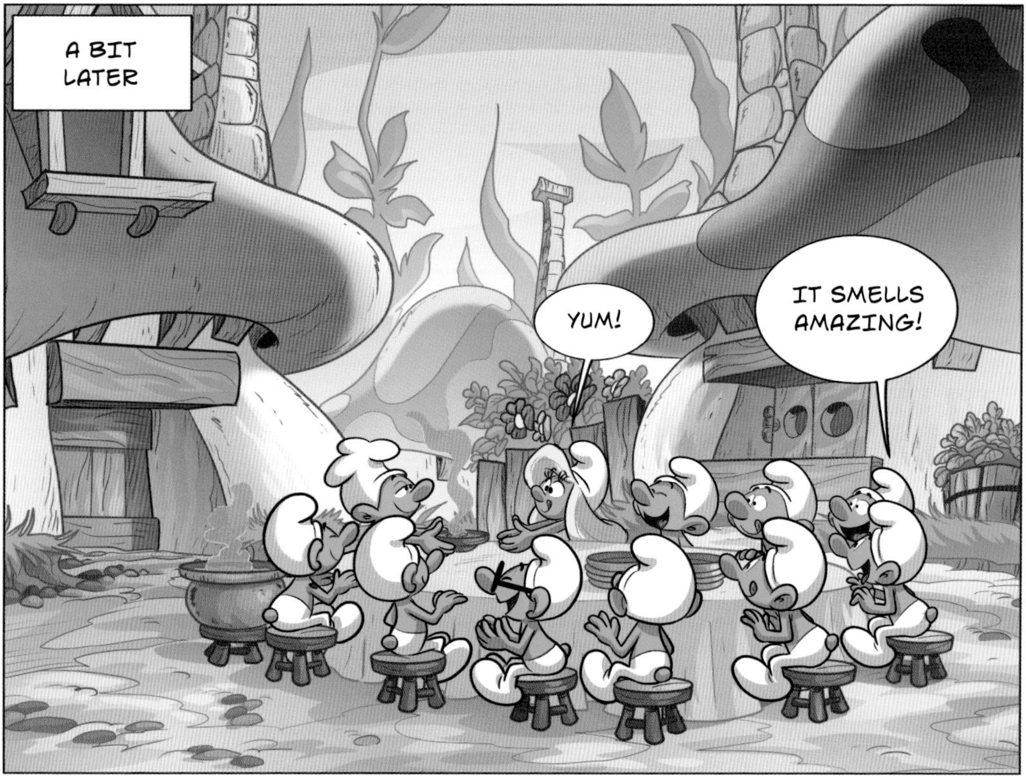
A BIT LATER
YUM!
IT SMELLS AMAZING!

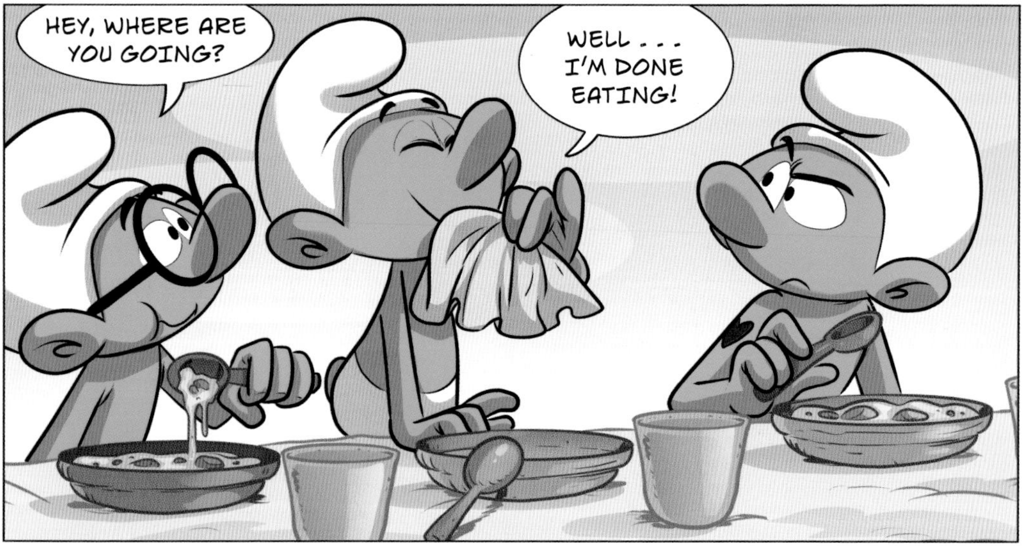
HEY, WHERE ARE YOU GOING?
WELL . . . I'M DONE EATING!

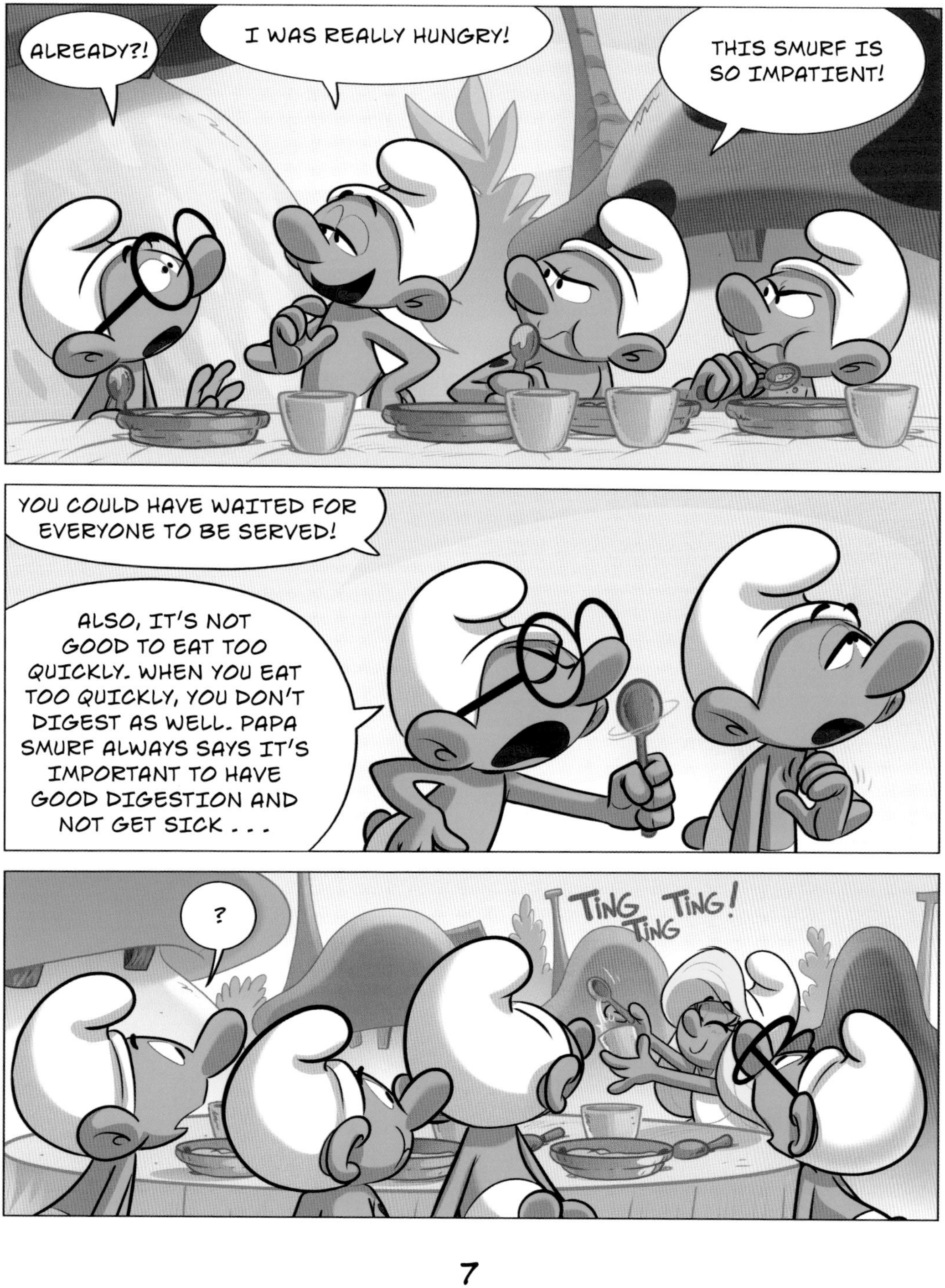
ALREADY?!
I WAS REALLY HUNGRY!
THIS SMURF IS SO IMPATIENT!
YOU COULD HAVE WAITED FOR EVERYONE TO BE SERVED!
ALSO, IT'S NOT GOOD TO EAT TOO QUICKLY. WHEN YOU EAT TOO QUICKLY, YOU DON'T DIGEST AS WELL. PAPA SMURF ALWAYS SAYS IT'S IMPORTANT TO HAVE GOOD DIGESTION AND NOT GET SICK . . .
?
TING TING TING!

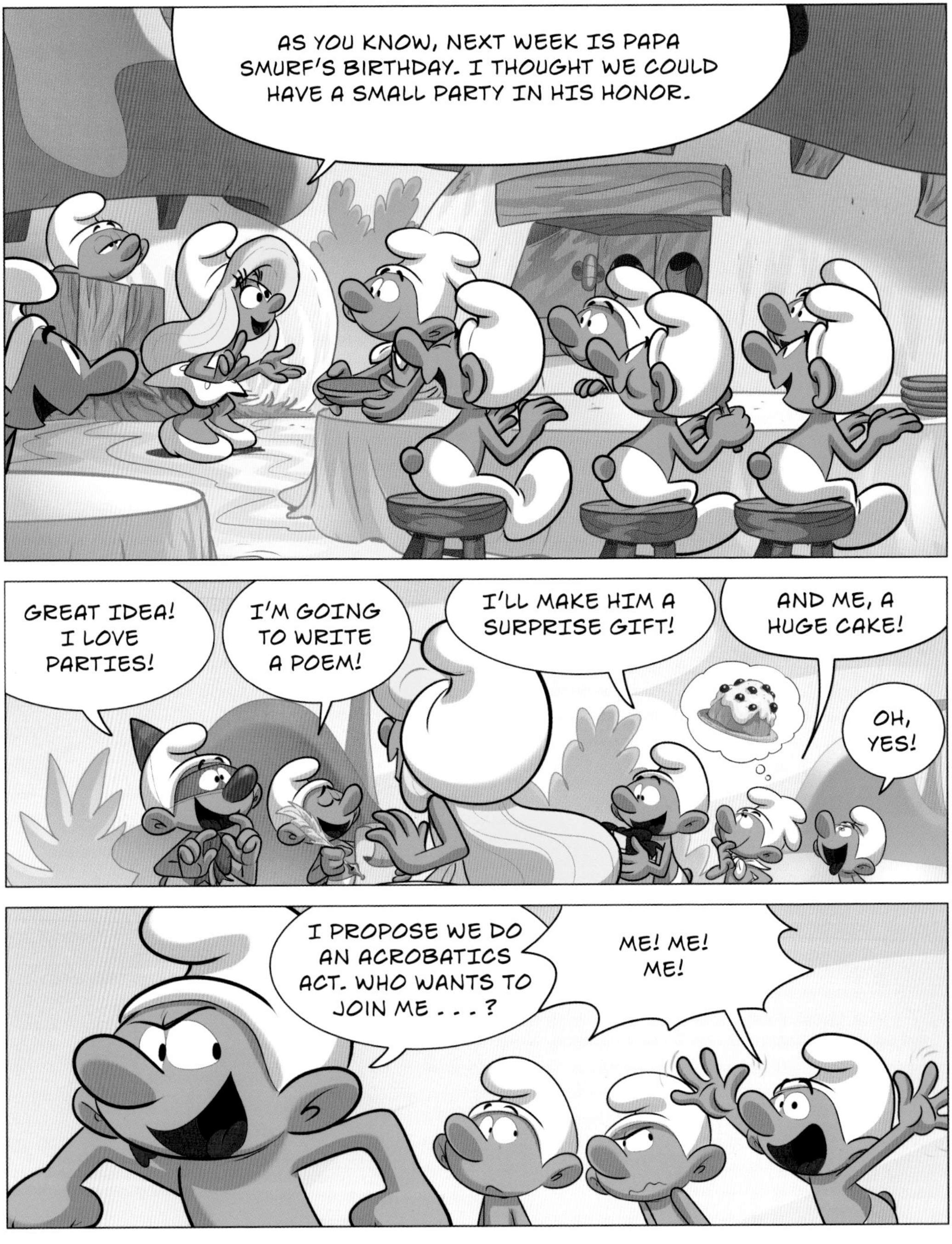
AS YOU KNOW, NEXT WEEK IS PAPA SMURF'S BIRTHDAY. I THOUGHT WE COULD HAVE A SMALL PARTY IN HIS HONOR.
GREAT IDEA! I LOVE PARTIES!
I'M GOING TO WRITE A POEM!
I'LL MAKE HIM A SURPRISE GIFT!
AND ME, A HUGE CAKE!
OH, YES!
I PROPOSE WE DO AN ACROBATICS ACT. WHO WANTS TO JOIN ME . . . ?
ME! ME! ME!

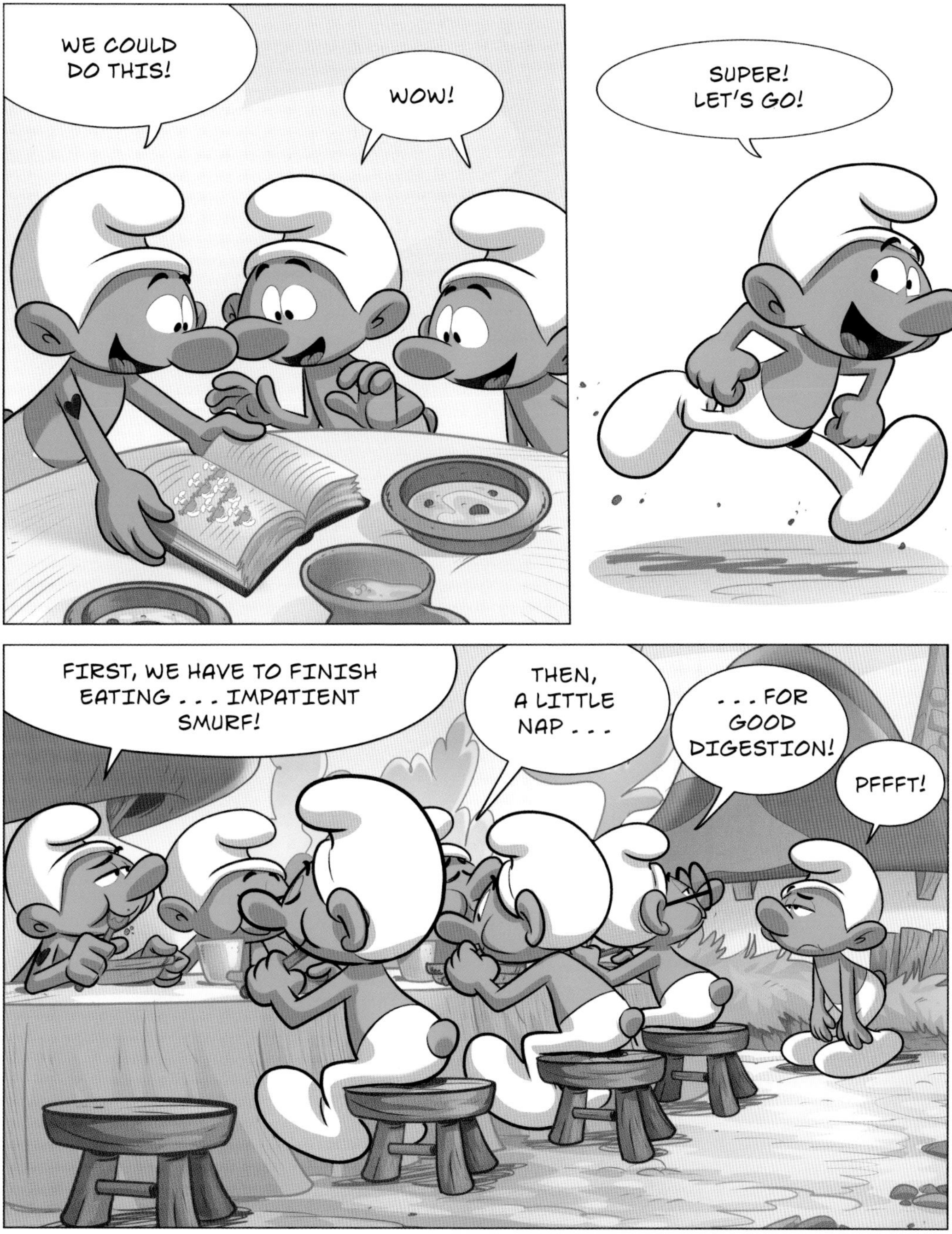
WE COULD DO THIS!
WOW!
SUPER! LET'S GO!
FIRST, WE HAVE TO FINISH EATING . . . IMPATIENT SMURF!
THEN, A LITTLE NAP . . .
. . . FOR GOOD DIGESTION!
PFFFT!

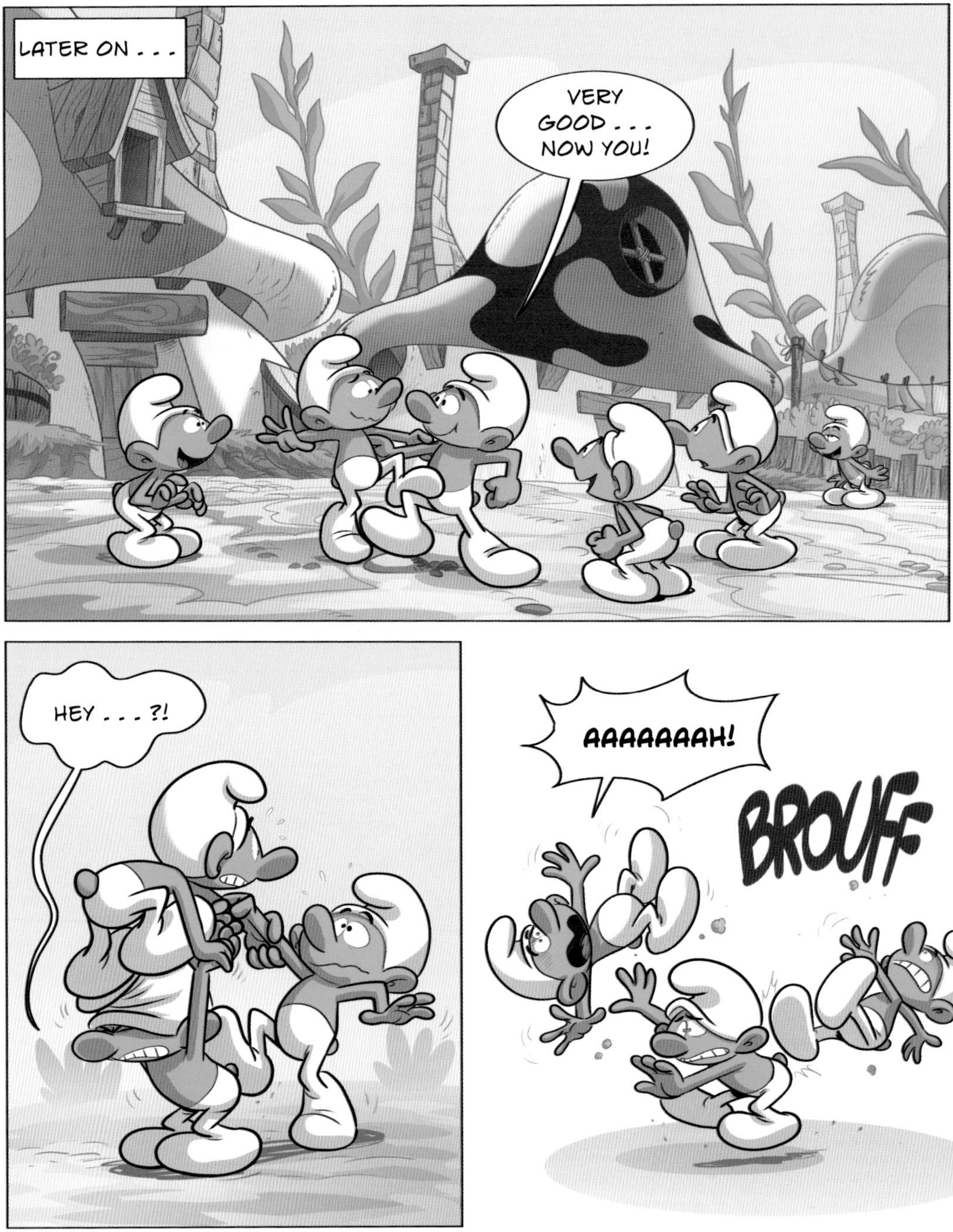
LATER ON . . .
VERY GOOD . . . NOW YOU!
HEY . . . ?!
AAAAAAAH!
BROUFF

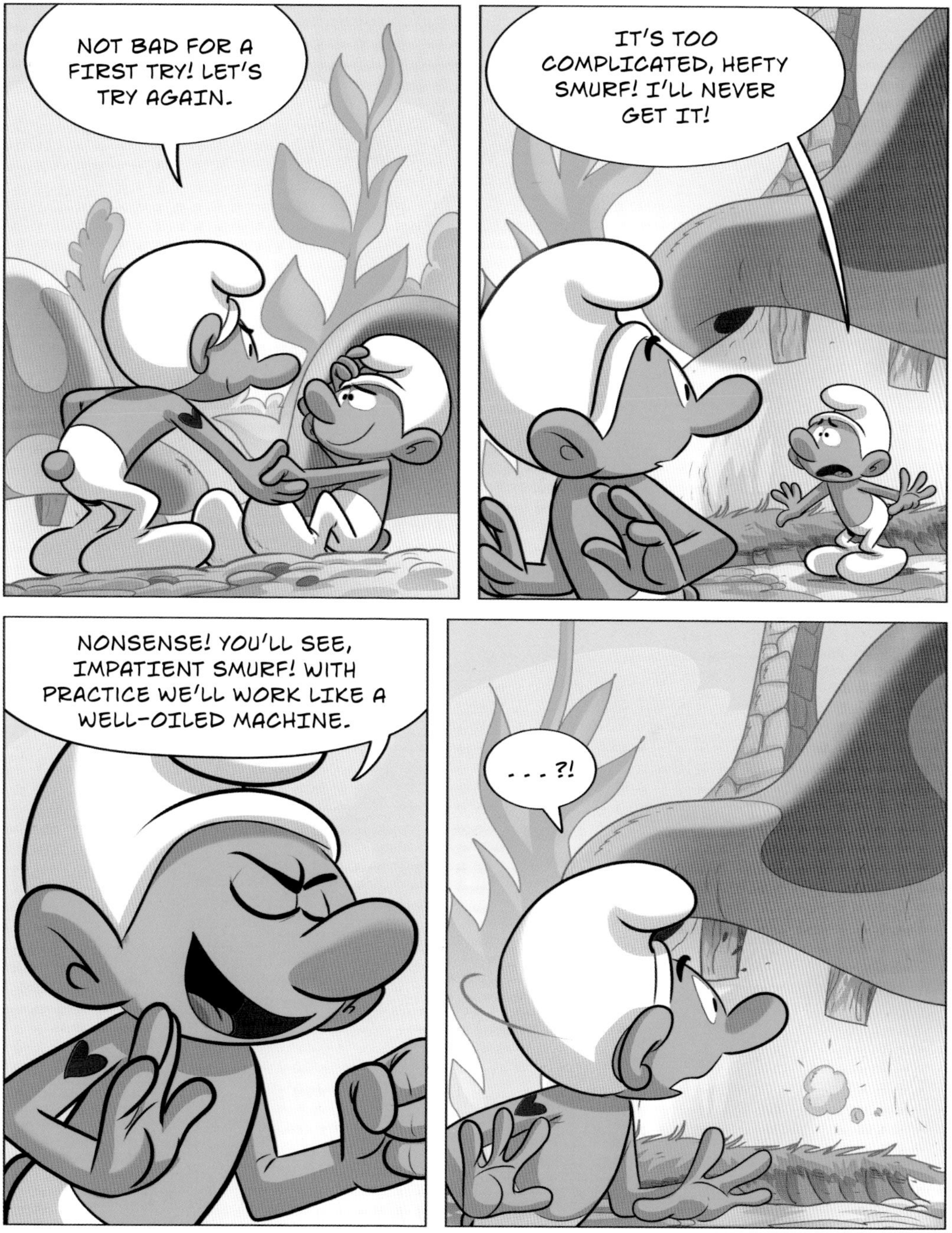
NOT BAD FOR A FIRST TRY! LET'S TRY AGAIN.
IT'S TOO COMPLICATED, HEFTY SMURF! I'LL NEVER GET IT!
NONSENSE! YOU'LL SEE, IMPATIENT SMURF! WITH PRACTICE WE'LL WORK LIKE A WELL-OILED MACHINE.
. . . ?!

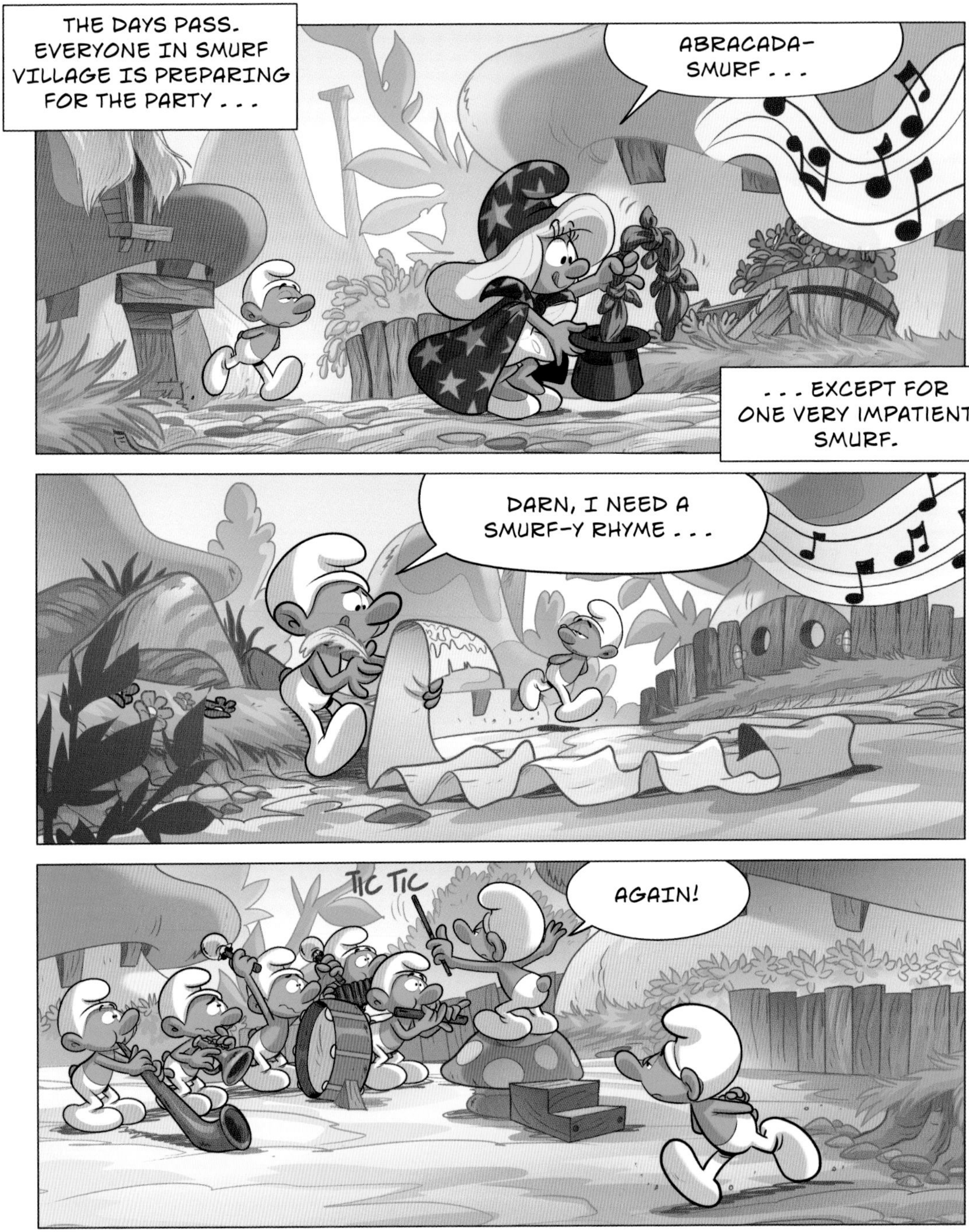
THE DAYS PASS. EVERYONE IN SMURF VILLAGE IS PREPARING FOR THE PARTY . . .
ABRACADA-SMURF . . .
. . . EXCEPT FOR ONE VERY IMPATIENT SMURF.
DARN, I NEED A SMURF-Y RHYME . . .
TIC TIC
AGAIN!

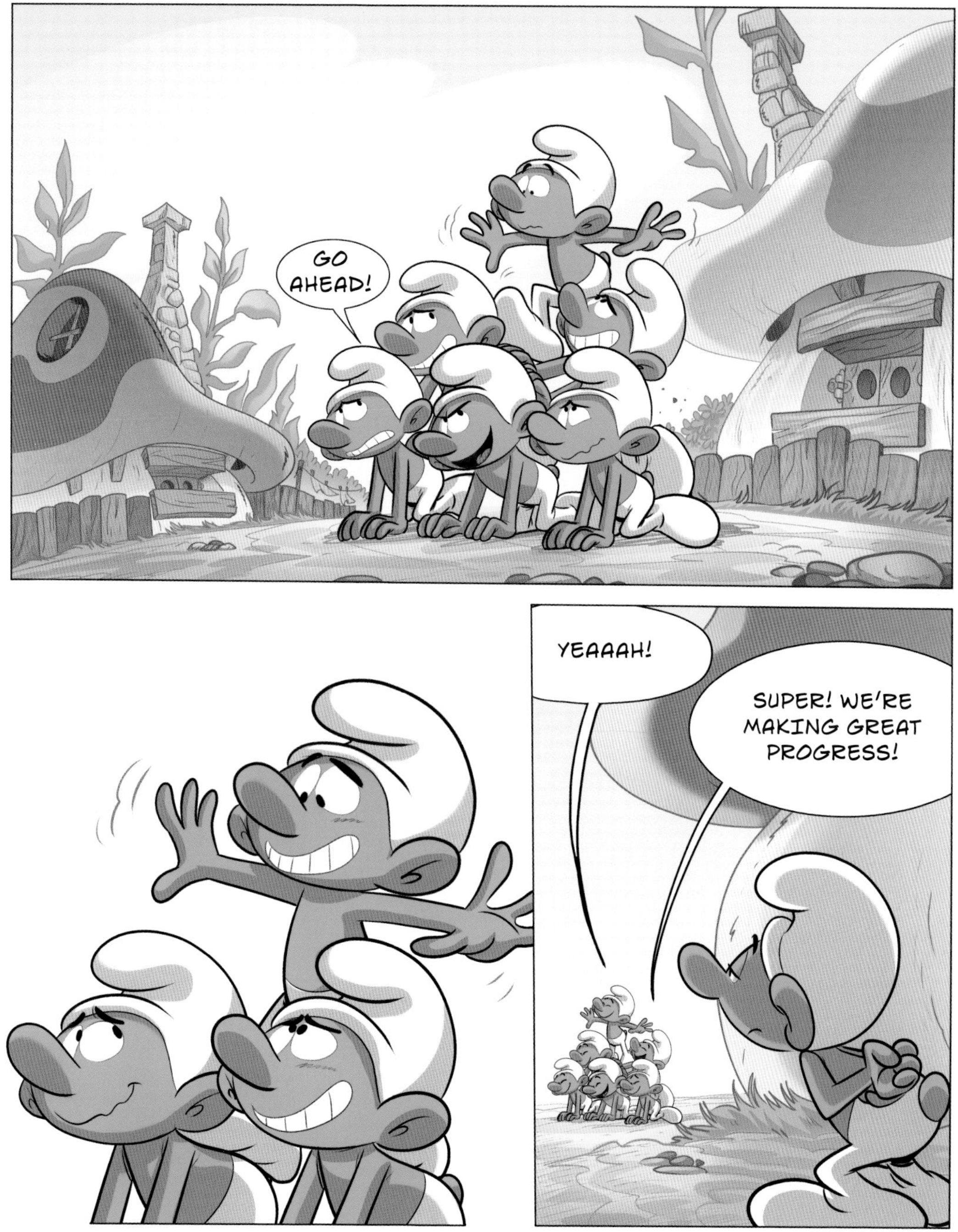
GO AHEAD!
YEAAAH!
SUPER! WE'RE MAKING GREAT PROGRESS!

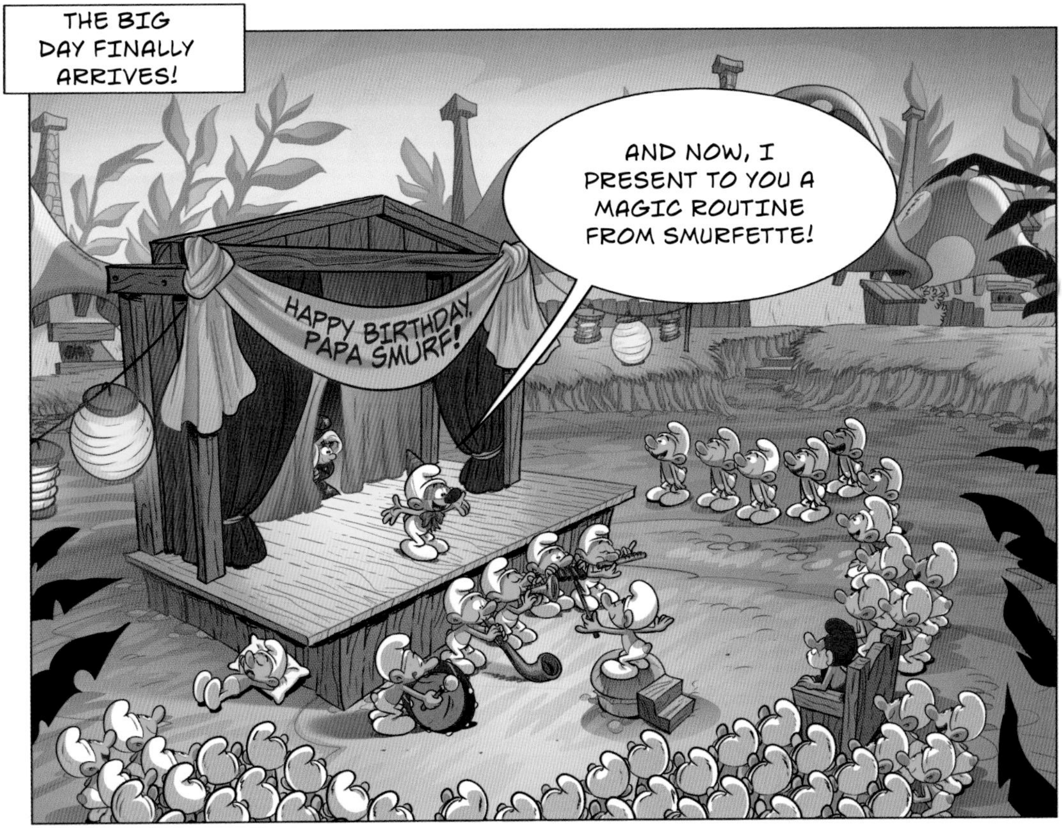
THE BIG DAY FINALLY ARRIVES!
AND NOW, I PRESENT TO YOU A MAGIC ROUTINE FROM SMURFETTE!
HAPPY BIRTHDAY, PAPA SMURF!

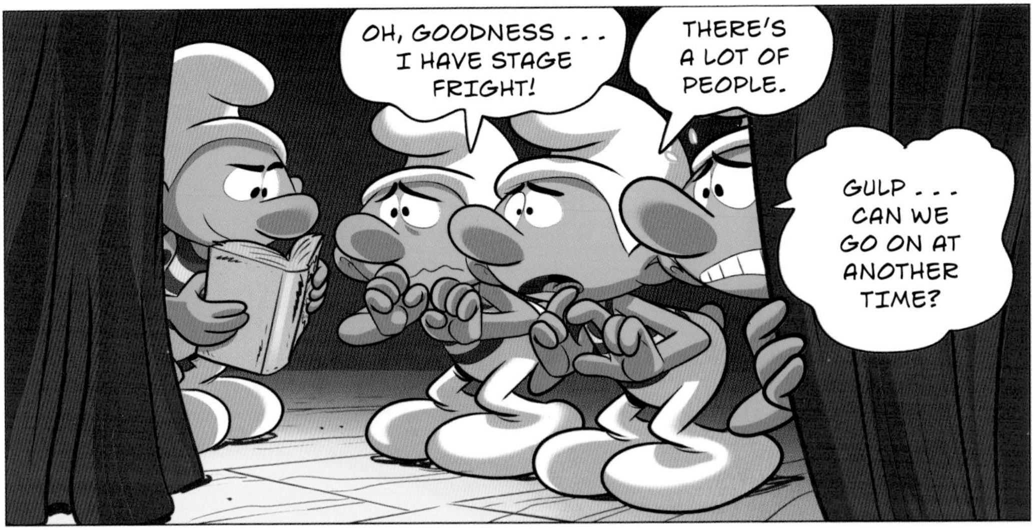
OH, GOODNESS . . . I HAVE STAGE FRIGHT!
THERE'S A LOT OF PEOPLE.
GULP . . . CAN WE GO ON AT ANOTHER TIME?

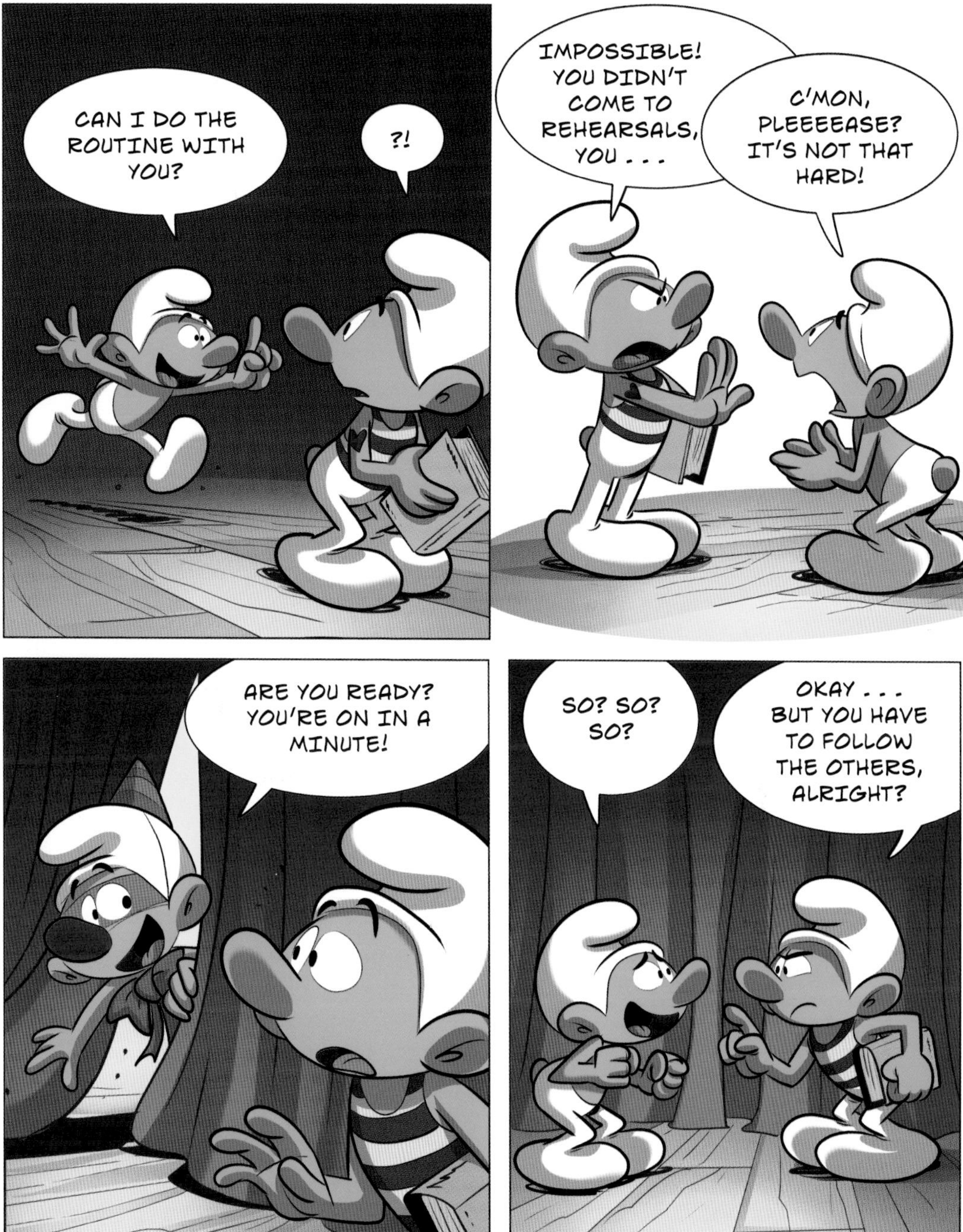
CAN I DO THE ROUTINE WITH YOU?
?!
IMPOSSIBLE! YOU DIDN'T COME TO REHEARSALS, YOU . . .
C'MON, PLEEEEASE? IT'S NOT THAT HARD!
ARE YOU READY? YOU'RE ON IN A MINUTE!
SO? SO? SO?
OKAY . . . BUT YOU HAVE TO FOLLOW THE OTHERS, ALRIGHT?

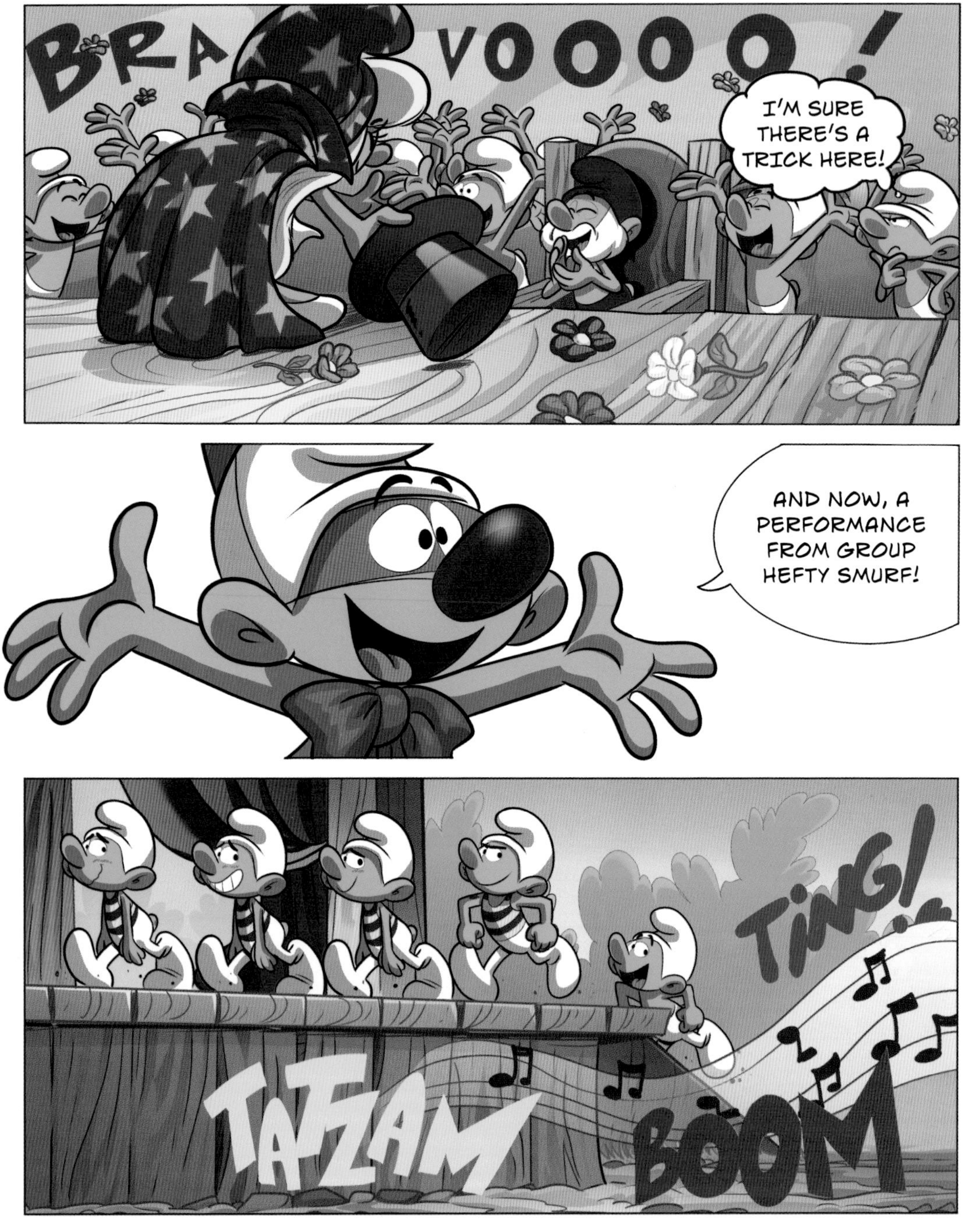
BRAVOOOO!
I'M SURE THERE'S A TRICK HERE!
AND NOW, A PERFORMANCE FROM GROUP HEFTY SMURF!
TING!
TATZAM
BOOM

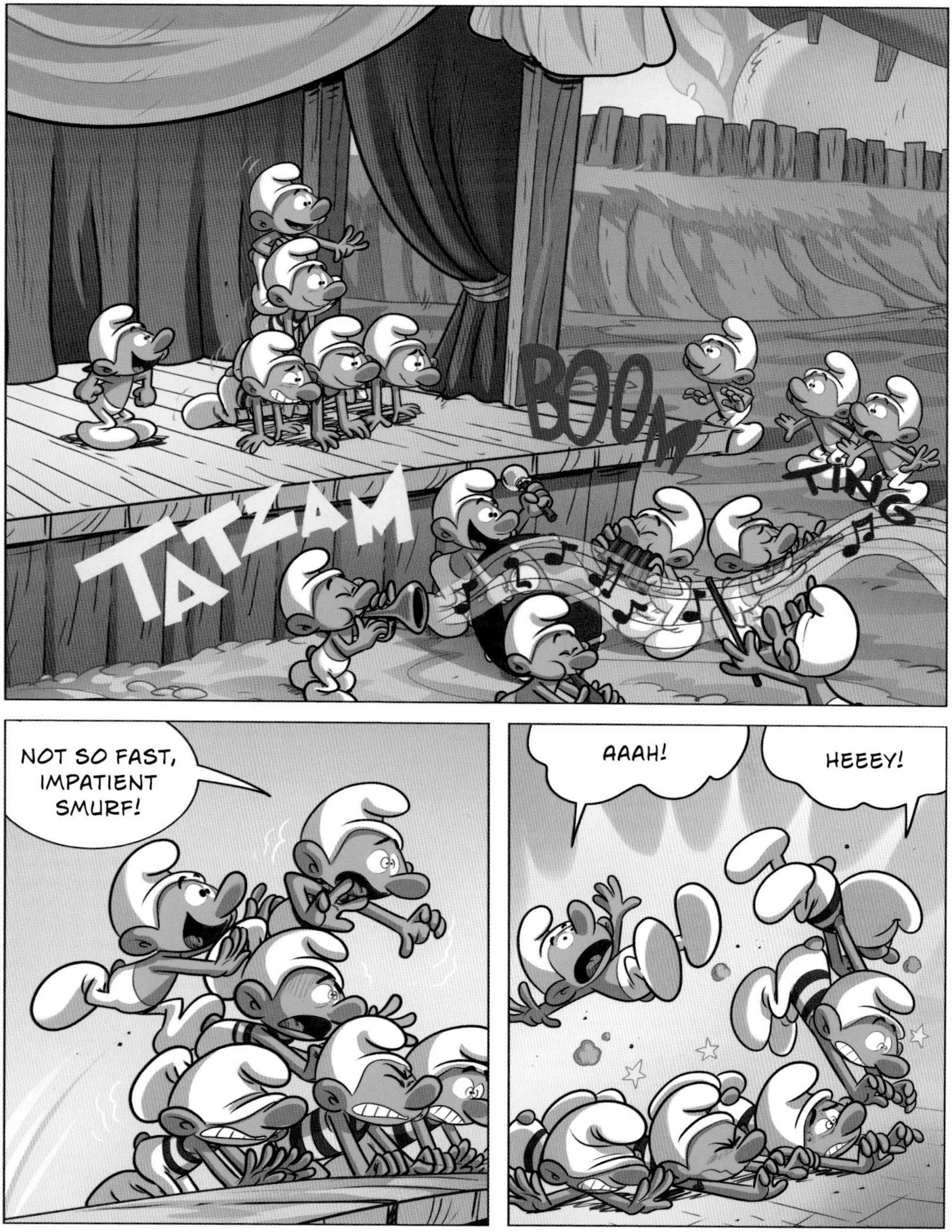
BOOM
TATZAM
TING
NOT SO FAST, IMPATIENT SMURF!
AAAH!
HEEEY!

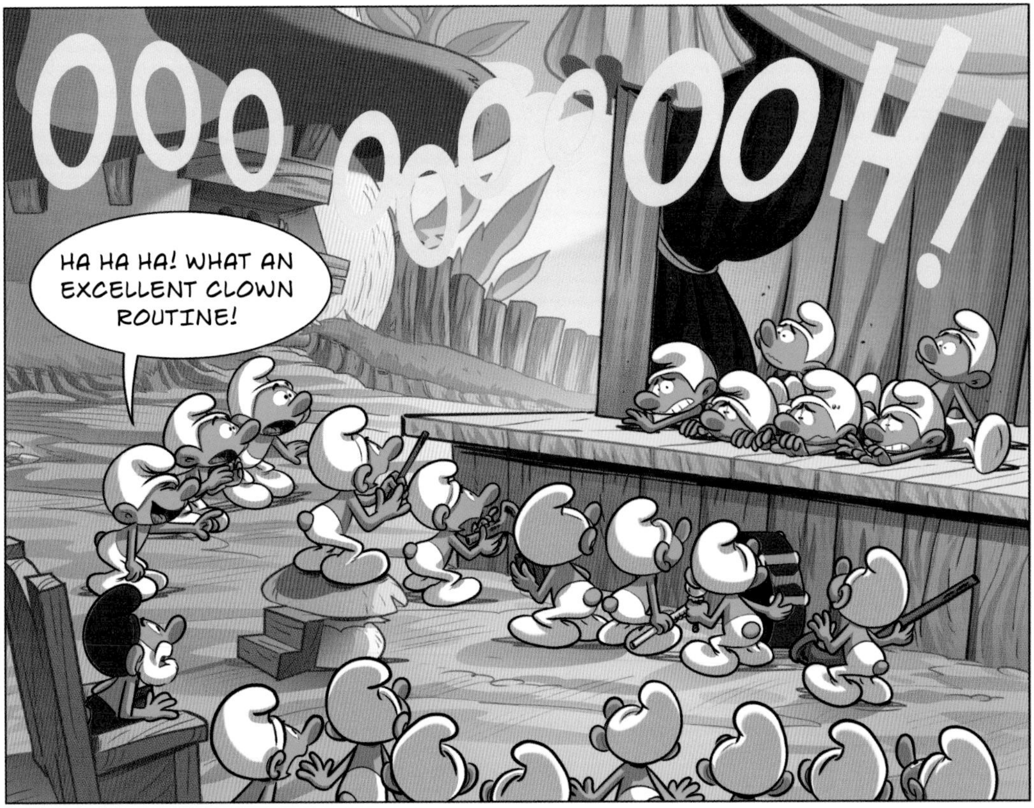
OOO OOOOOOOH!
HA HA HA! WHAT AN EXCELLENT CLOWN ROUTINE!

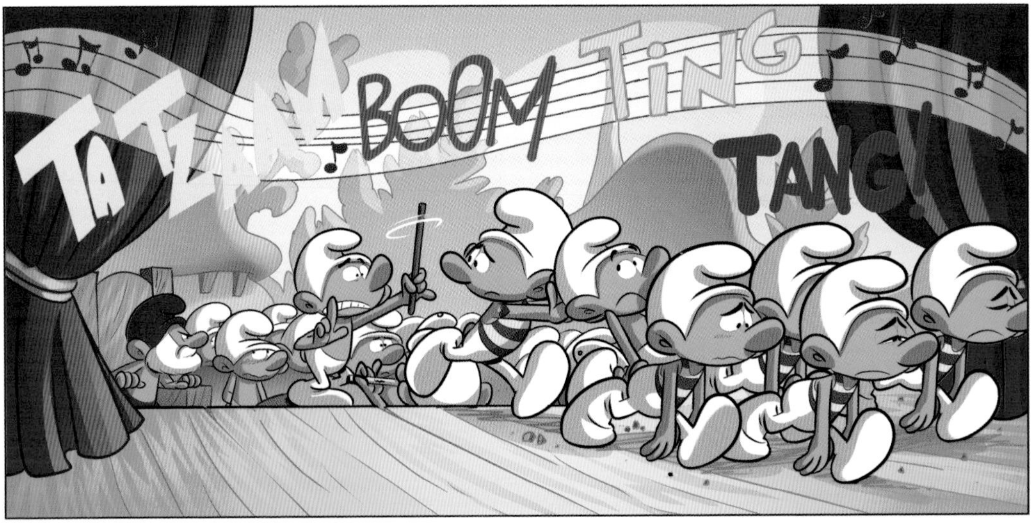
BOOM
TING
TANG!

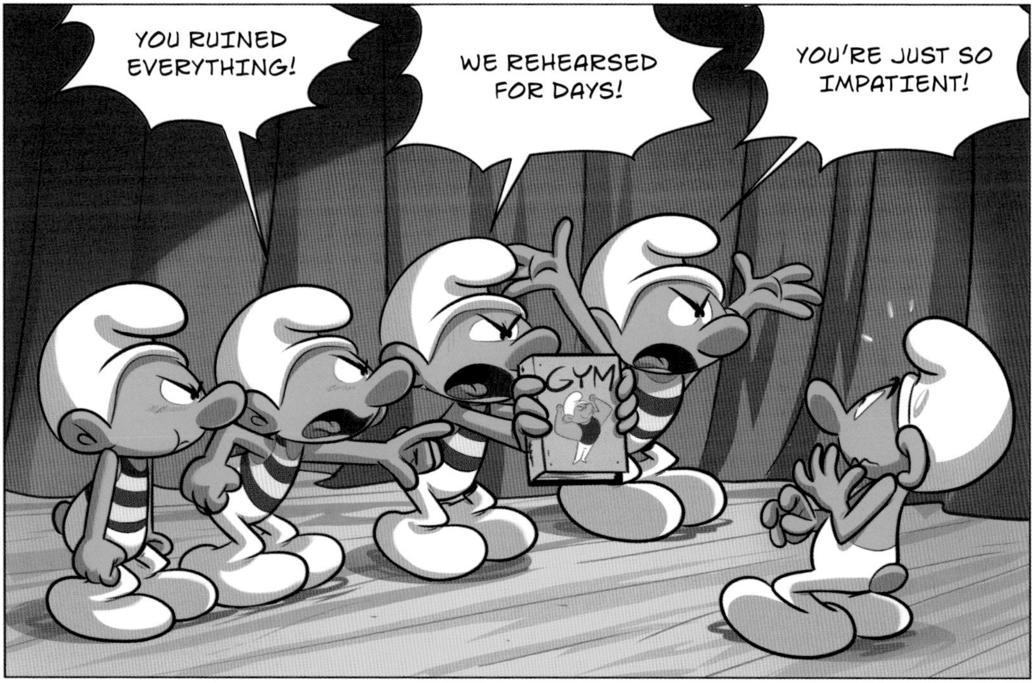

YOU RUINED EVERYTHING!
WE REHEARSED FOR DAYS!
YOU'RE JUST SO IMPATIENT!
GYM

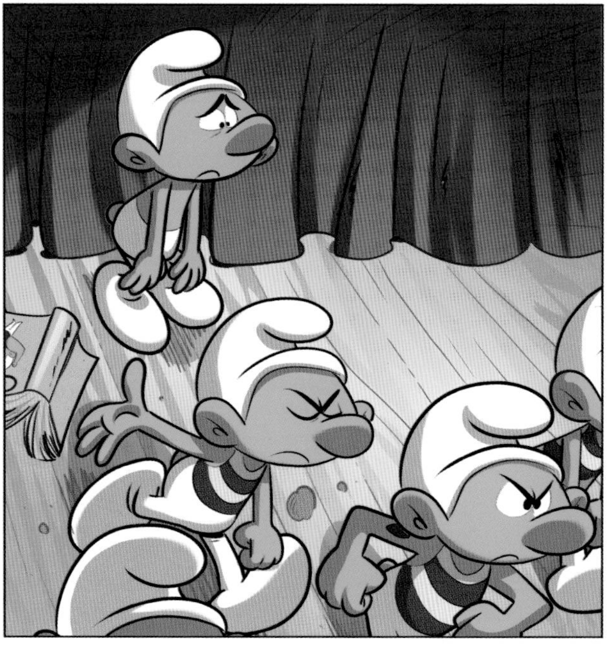

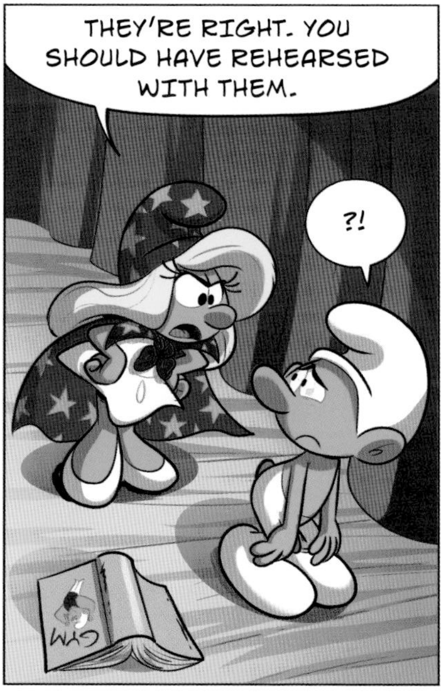

THEY'RE RIGHT. YOU SHOULD HAVE REHEARSED WITH THEM.
?!
GYM

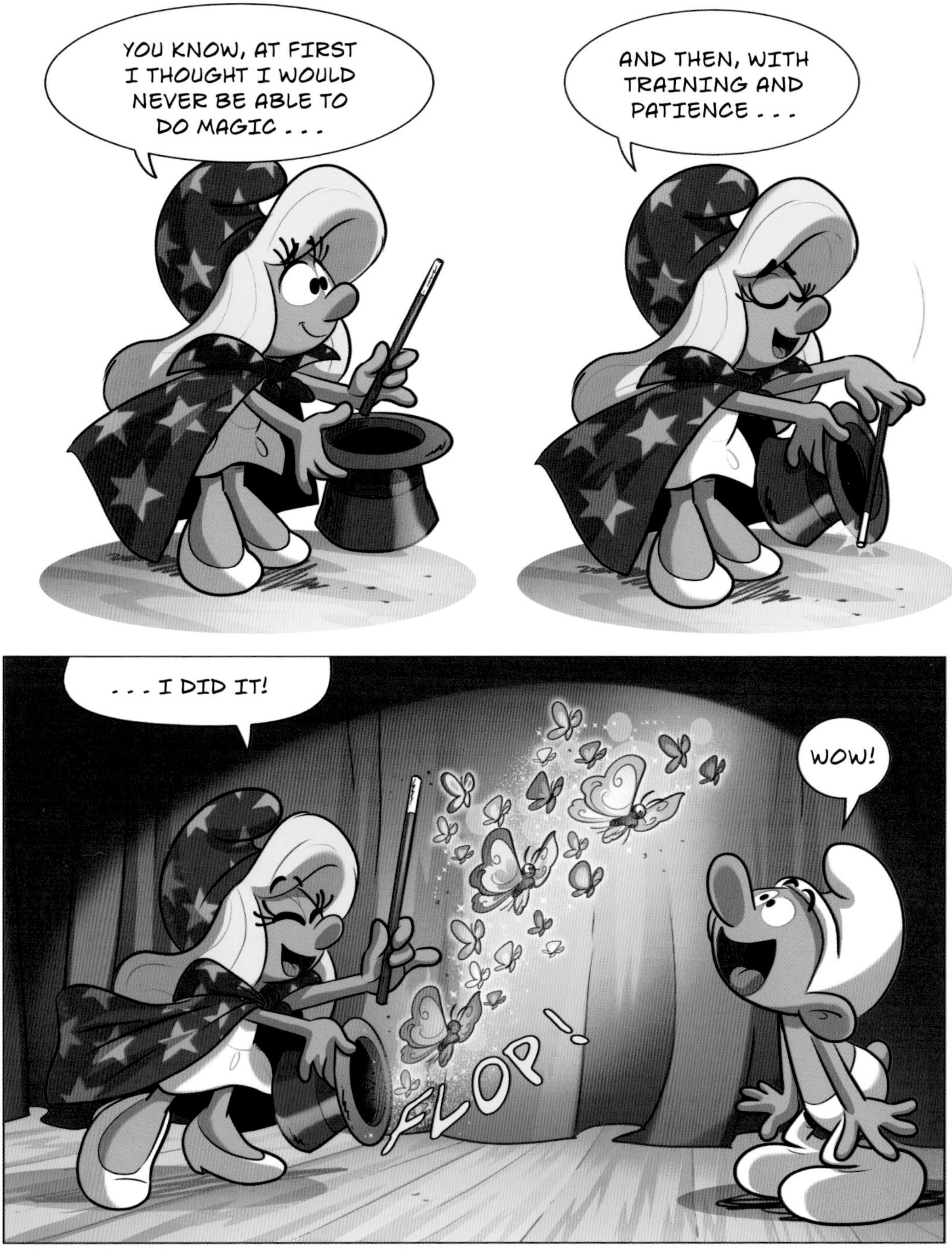
YOU KNOW, AT FIRST I THOUGHT I WOULD NEVER BE ABLE TO DO MAGIC . . .
AND THEN, WITH TRAINING AND PATIENCE . . .
. . . I DID IT!
WOW!
FLOP!

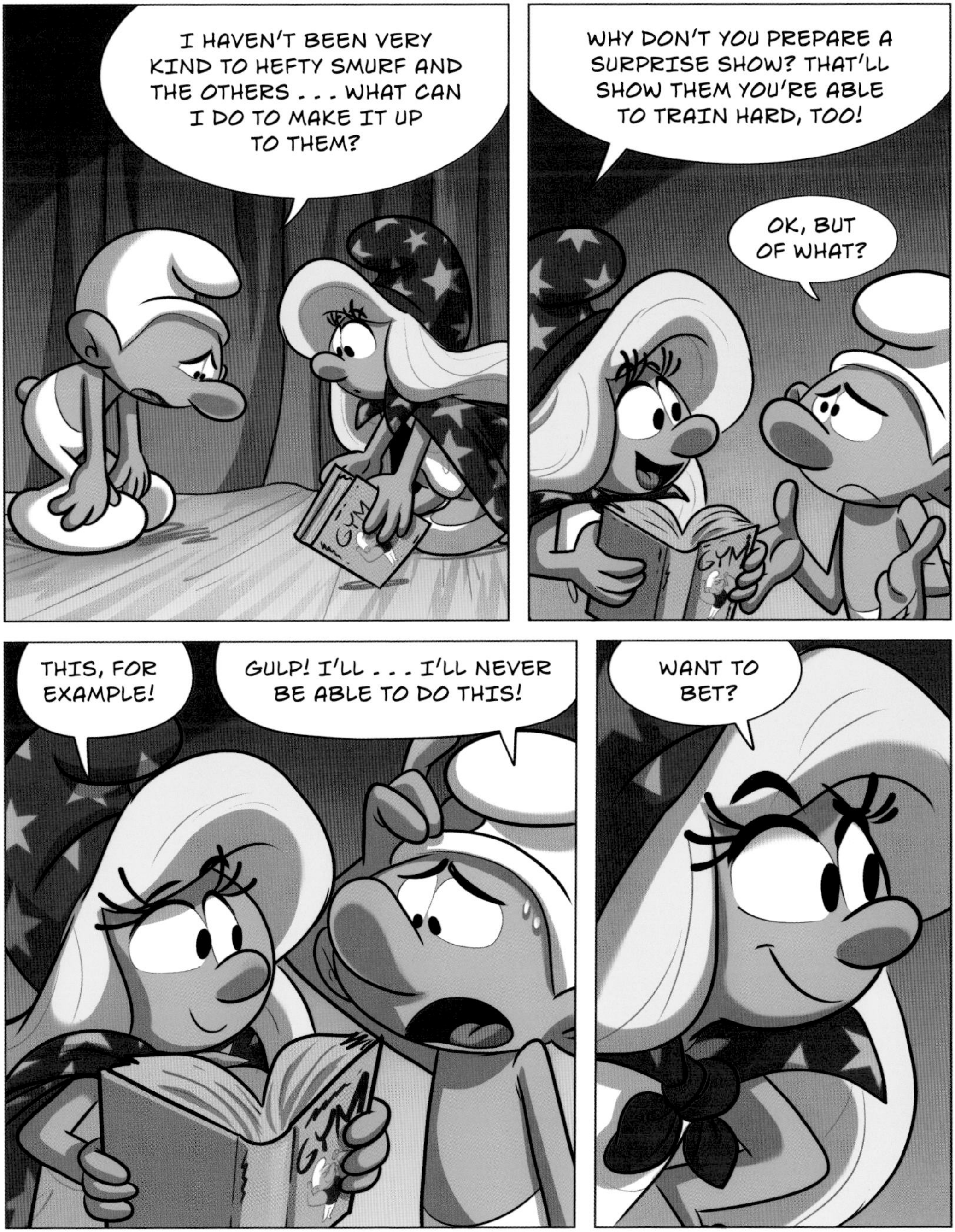
I HAVEN'T BEEN VERY KIND TO HEFTY SMURF AND THE OTHERS . . . WHAT CAN I DO TO MAKE IT UP TO THEM?
WHY DON'T YOU PREPARE A SURPRISE SHOW? THAT'LL SHOW THEM YOU'RE ABLE TO TRAIN HARD, TOO!
OK, BUT OF WHAT?
THIS, FOR EXAMPLE!
GULP! I'LL . . . I'LL NEVER BE ABLE TO DO THIS!
WANT TO BET?

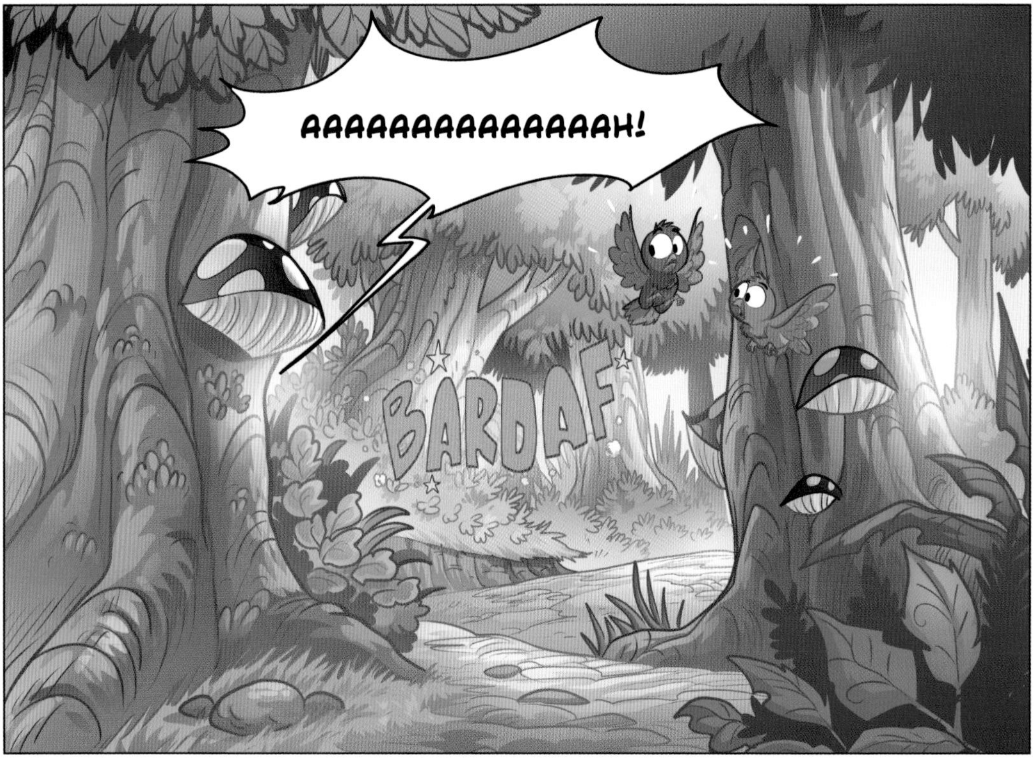
AAAAAAAAAAAAAAAH!
BARDAF

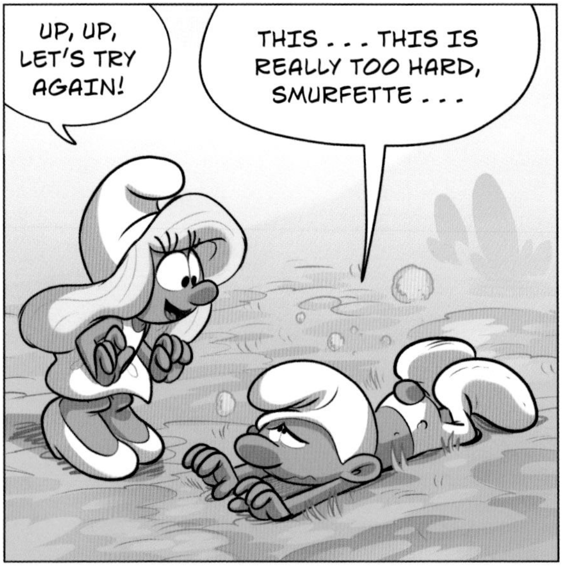
UP, UP, LET'S TRY AGAIN!
THIS . . . THIS IS REALLY TOO HARD, SMURFETTE . . .

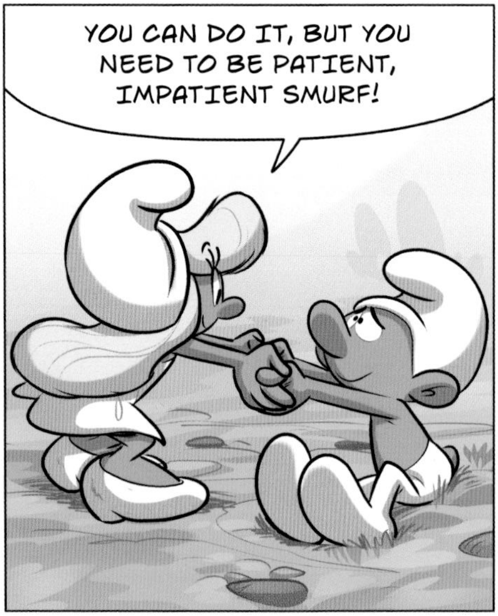
YOU CAN DO IT, BUT YOU NEED TO BE PATIENT, IMPATIENT SMURF!

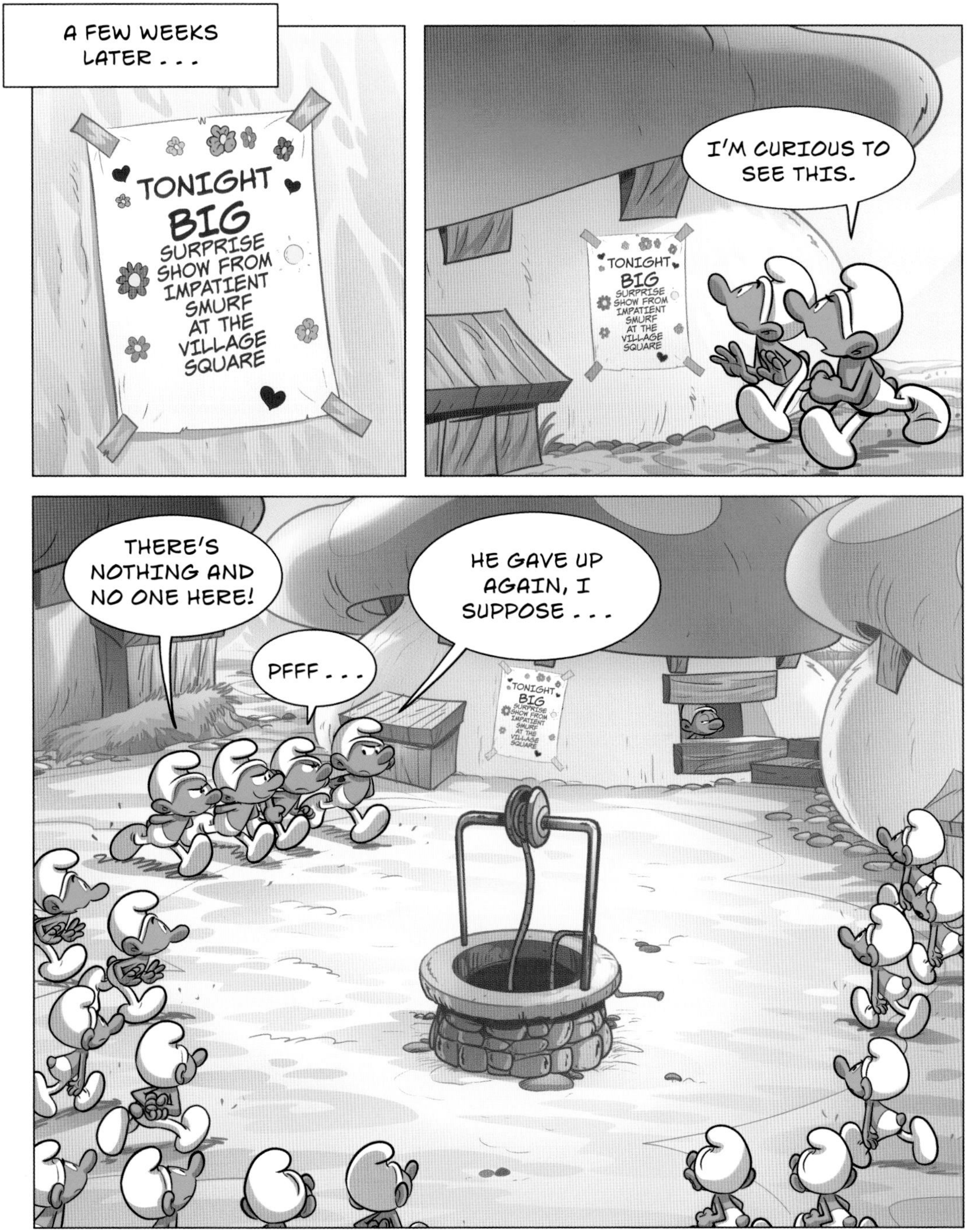
A FEW WEEKS LATER . . .
TONIGHT BIG SURPRISE SHOW FROM IMPATIENT SMURF AT THE VILLAGE SQUARE
I'M CURIOUS TO SEE THIS.
THERE'S NOTHING AND NO ONE HERE!
PFFF . . .
HE GAVE UP AGAIN, I SUPPOSE . . .

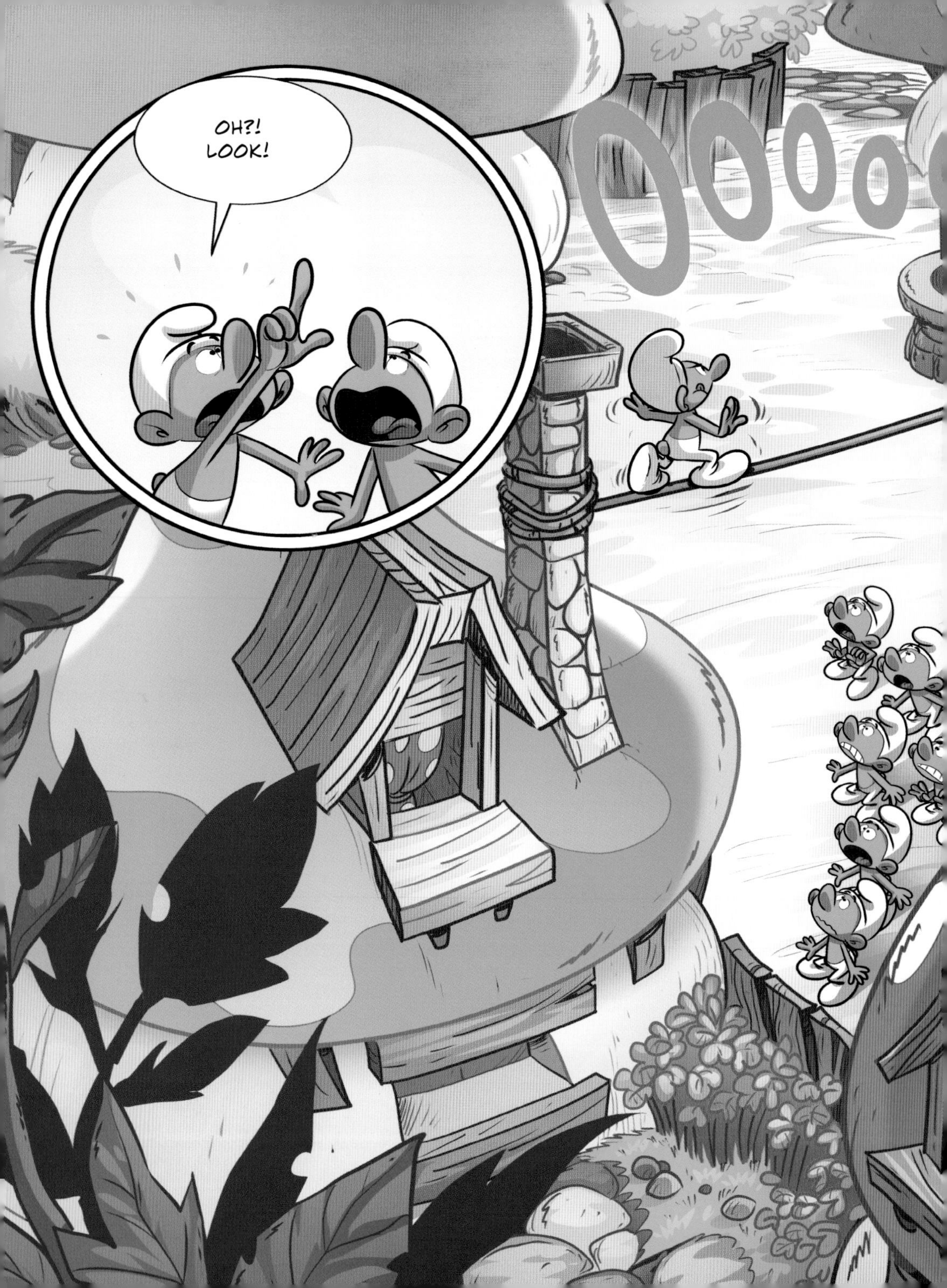
OH?!
LOOK!
OOOOO

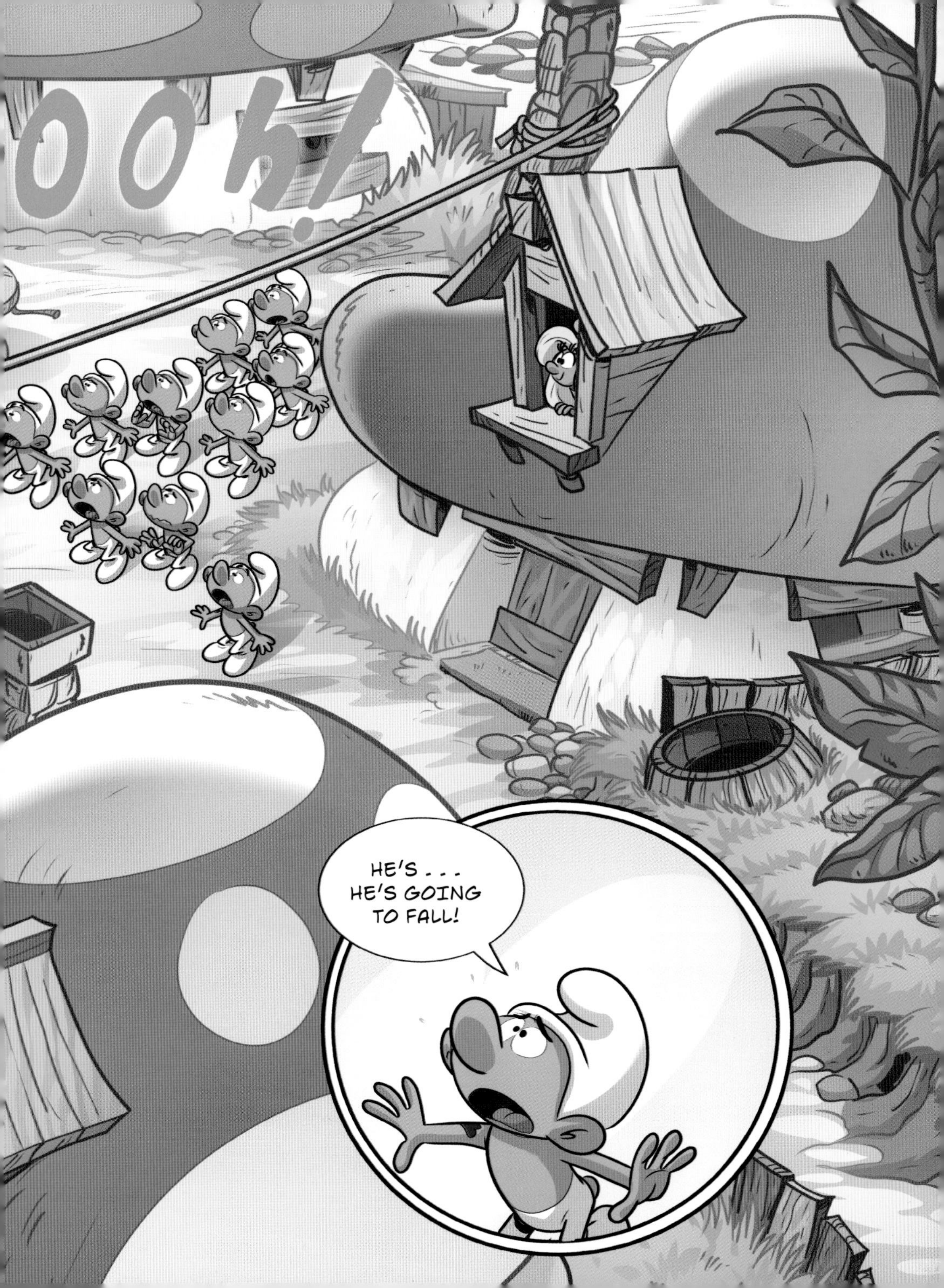
OOOh!
HE'S . . . HE'S GOING TO FALL!

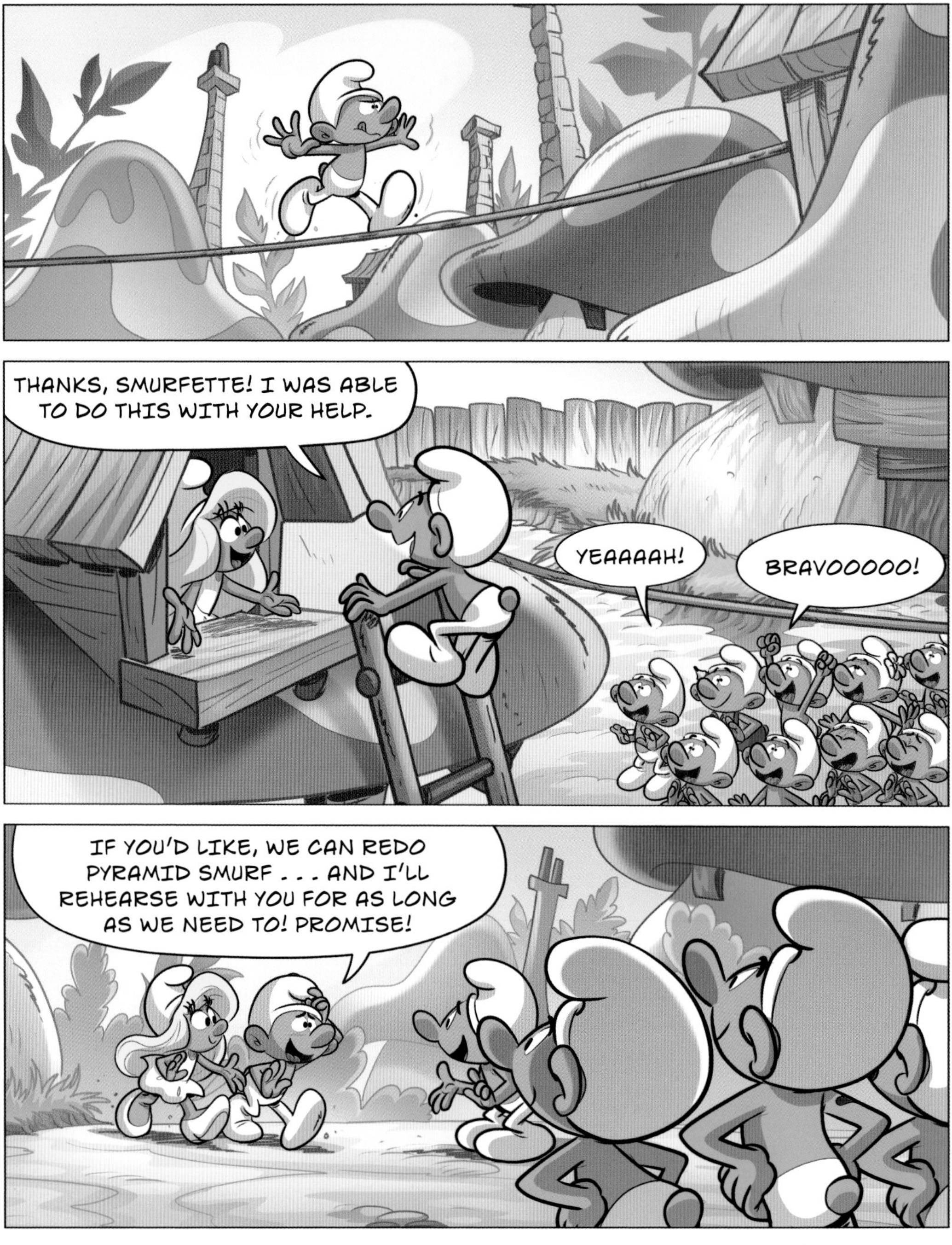
THANKS, SMURFETTE! I WAS ABLE TO DO THIS WITH YOUR HELP.
YEAAAAH!
BRAVOOOOO!
IF YOU'D LIKE, WE CAN REDO PYRAMID SMURF . . . AND I'LL REHEARSE WITH YOU FOR AS LONG AS WE NEED TO! PROMISE!

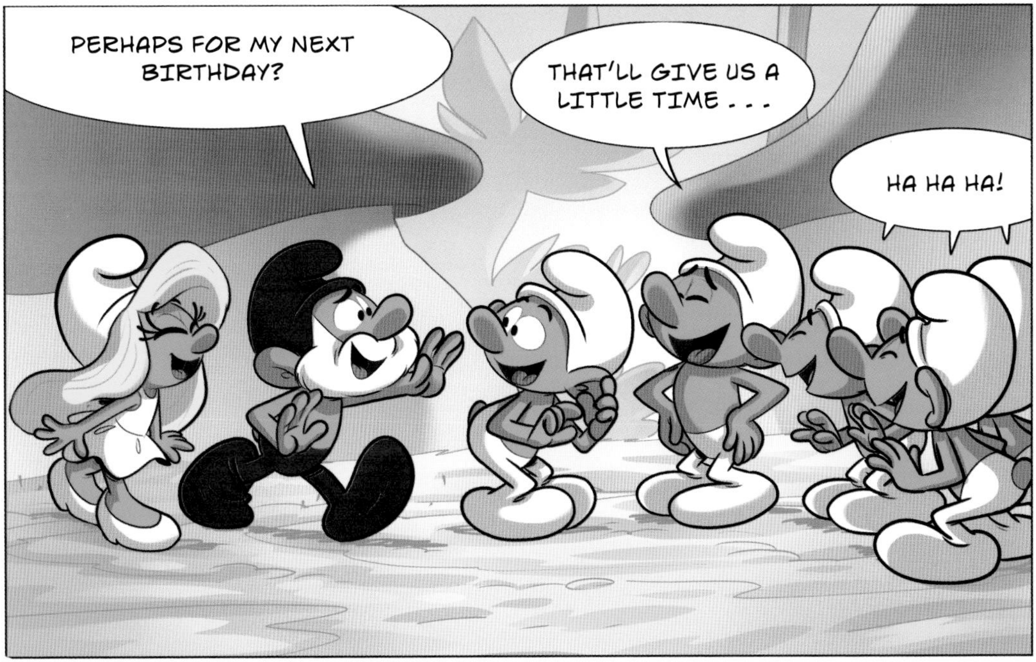
PERHAPS FOR MY NEXT BIRTHDAY?
THAT'LL GIVE US A LITTLE TIME . . .
HA HA HA!

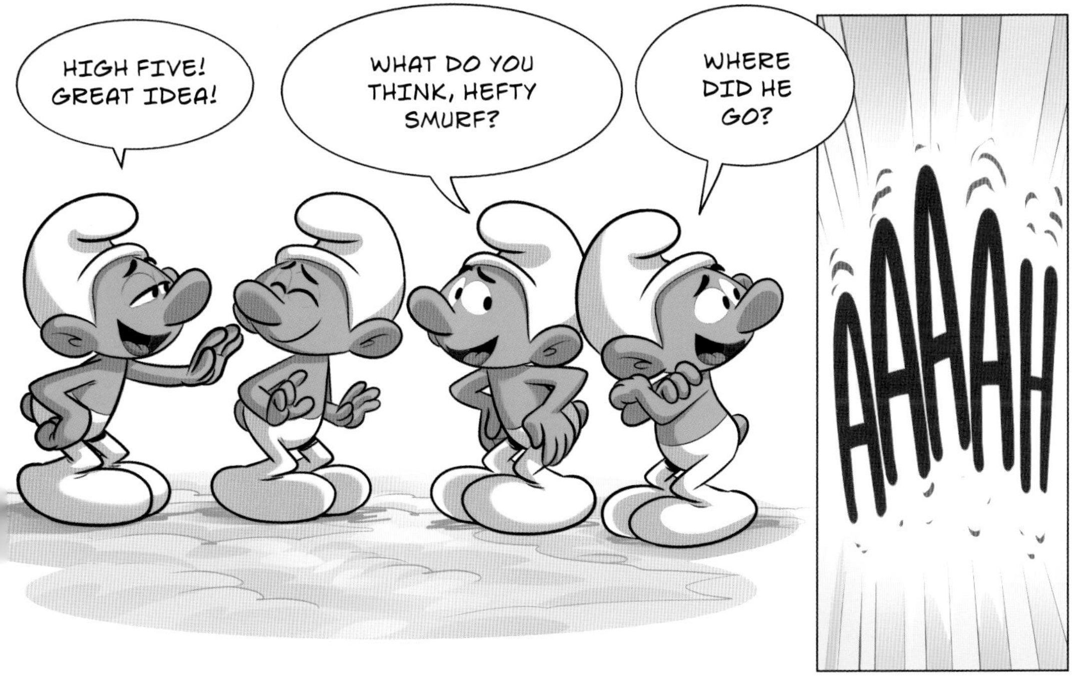
HIGH FIVE! GREAT IDEA!
WHAT DO YOU THINK, HEFTY SMURF?
WHERE DID HE GO?
AAAAH

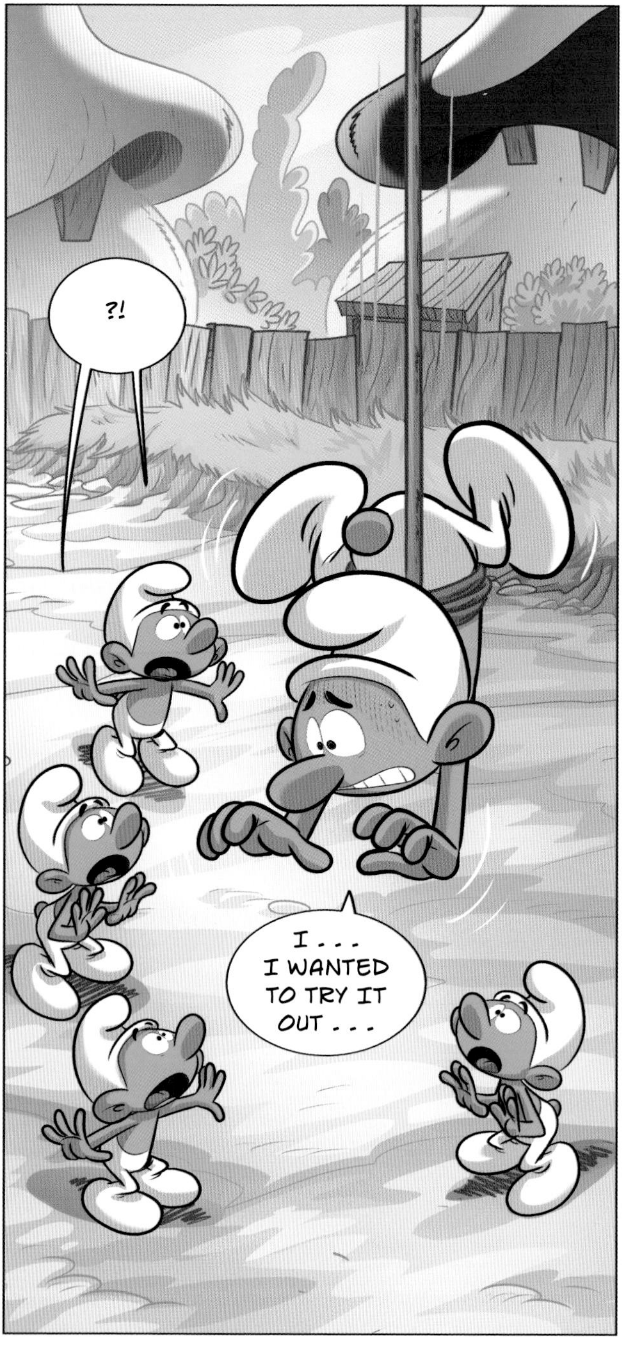
?!
I . . .
I WANTED
TO TRY IT
OUT . . .

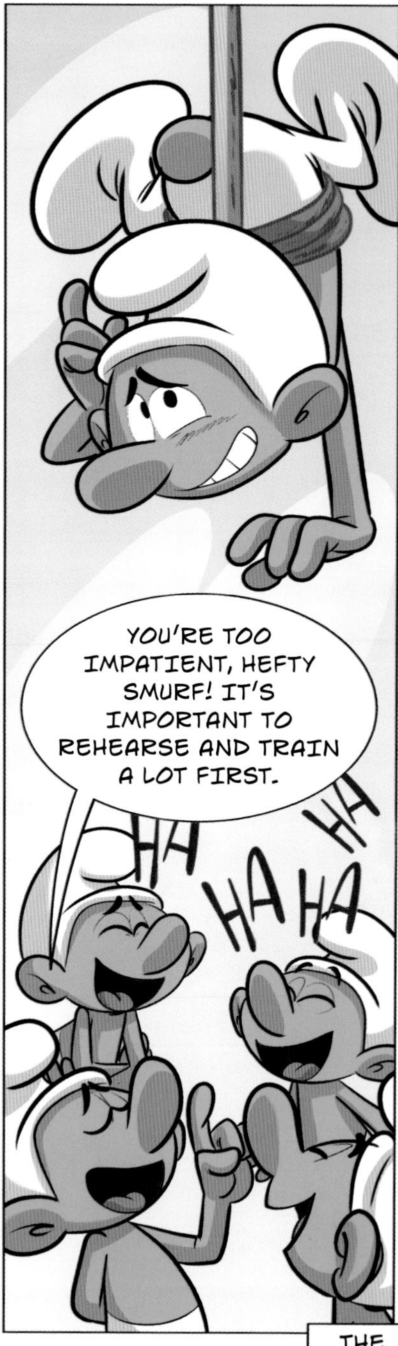
YOU'RE TOO
IMPATIENT, HEFTY
SMURF! IT'S
IMPORTANT TO
REHEARSE AND TRAIN
A LOT FIRST.
HA
HA
HA
HA

THE END

THE LITTERBUG SMURF

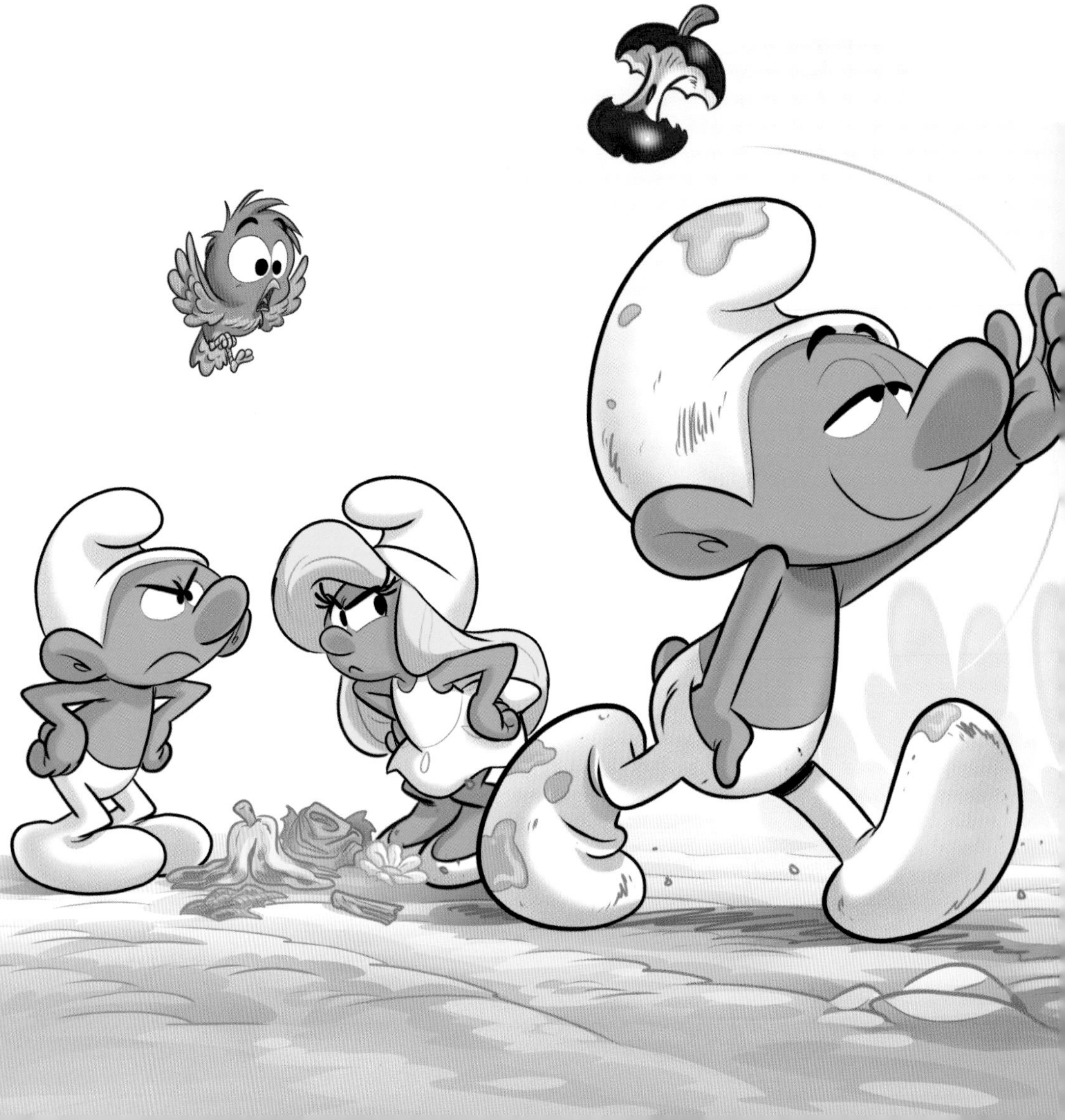

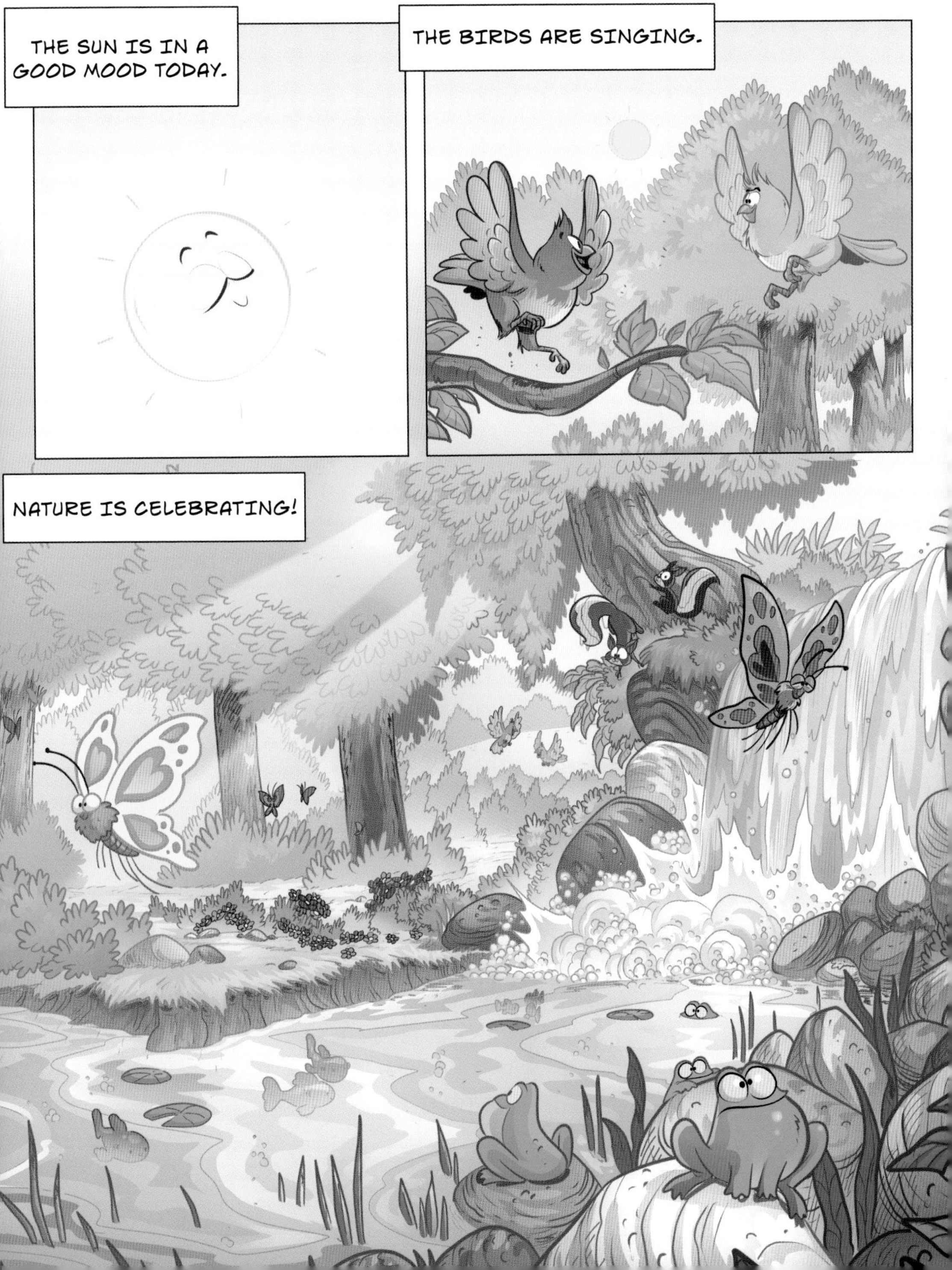
THE SUN IS IN A GOOD MOOD TODAY.
THE BIRDS ARE SINGING.
NATURE IS CELEBRATING!

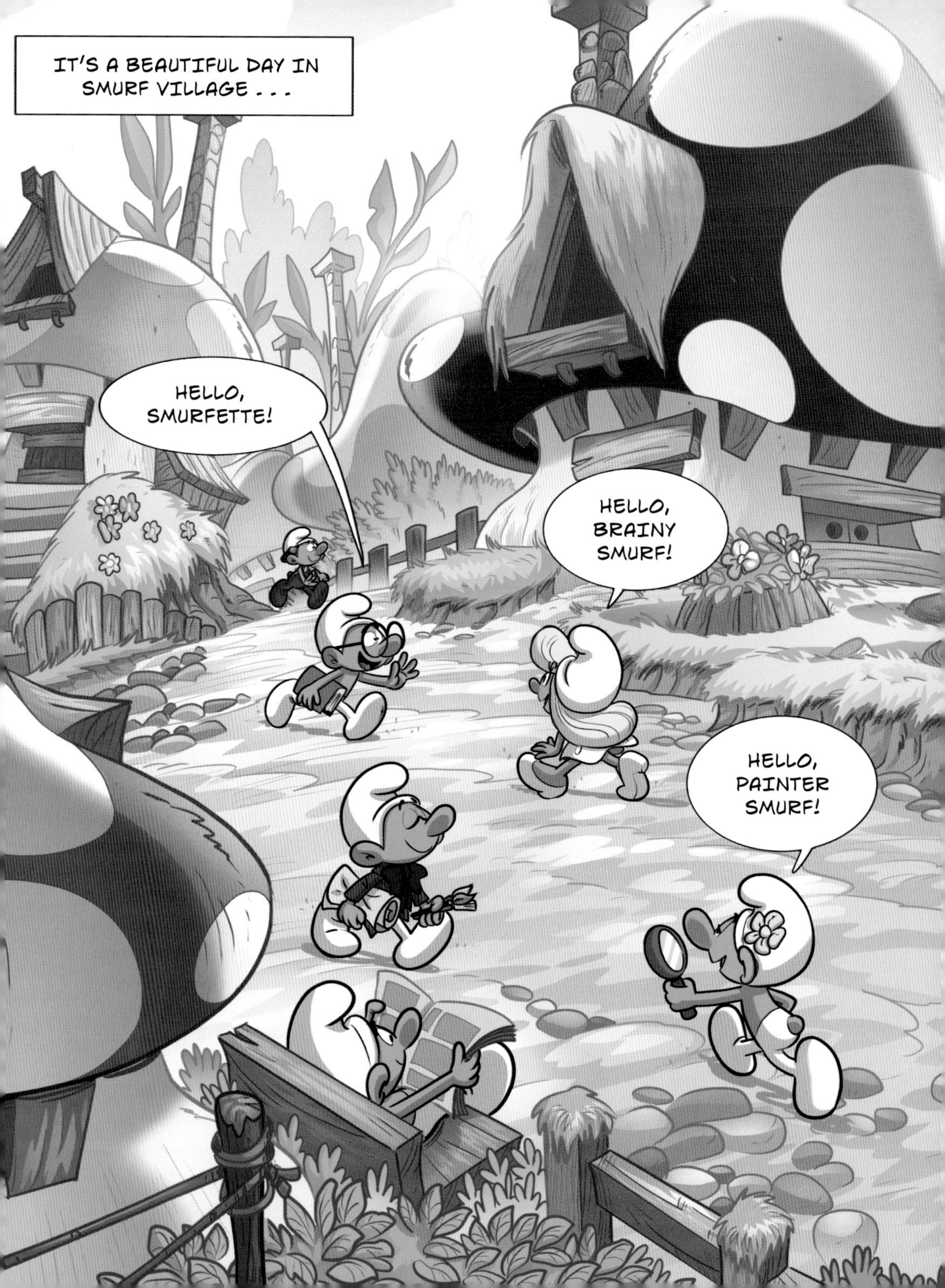
IT'S A BEAUTIFUL DAY IN SMURF VILLAGE . . .
HELLO, SMURFETTE!
HELLO, BRAINY SMURF!
HELLO, PAINTER SMURF!

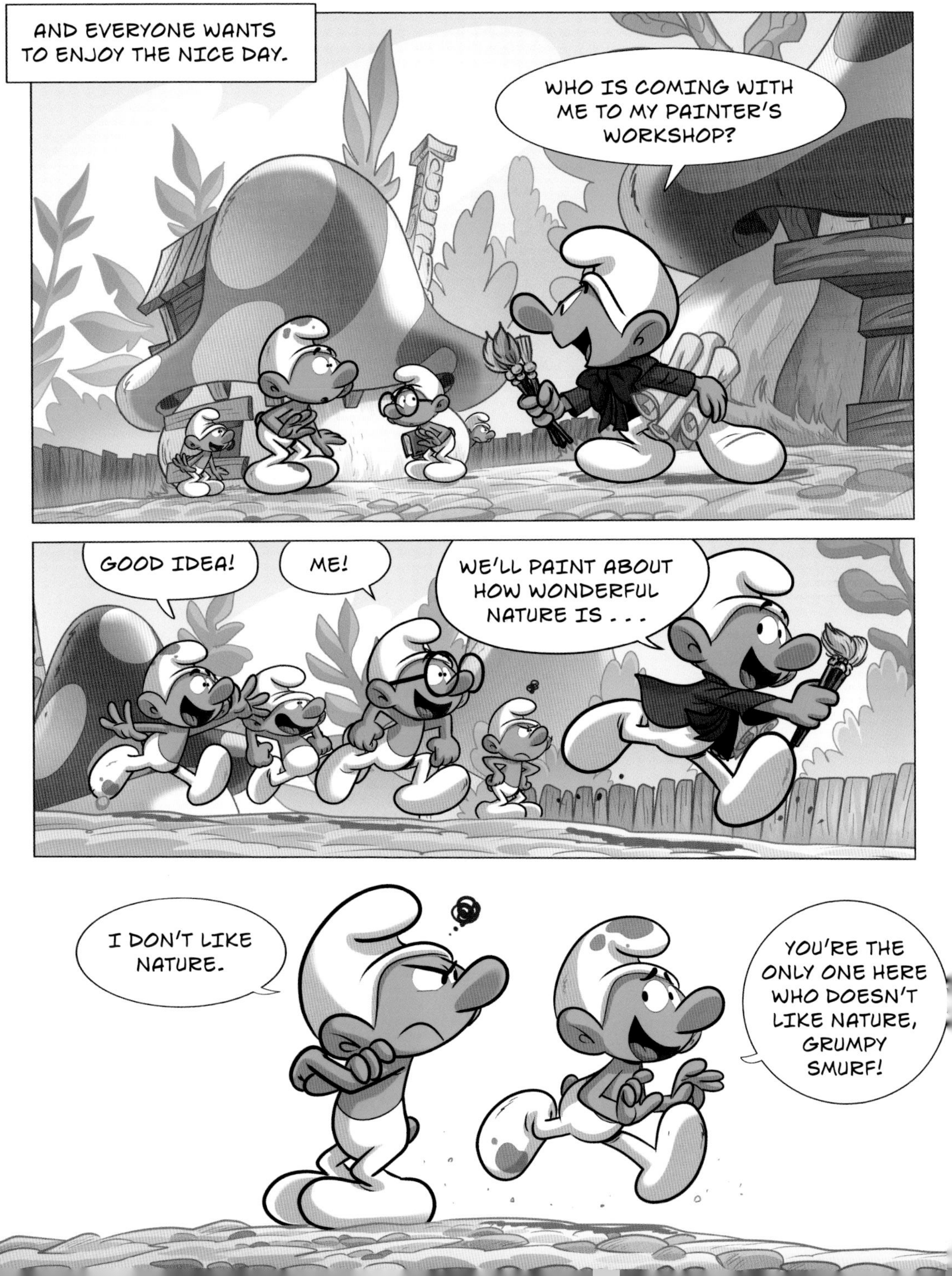
AND EVERYONE WANTS TO ENJOY THE NICE DAY.
WHO IS COMING WITH ME TO MY PAINTER'S WORKSHOP?
GOOD IDEA!
ME!
WE'LL PAINT ABOUT HOW WONDERFUL NATURE IS . . .
I DON'T LIKE NATURE.
YOU'RE THE ONLY ONE HERE WHO DOESN'T LIKE NATURE, GRUMPY SMURF!

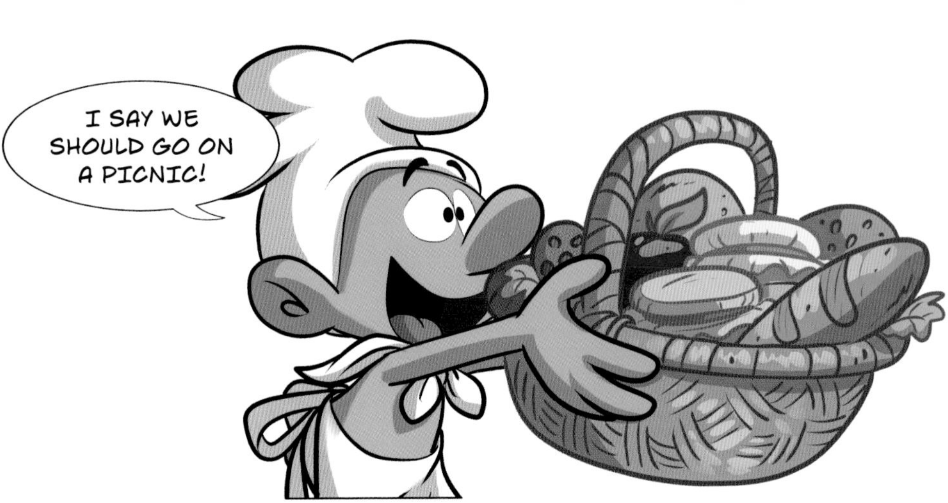
I SAY WE SHOULD GO ON A PICNIC!

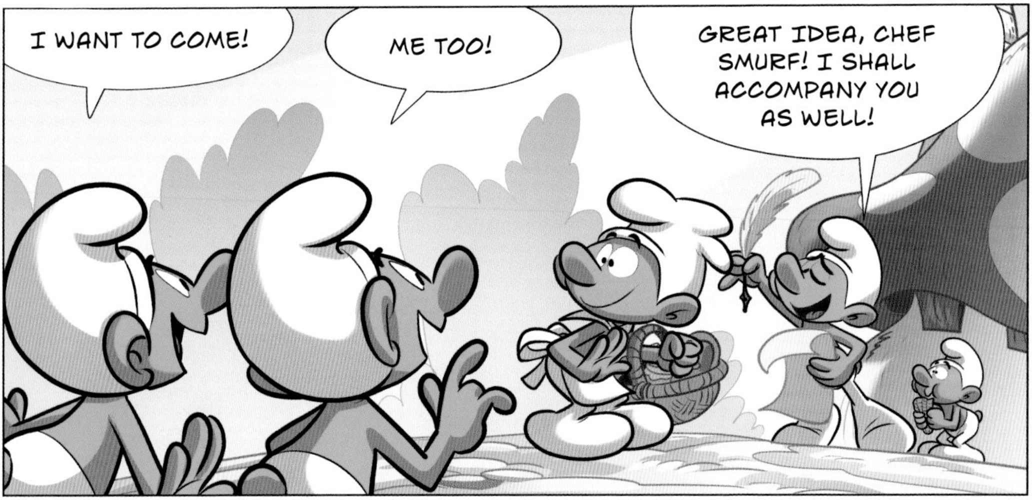
I WANT TO COME!
ME TOO!
GREAT IDEA, CHEF SMURF! I SHALL ACCOMPANY YOU AS WELL!

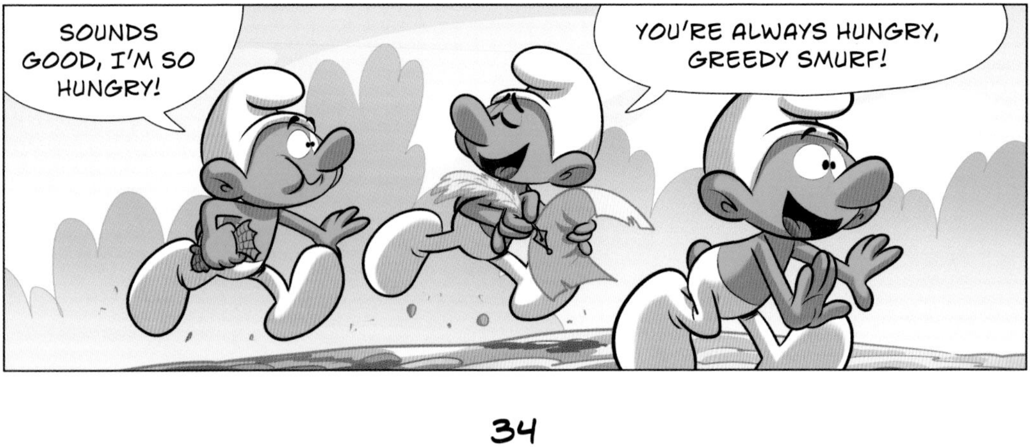
SOUNDS GOOD, I'M SO HUNGRY!
YOU'RE ALWAYS HUNGRY, GREEDY SMURF!

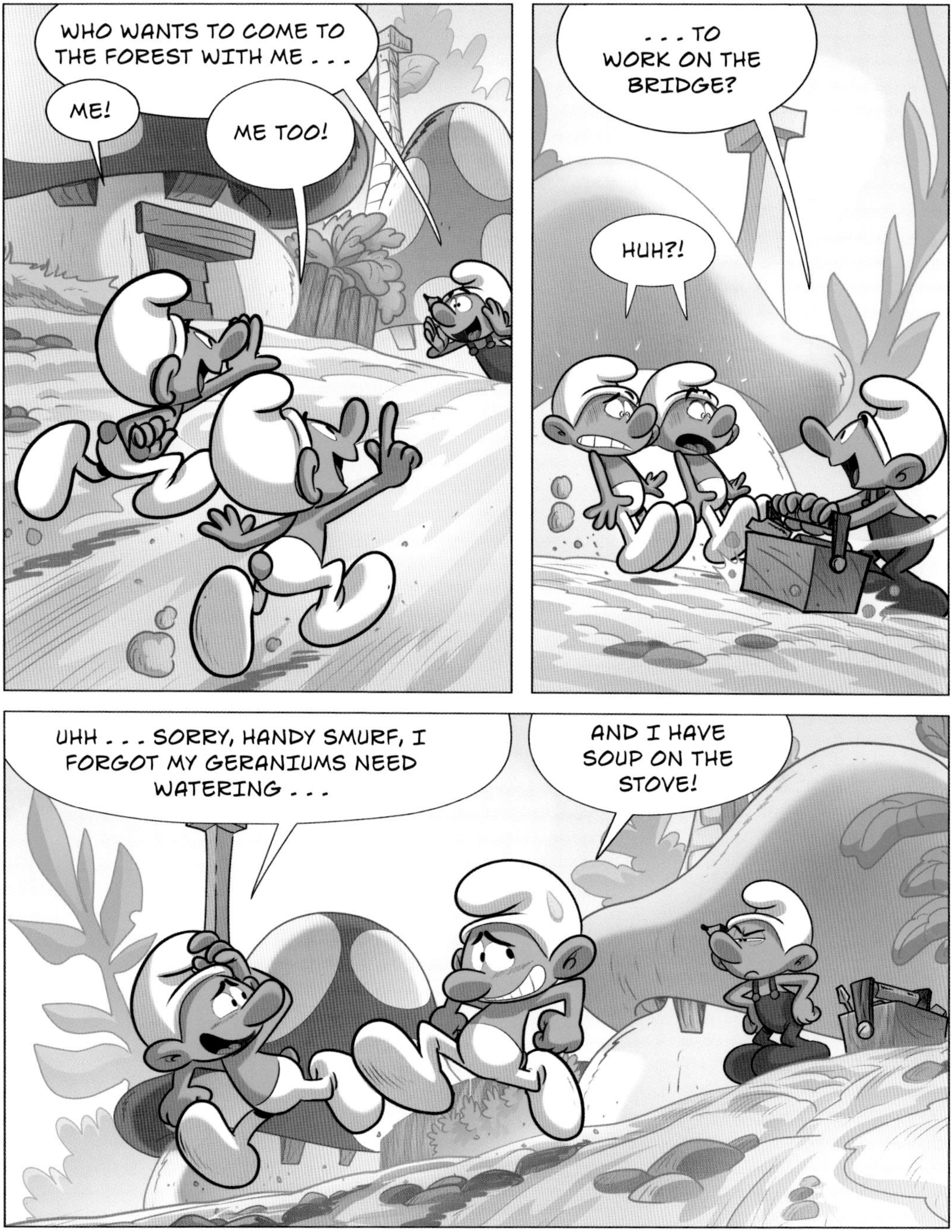
WHO WANTS TO COME TO THE FOREST WITH ME . . .
ME!
ME TOO!
. . . TO WORK ON THE BRIDGE?
HUH?!
UHH . . . SORRY, HANDY SMURF, I FORGOT MY GERANIUMS NEED WATERING . . .
AND I HAVE SOUP ON THE STOVE!

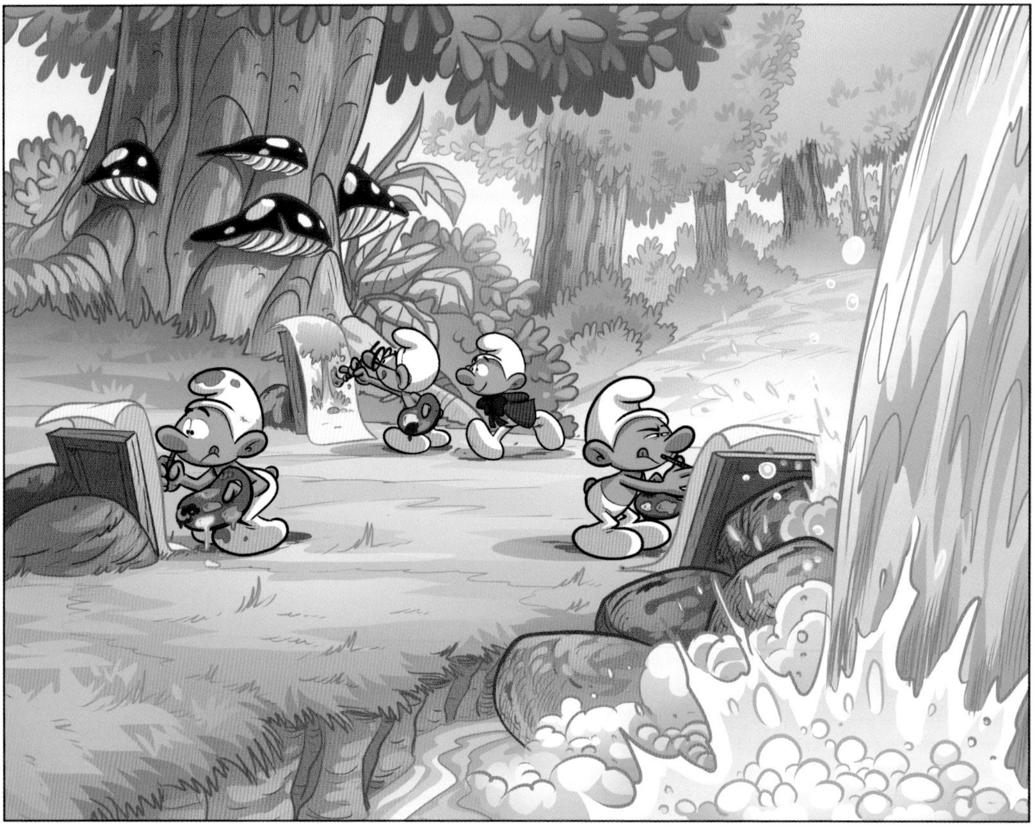

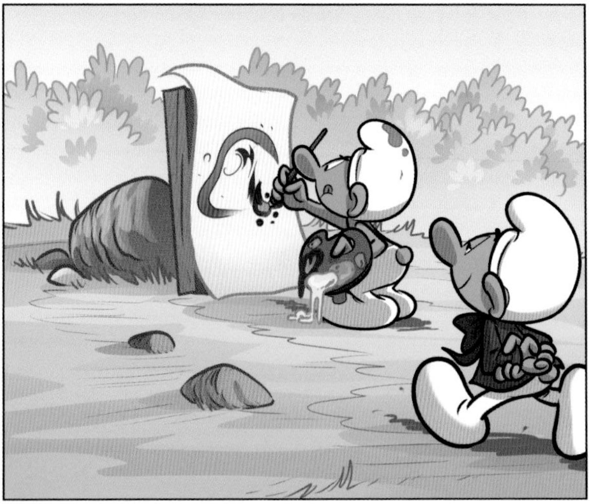

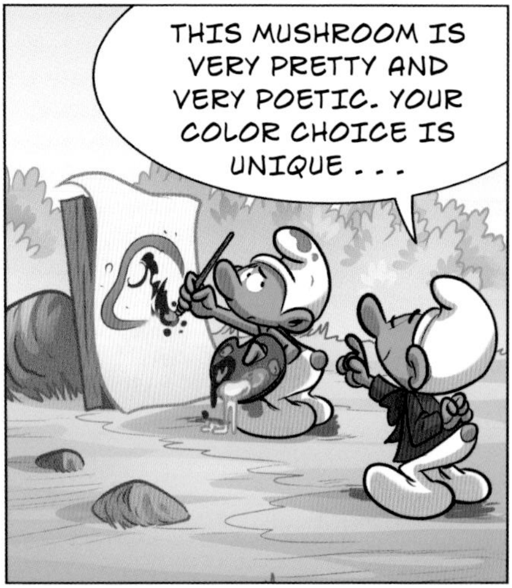
THIS MUSHROOM IS VERY PRETTY AND VERY POETIC. YOUR COLOR CHOICE IS UNIQUE . . .

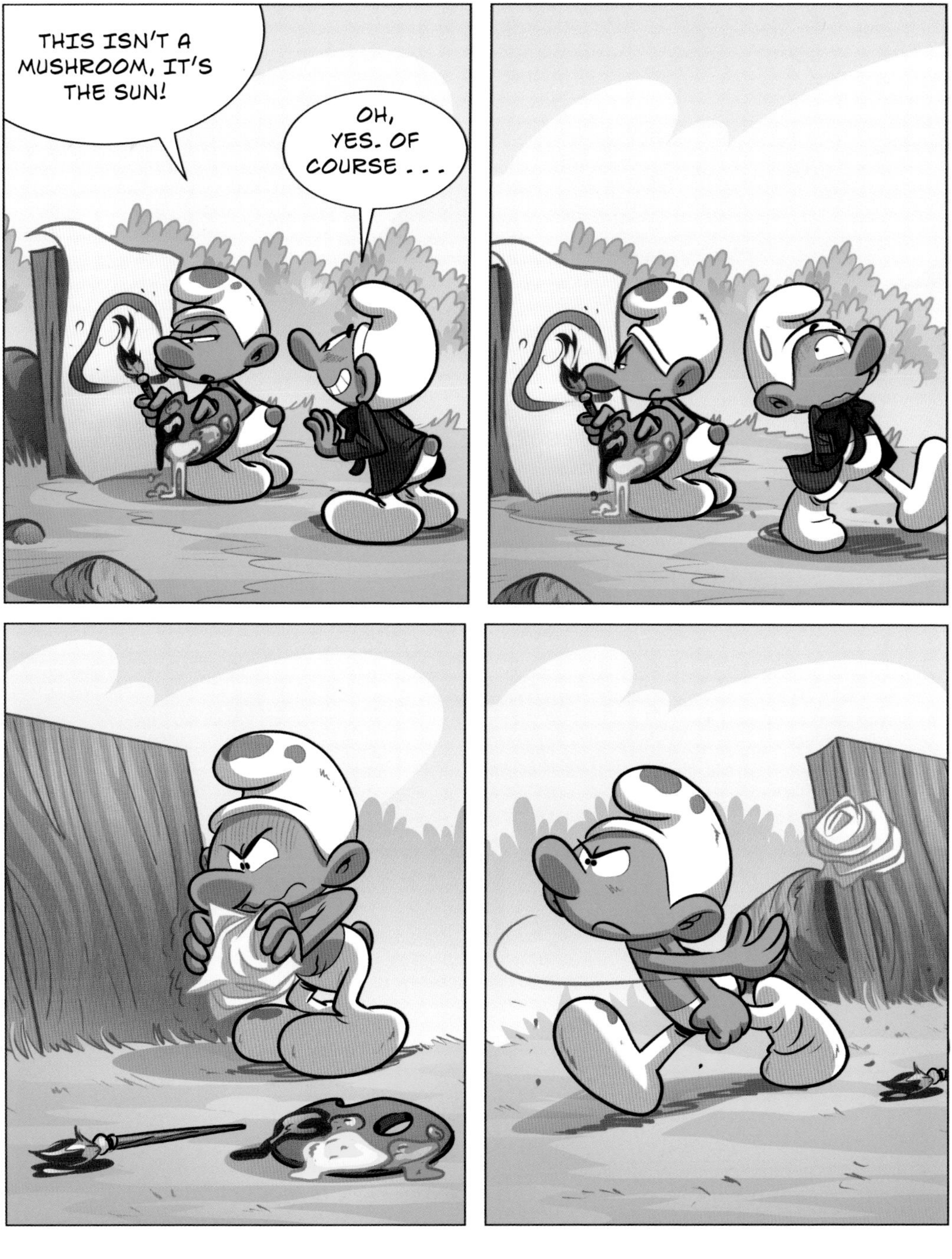
THIS ISN'T A MUSHROOM, IT'S THE SUN!
OH, YES. OF COURSE . . .

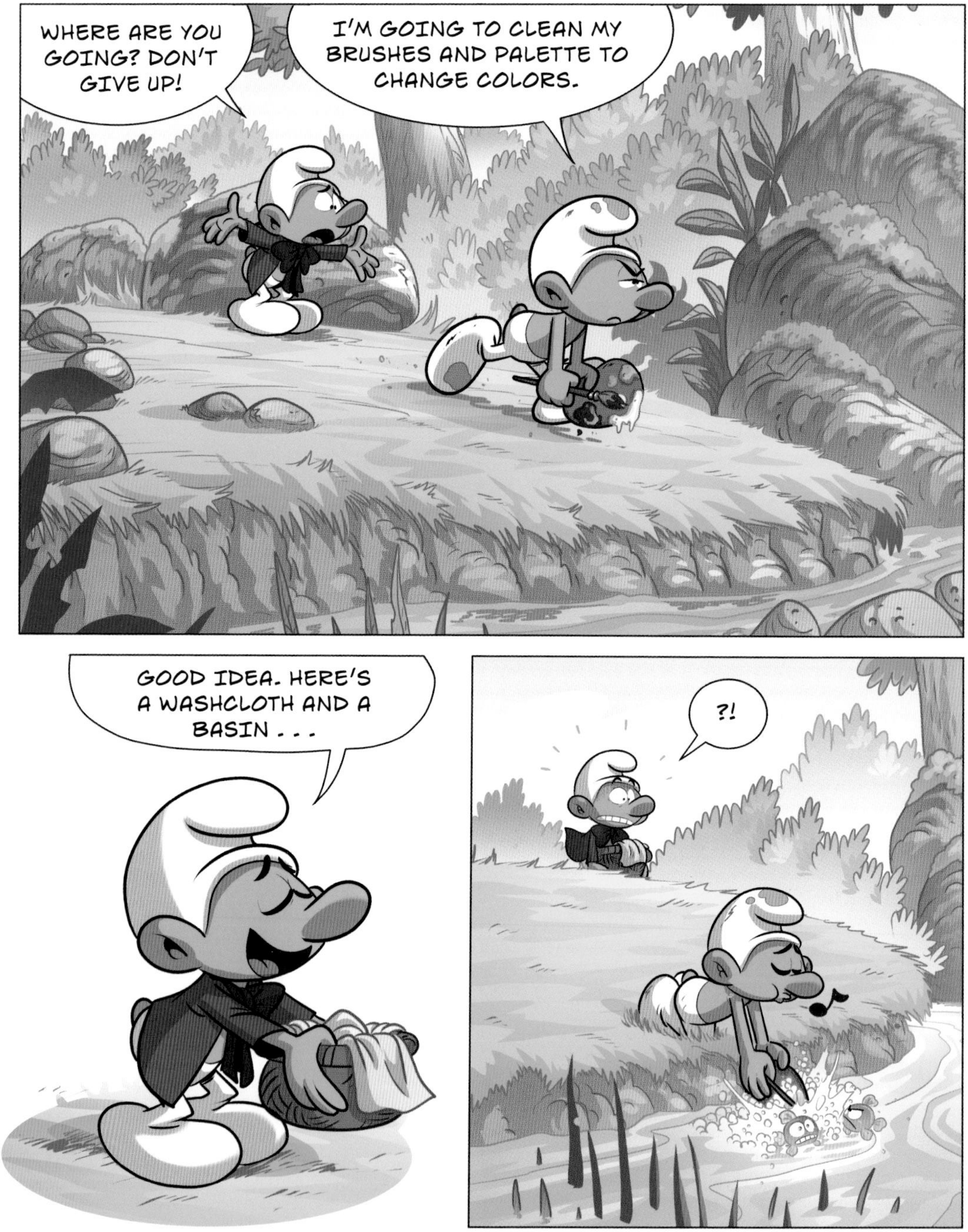
WHERE ARE YOU GOING? DON'T GIVE UP!
I'M GOING TO CLEAN MY BRUSHES AND PALETTE TO CHANGE COLORS.
GOOD IDEA. HERE'S A WASHCLOTH AND A BASIN . . .
?!

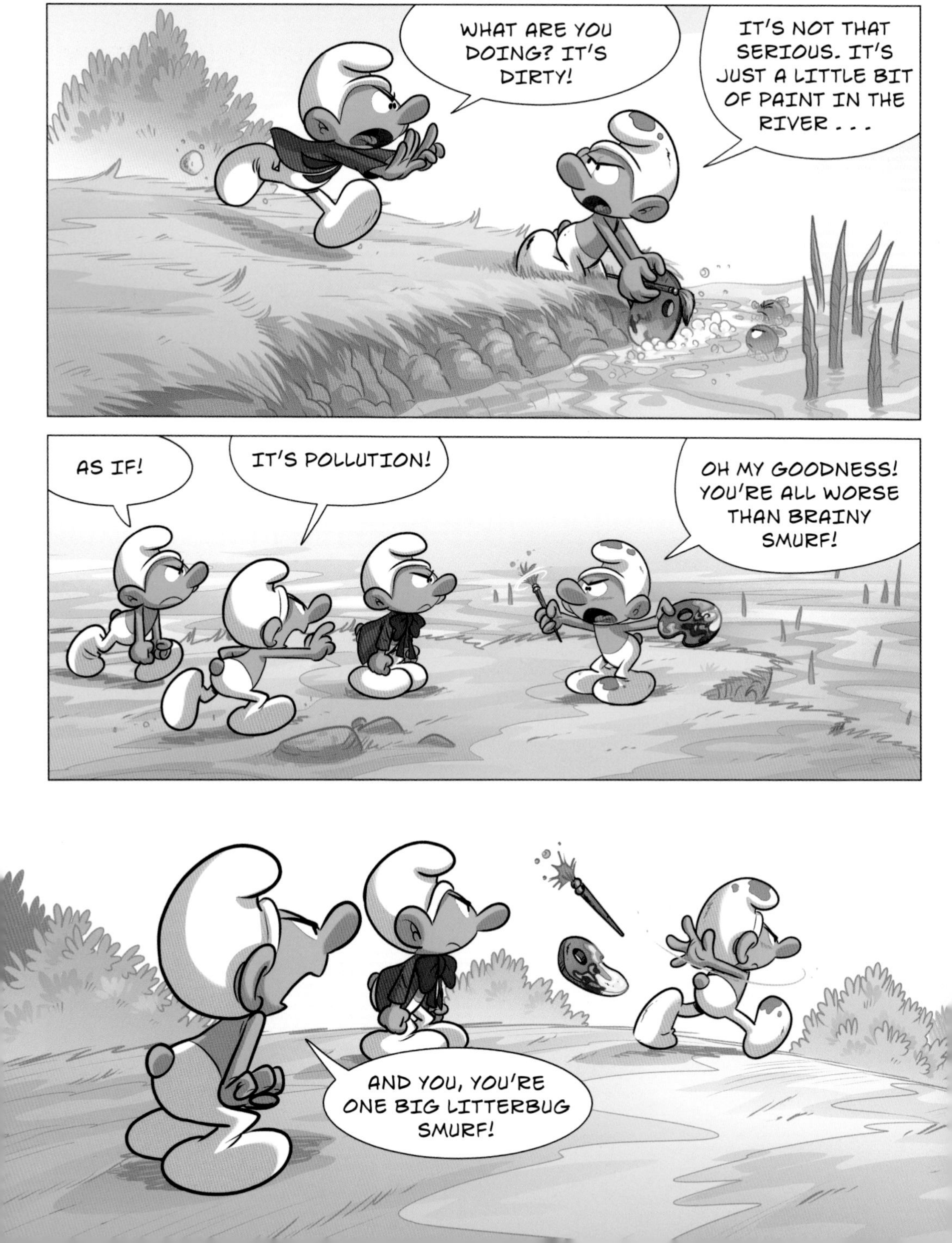
WHAT ARE YOU DOING? IT'S DIRTY!
IT'S NOT THAT SERIOUS. IT'S JUST A LITTLE BIT OF PAINT IN THE RIVER . . .
AS IF!
IT'S POLLUTION!
OH MY GOODNESS! YOU'RE ALL WORSE THAN BRAINY SMURF!
AND YOU, YOU'RE ONE BIG LITTERBUG SMURF!

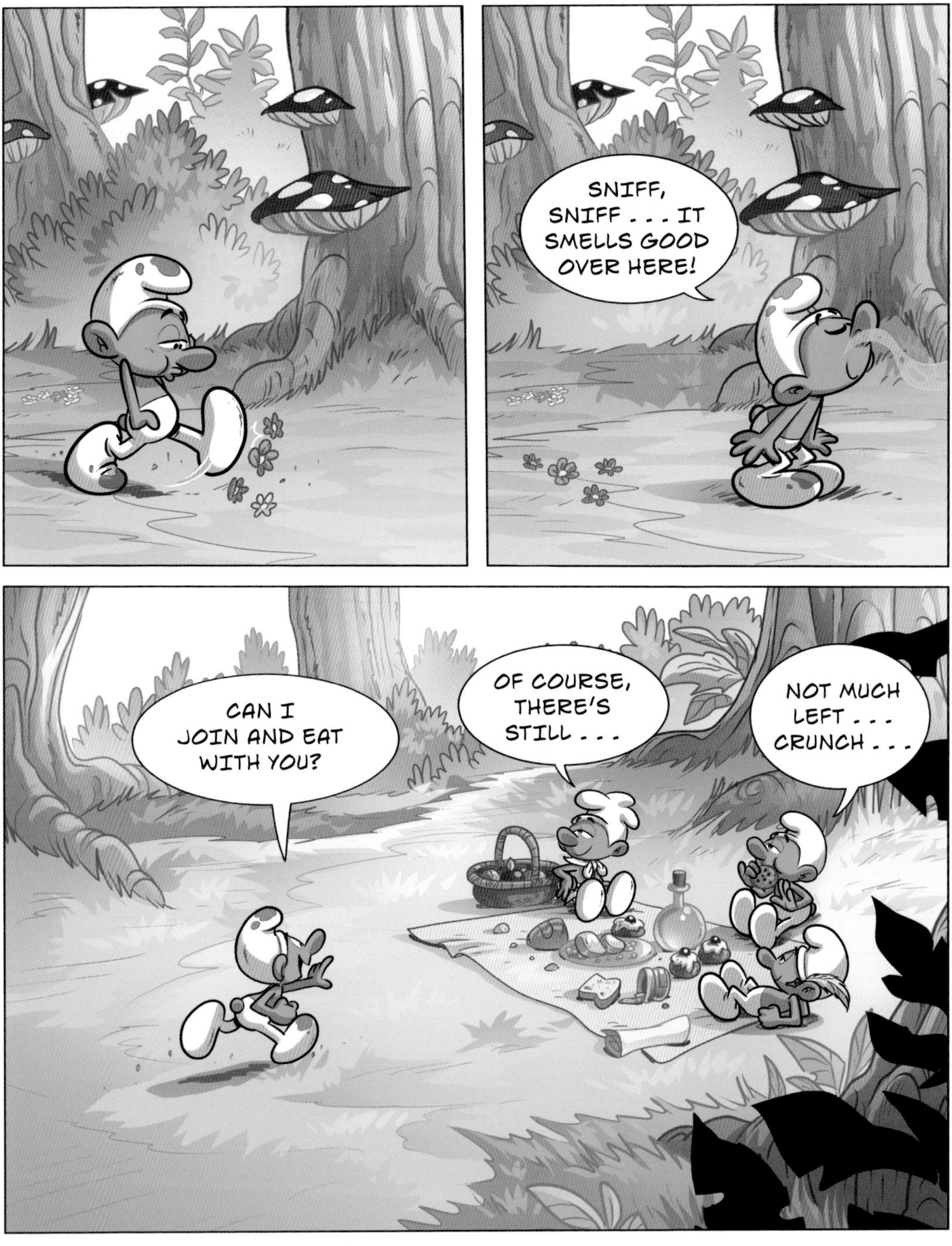
SNIFF, SNIFF . . . IT SMELLS GOOD OVER HERE!
CAN I JOIN AND EAT WITH YOU?
OF COURSE, THERE'S STILL . . .
NOT MUCH LEFT . . . CRUNCH . . .

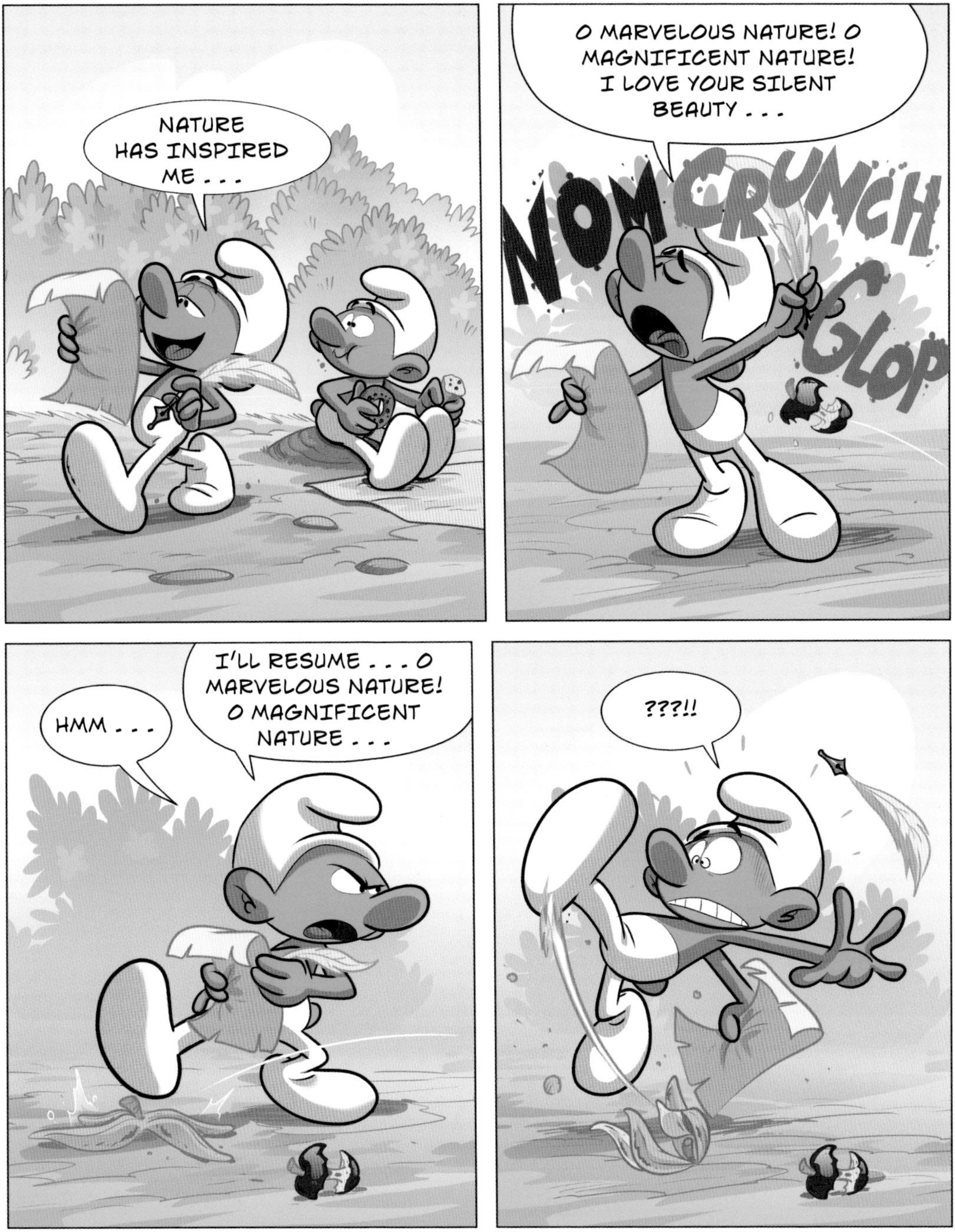
NATURE HAS INSPIRED ME . . .
O MARVELOUS NATURE! O MAGNIFICENT NATURE! I LOVE YOUR SILENT BEAUTY . . .
NOM
CRUNCH
GLOP
HMM . . .
I'LL RESUME . . . O MARVELOUS NATURE! O MAGNIFICENT NATURE . . .
???!!

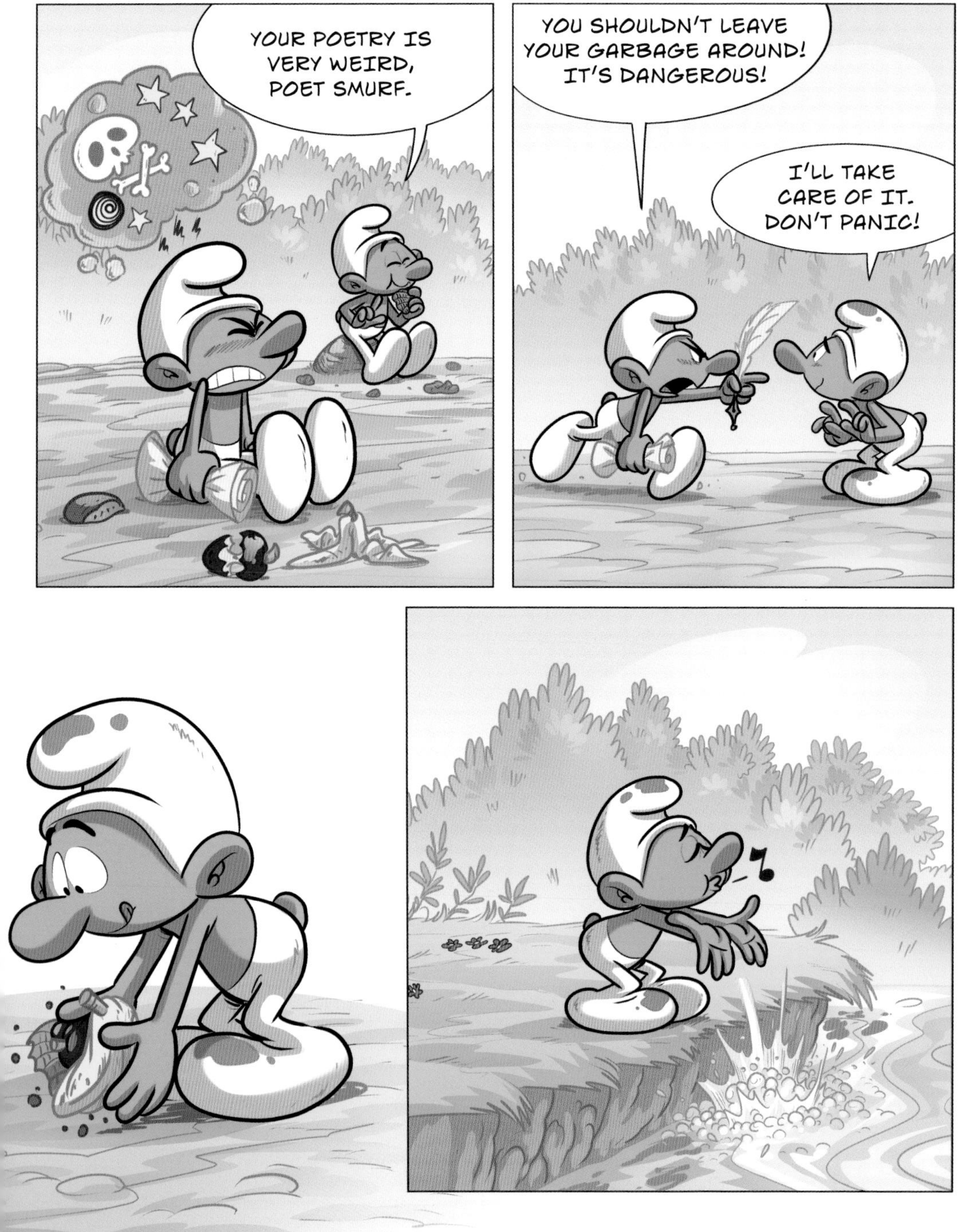
YOUR POETRY IS VERY WEIRD, POET SMURF.
YOU SHOULDN'T LEAVE YOUR GARBAGE AROUND! IT'S DANGEROUS!
I'LL TAKE CARE OF IT. DON'T PANIC!

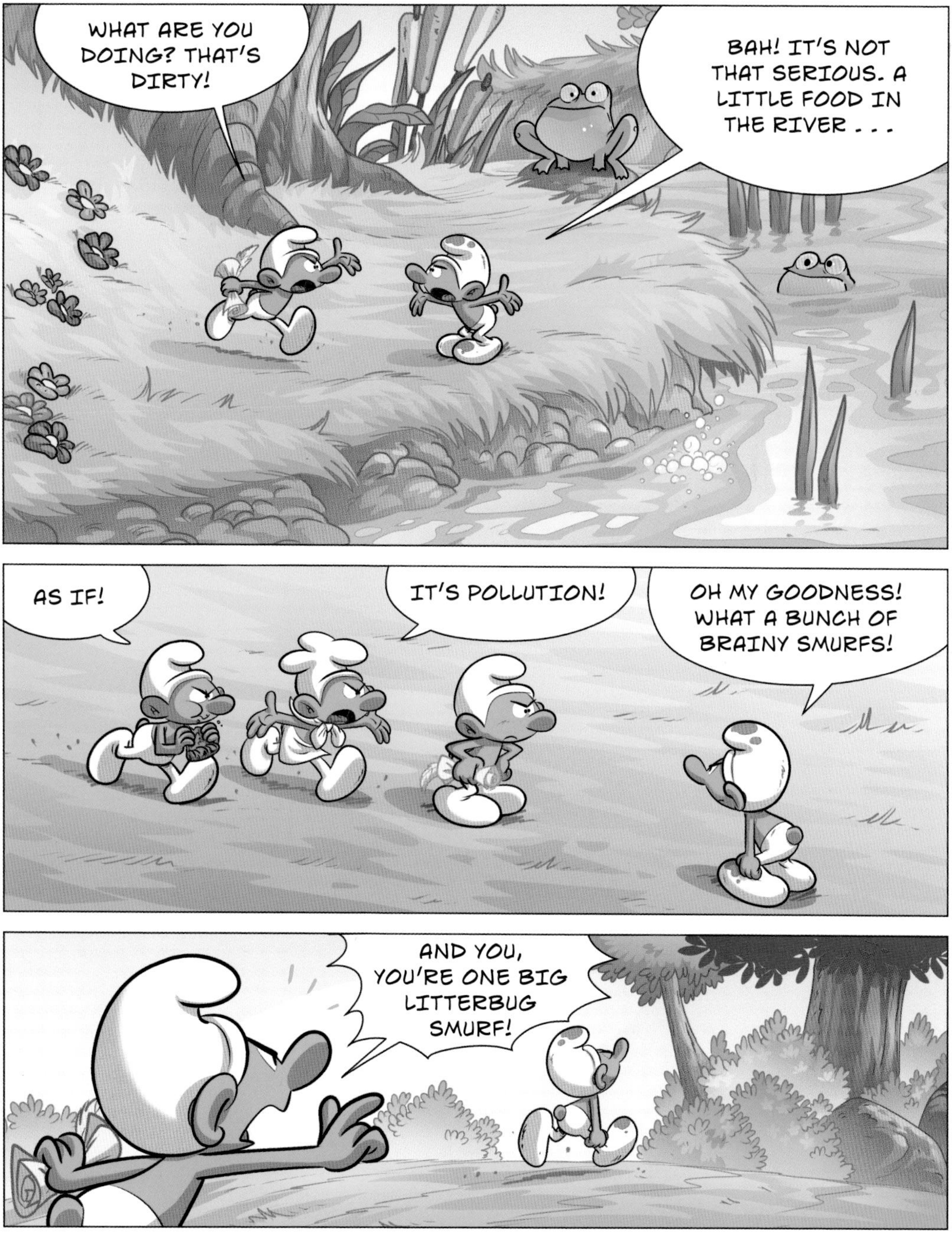
WHAT ARE YOU DOING? THAT'S DIRTY!
BAH! IT'S NOT THAT SERIOUS. A LITTLE FOOD IN THE RIVER . . .
AS IF!
IT'S POLLUTION!
OH MY GOODNESS! WHAT A BUNCH OF BRAINY SMURFS!
AND YOU, YOU'RE ONE BIG LITTERBUG SMURF!

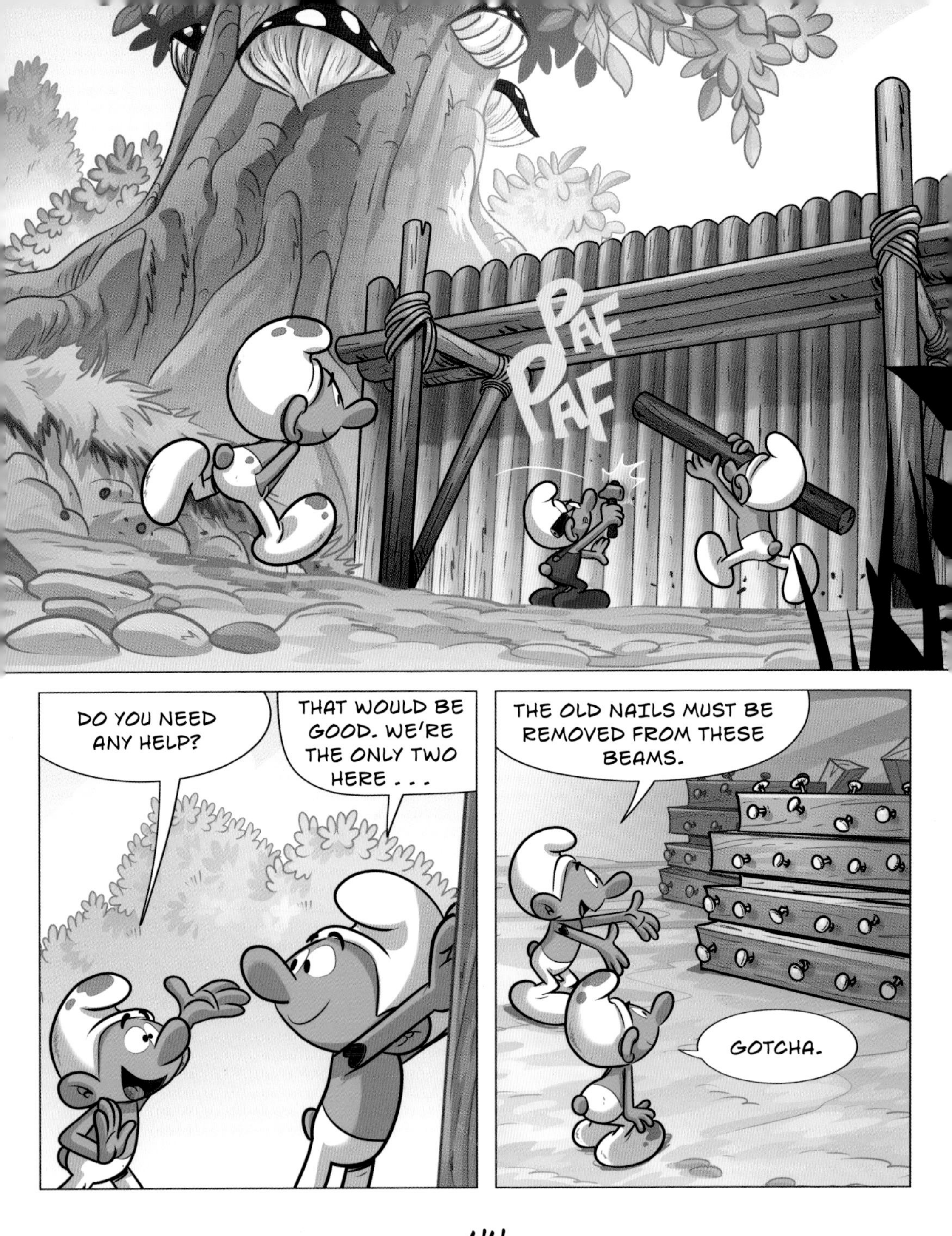
PAF
PAF
DO YOU NEED ANY HELP?
THAT WOULD BE GOOD. WE'RE THE ONLY TWO HERE . . .
THE OLD NAILS MUST BE REMOVED FROM THESE BEAMS.
GOTCHA.

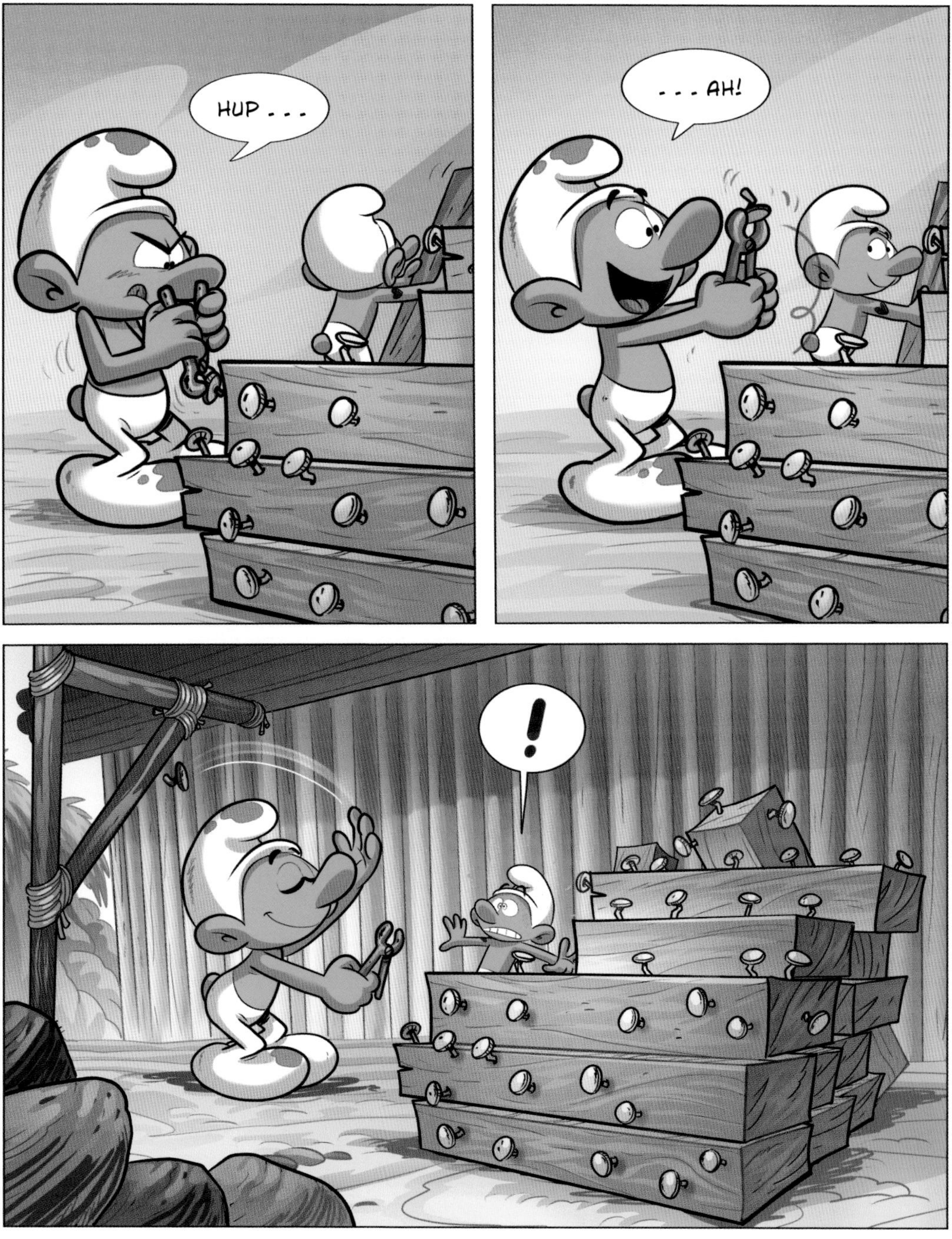
HUP . . .
. . . AH!
!

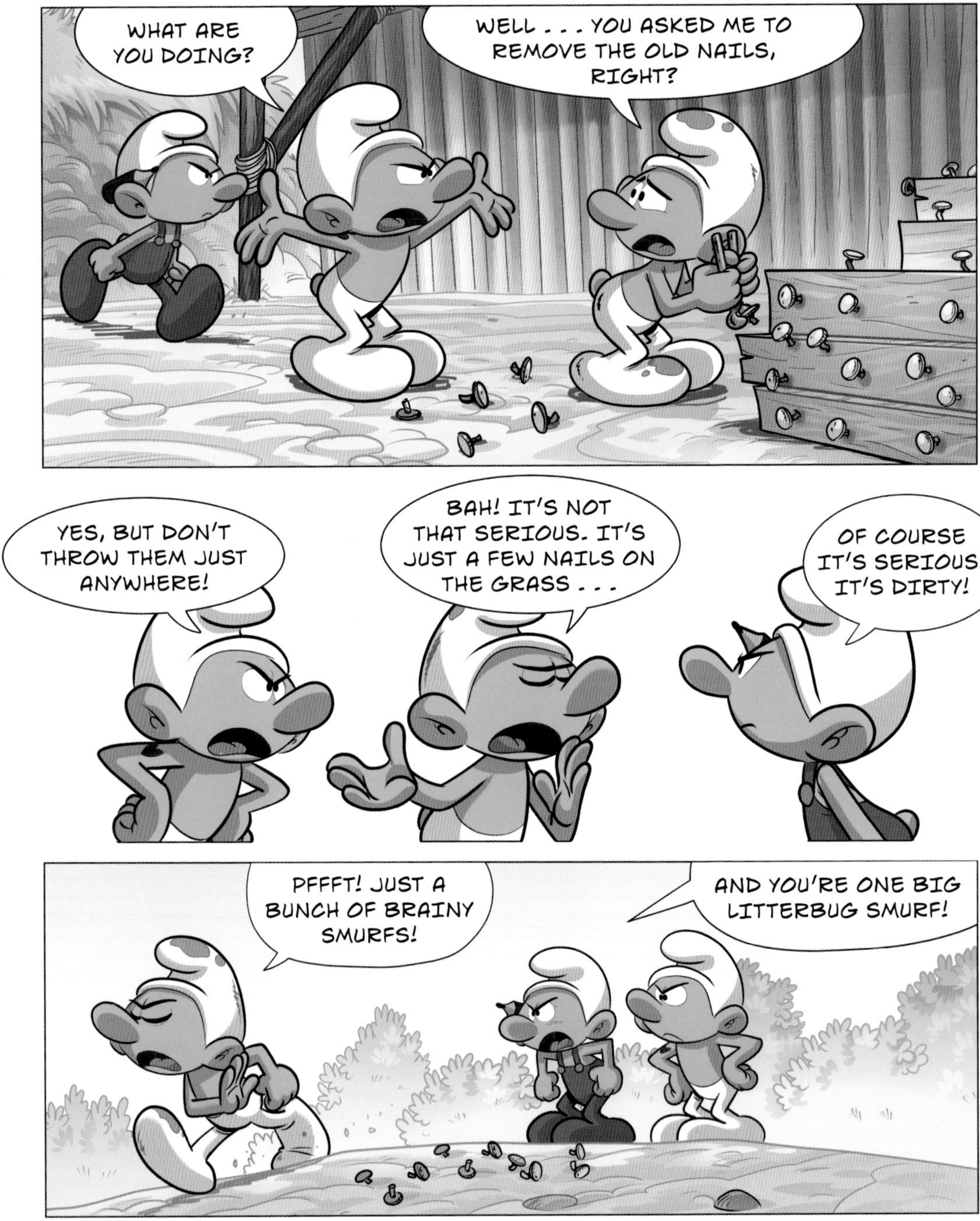
WHAT ARE YOU DOING?
WELL . . . YOU ASKED ME TO REMOVE THE OLD NAILS, RIGHT?
YES, BUT DON'T THROW THEM JUST ANYWHERE!
BAH! IT'S NOT THAT SERIOUS. IT'S JUST A FEW NAILS ON THE GRASS . . .
OF COURSE IT'S SERIOUS! IT'S DIRTY!
PFFFT! JUST A BUNCH OF BRAINY SMURFS!
AND YOU'RE ONE BIG LITTERBUG SMURF!

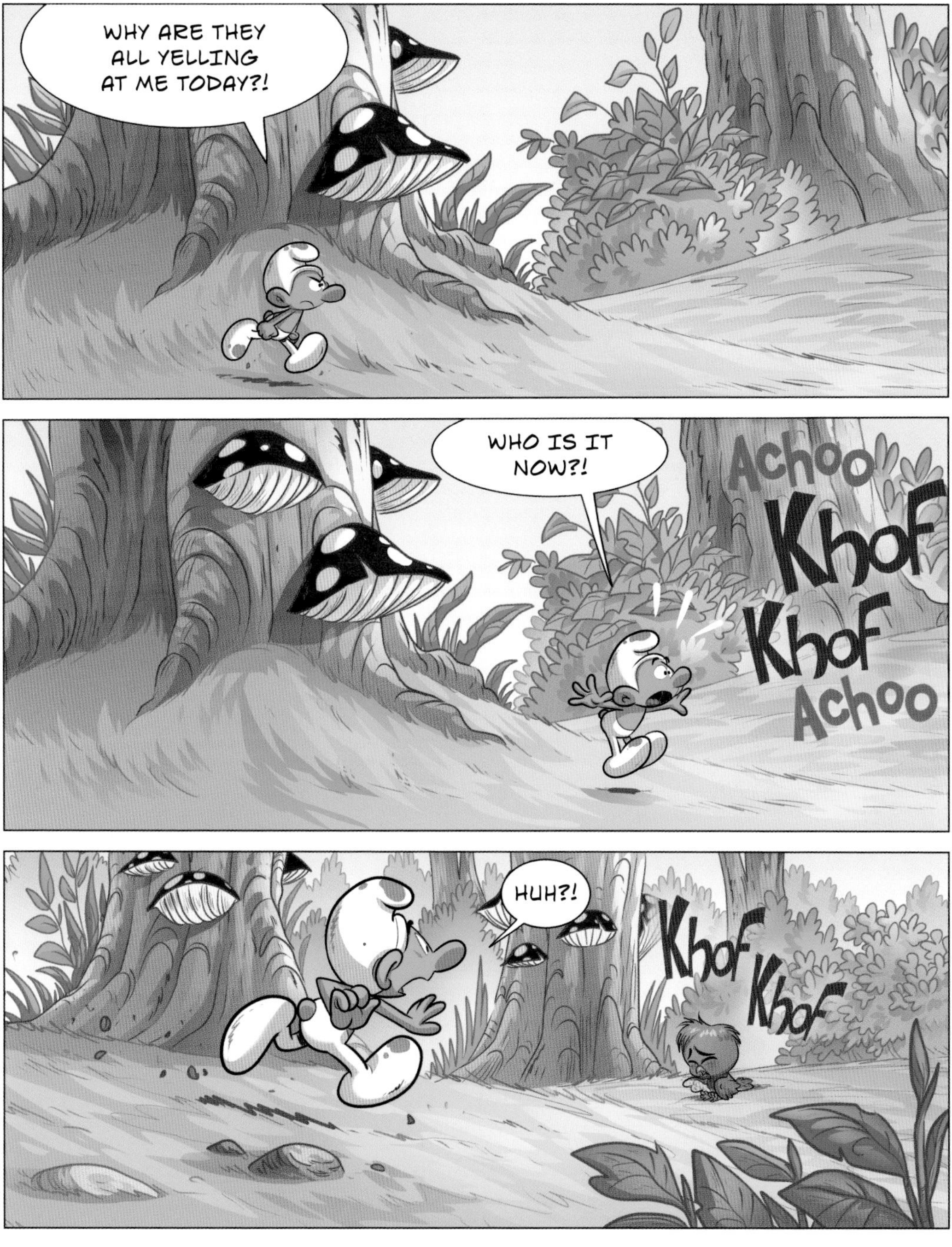
WHY ARE THEY ALL YELLING AT ME TODAY?!
WHO IS IT NOW?!
Achoo
Khof
Khof
Achoo
HUH?!
Khof
Khof

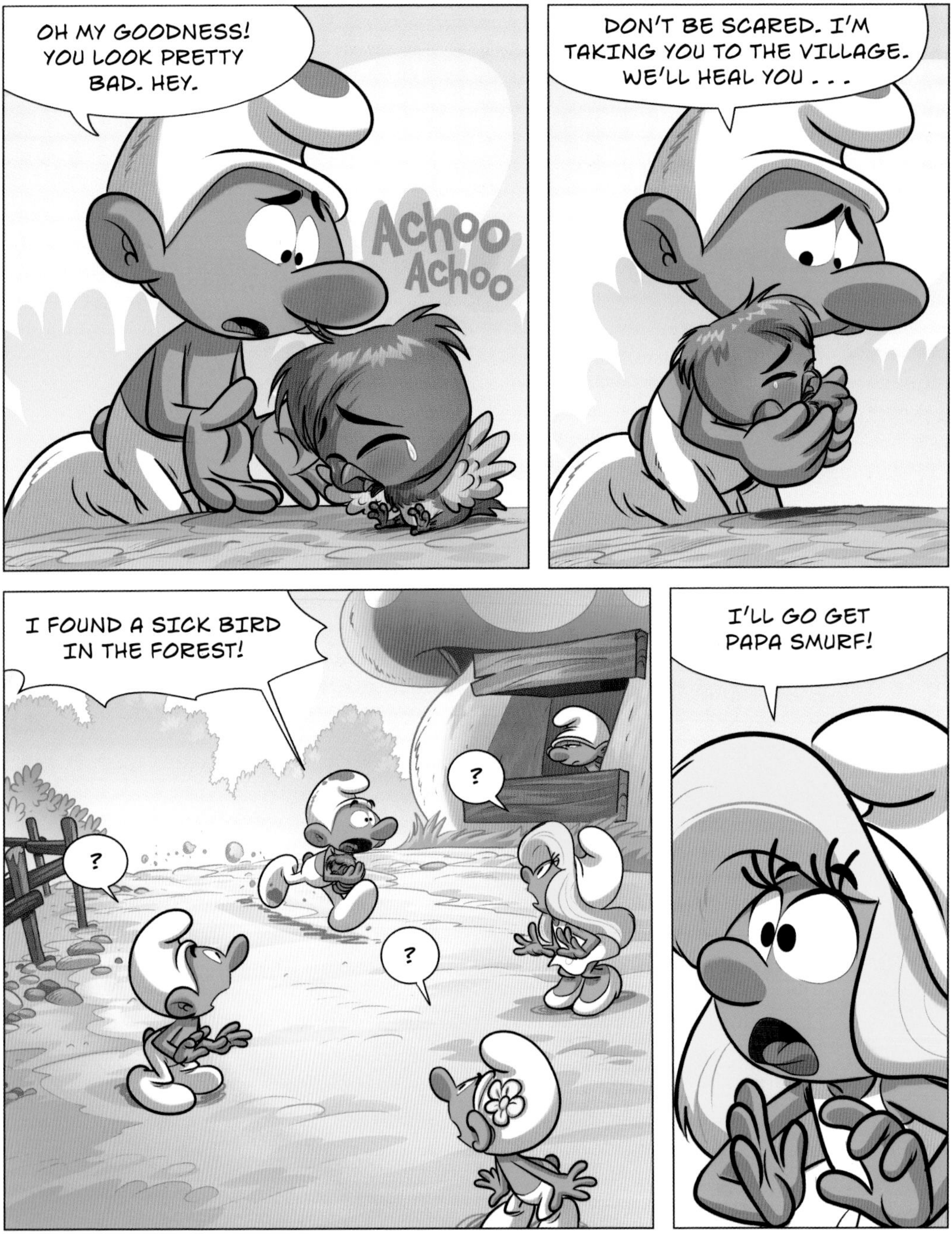
OH MY GOODNESS! YOU LOOK PRETTY BAD. HEY.
Achoo Achoo
DON'T BE SCARED. I'M TAKING YOU TO THE VILLAGE. WE'LL HEAL YOU . . .
I FOUND A SICK BIRD IN THE FOREST!
?
?
?
I'LL GO GET PAPA SMURF!

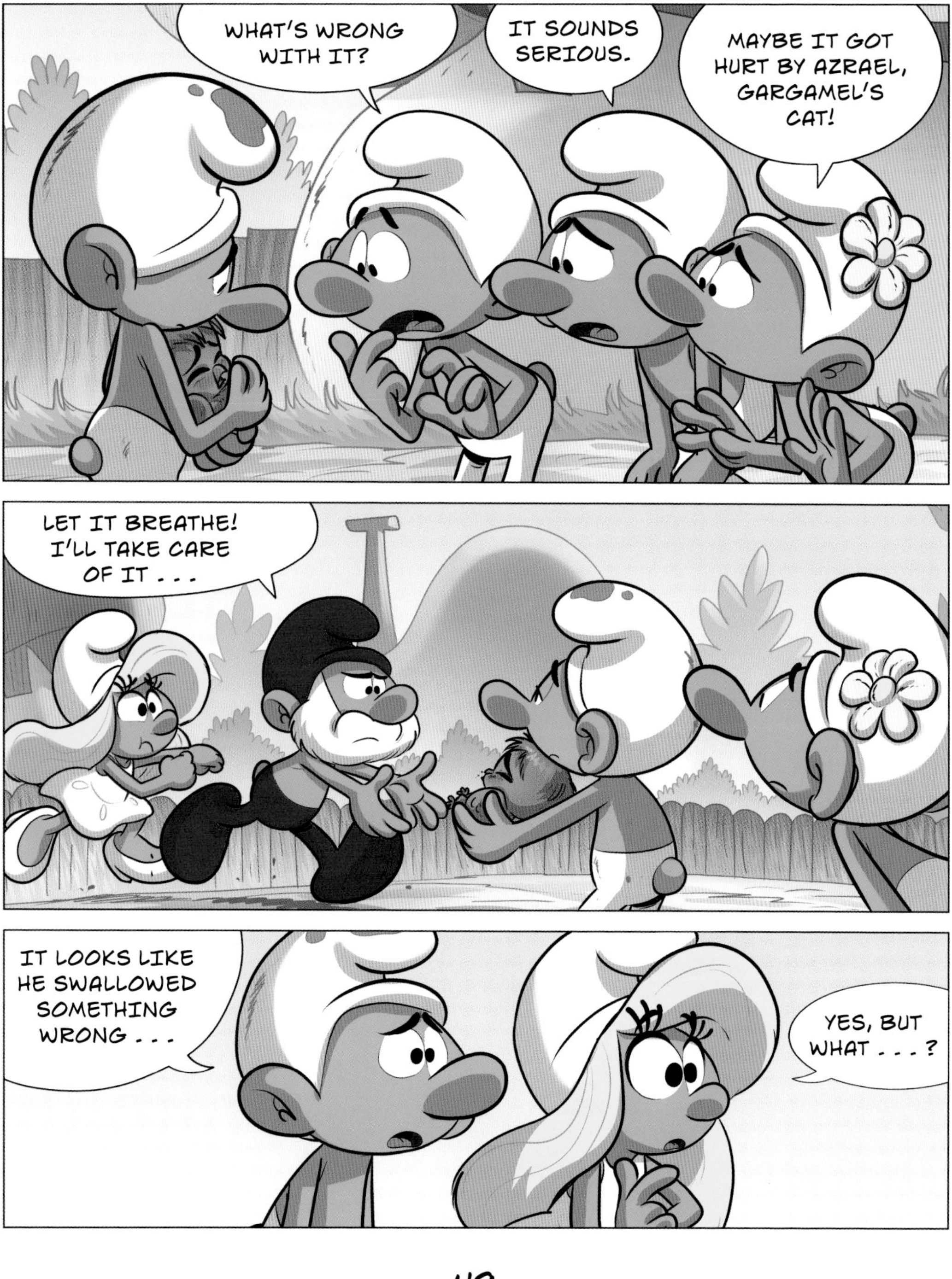
WHAT'S WRONG WITH IT?
IT SOUNDS SERIOUS.
MAYBE IT GOT HURT BY AZRAEL, GARGAMEL'S CAT!
LET IT BREATHE! I'LL TAKE CARE OF IT . . .
IT LOOKS LIKE HE SWALLOWED SOMETHING WRONG . . .
YES, BUT WHAT . . . ?

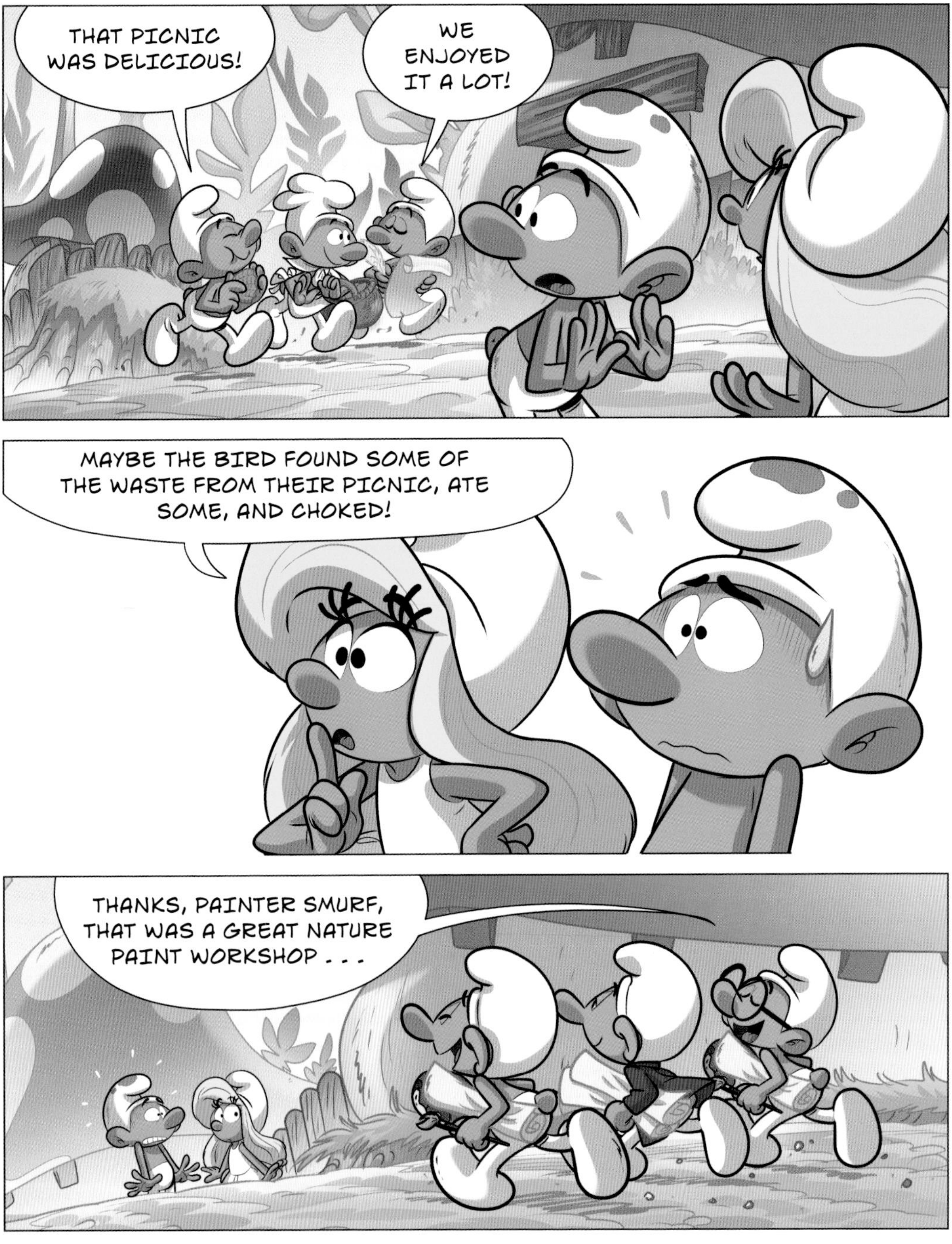
THAT PICNIC WAS DELICIOUS!
WE ENJOYED IT A LOT!
MAYBE THE BIRD FOUND SOME OF THE WASTE FROM THEIR PICNIC, ATE SOME, AND CHOKED!
THANKS, PAINTER SMURF, THAT WAS A GREAT NATURE PAINT WORKSHOP . . .

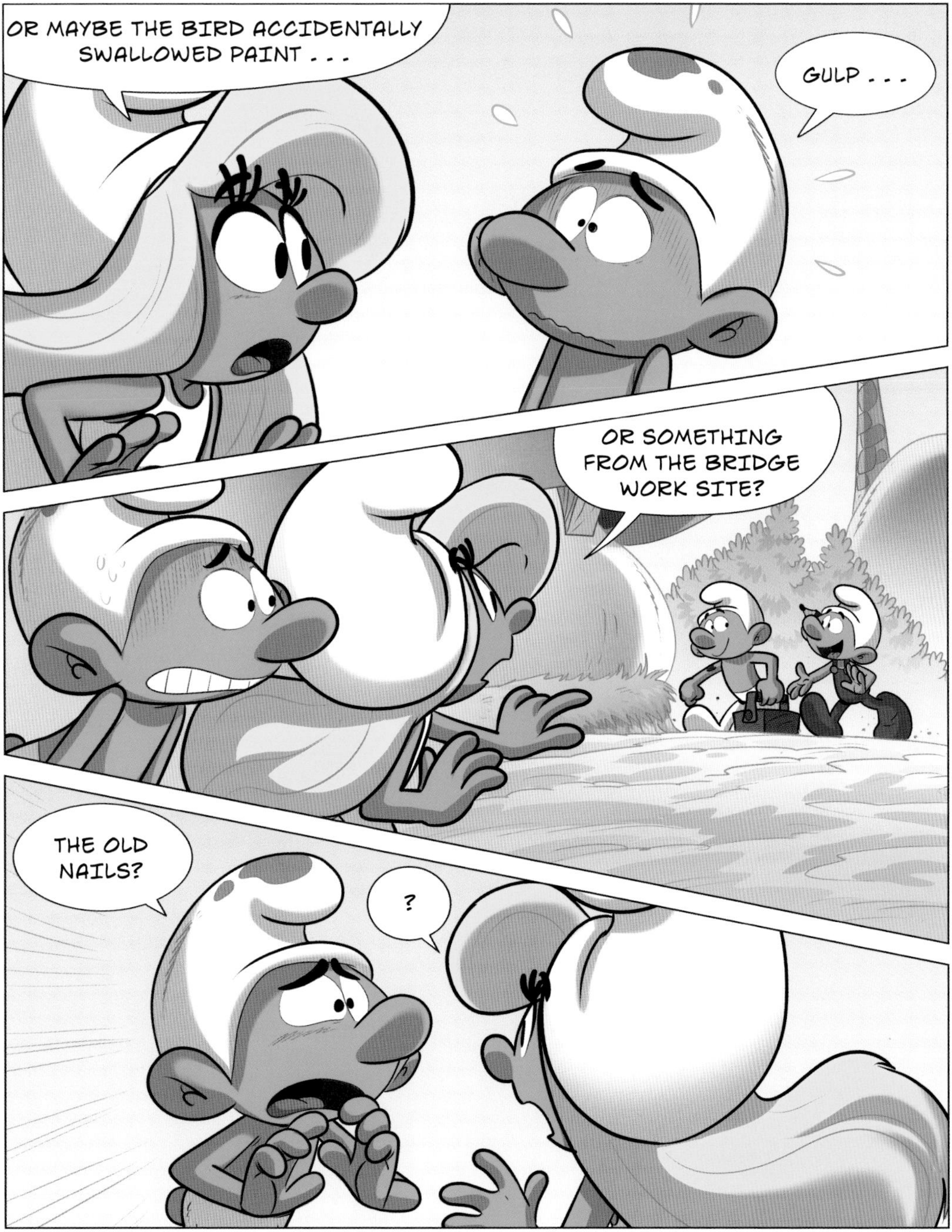
OR MAYBE THE BIRD ACCIDENTALLY SWALLOWED PAINT . . .
GULP . . .
OR SOMETHING FROM THE BRIDGE WORK SITE?
THE OLD NAILS?
?

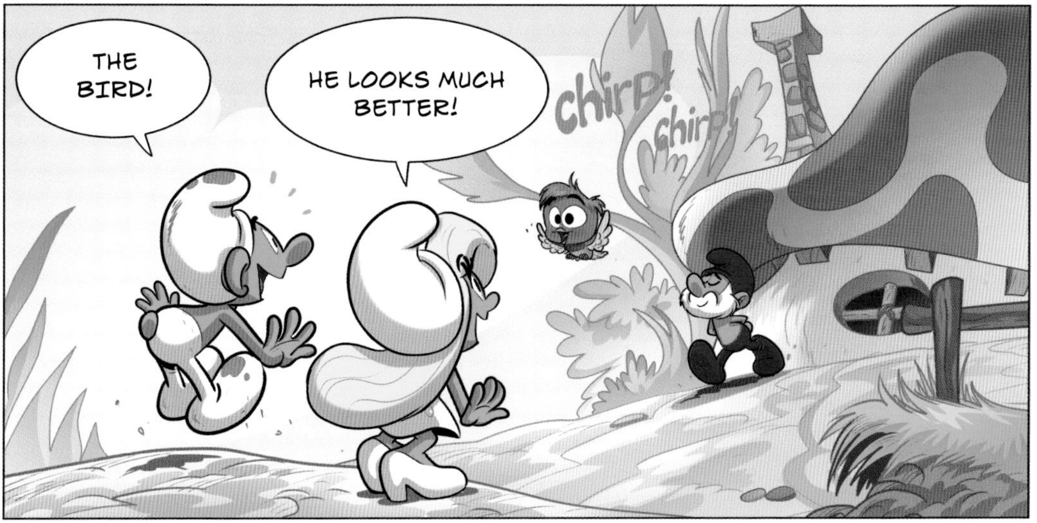
THE BIRD!
HE LOOKS MUCH BETTER!
Chirp!
Chirp!

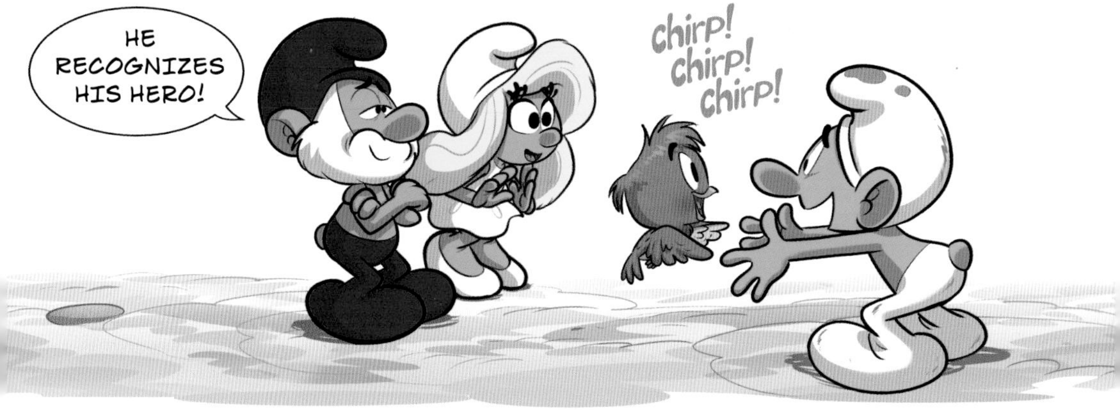
HE RECOGNIZES HIS HERO!
Chirp! Chirp! Chirp!

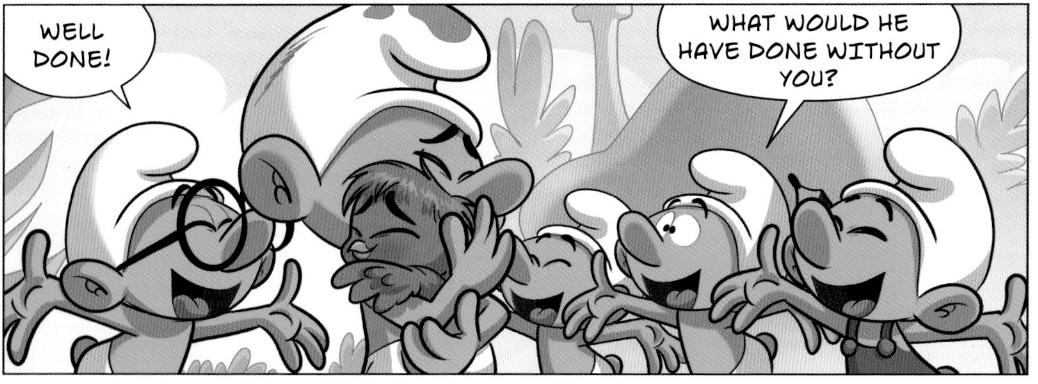
WELL DONE!
WHAT WOULD HE HAVE DONE WITHOUT YOU?

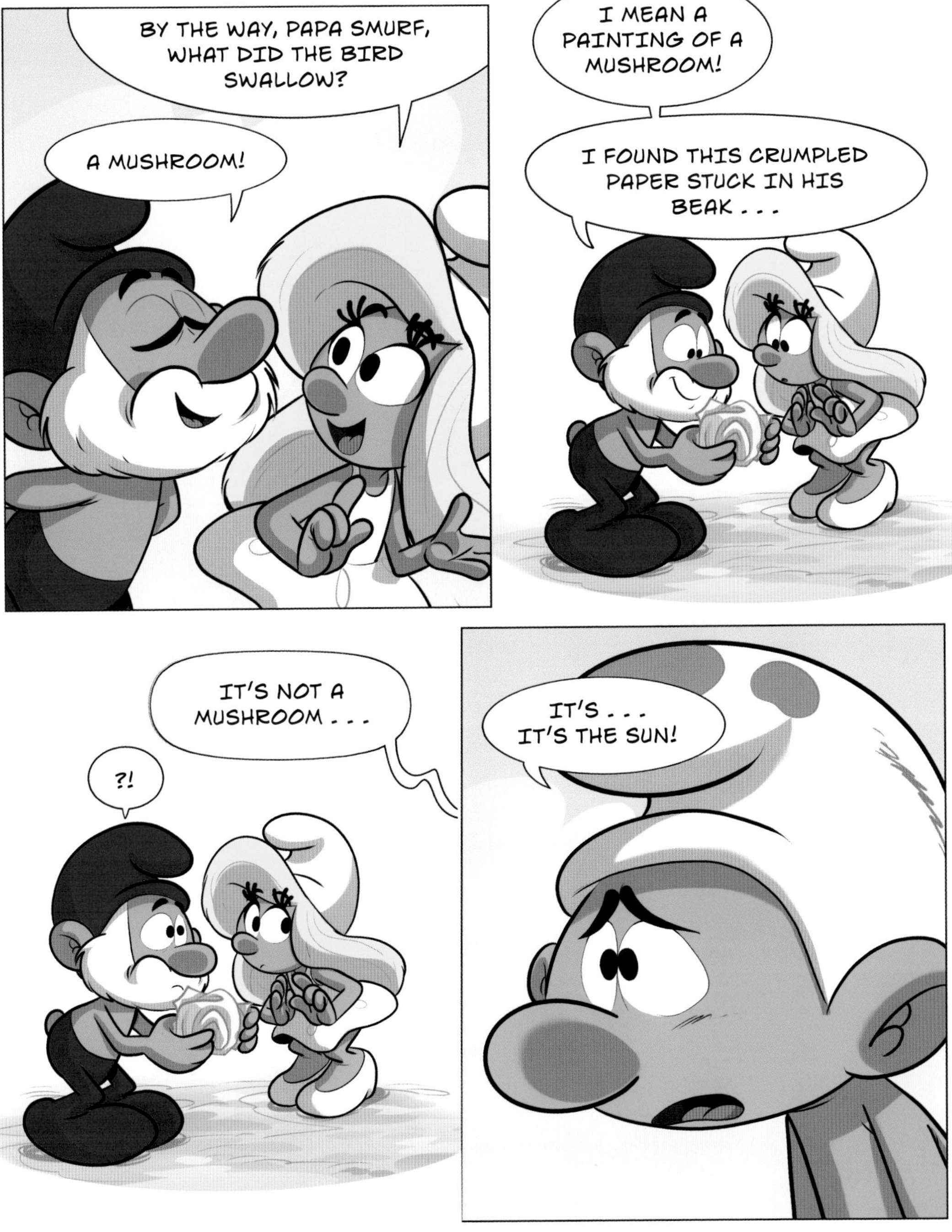
BY THE WAY, PAPA SMURF, WHAT DID THE BIRD SWALLOW?
A MUSHROOM!
I MEAN A PAINTING OF A MUSHROOM!
I FOUND THIS CRUMPLED PAPER STUCK IN HIS BEAK . . .
IT'S NOT A MUSHROOM . . .
?!
IT'S . . . IT'S THE SUN!

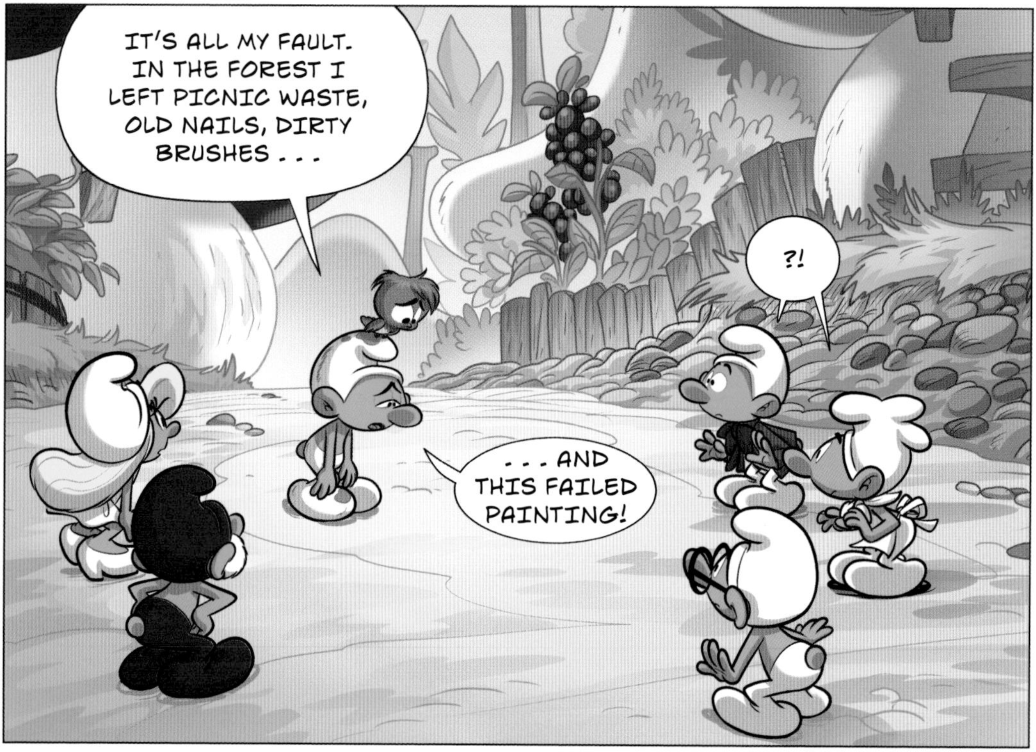
IT'S ALL MY FAULT. IN THE FOREST I LEFT PICNIC WASTE, OLD NAILS, DIRTY BRUSHES . . .
?!
. . . AND THIS FAILED PAINTING!

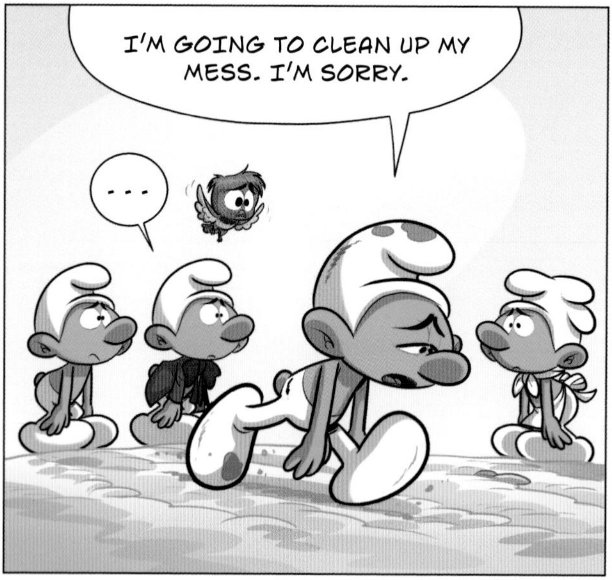
I'M GOING TO CLEAN UP MY MESS. I'M SORRY.
. . .

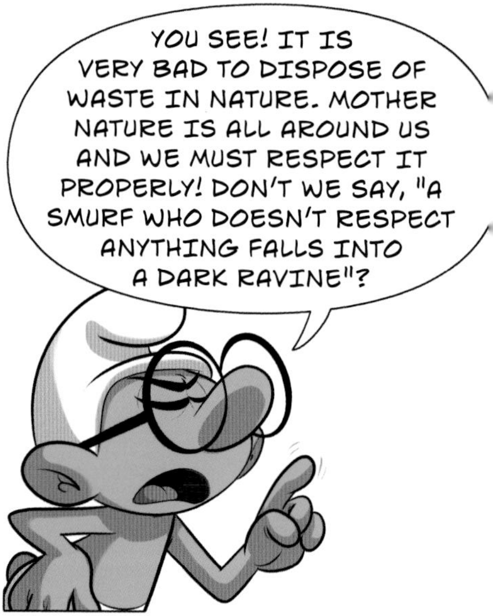
YOU SEE! IT IS VERY BAD TO DISPOSE OF WASTE IN NATURE. MOTHER NATURE IS ALL AROUND US AND WE MUST RESPECT IT PROPERLY! DON'T WE SAY, "A SMURF WHO DOESN'T RESPECT ANYTHING FALLS INTO A DARK RAVINE"?

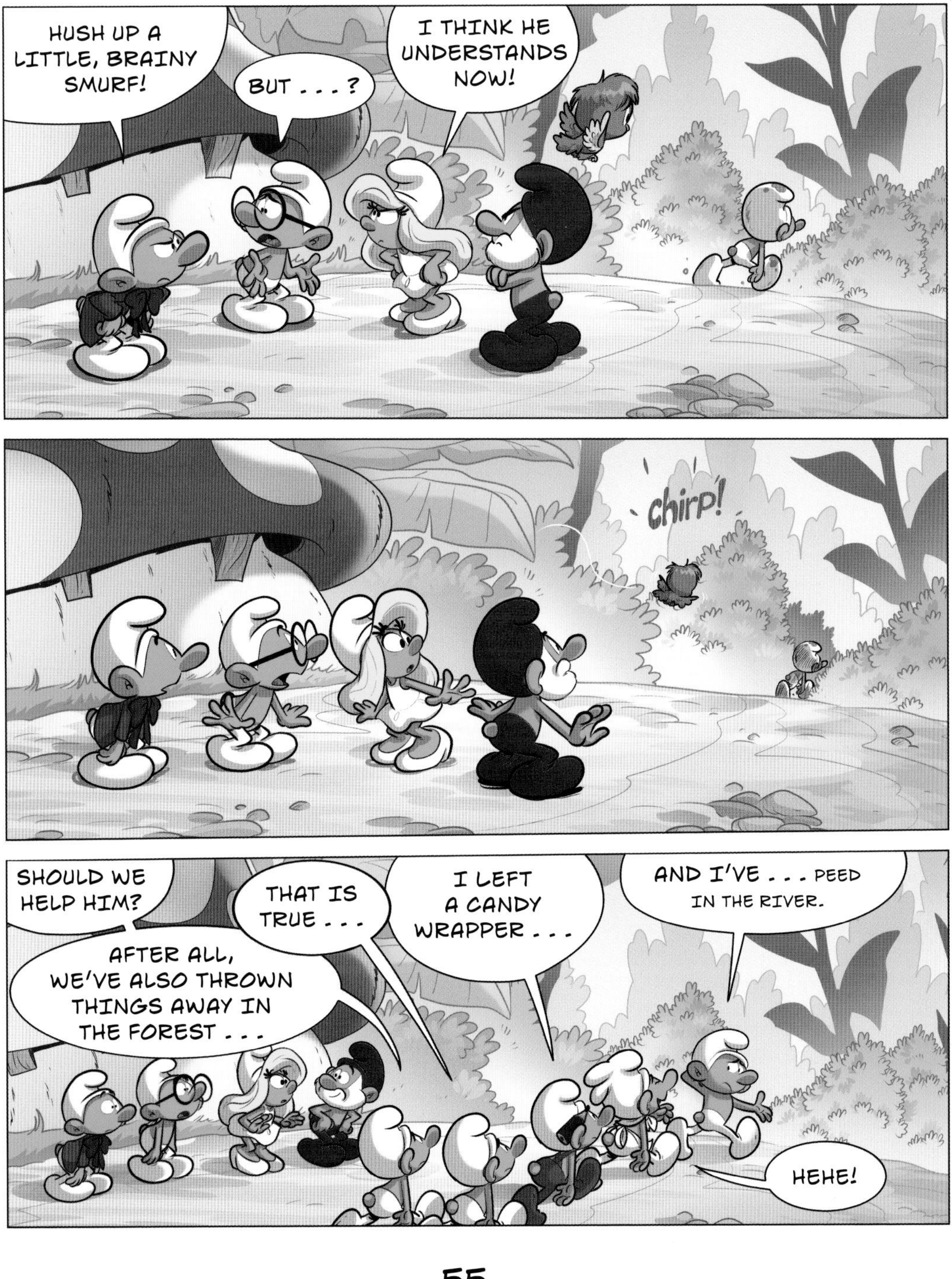
HUSH UP A LITTLE, BRAINY SMURF!
BUT . . . ?
I THINK HE UNDERSTANDS NOW!
CHIRP!
SHOULD WE HELP HIM?
AFTER ALL, WE'VE ALSO THROWN THINGS AWAY IN THE FOREST . . .
THAT IS TRUE . . .
I LEFT A CANDY WRAPPER . . .
AND I'VE . . . PEED IN THE RIVER.
HEHE!

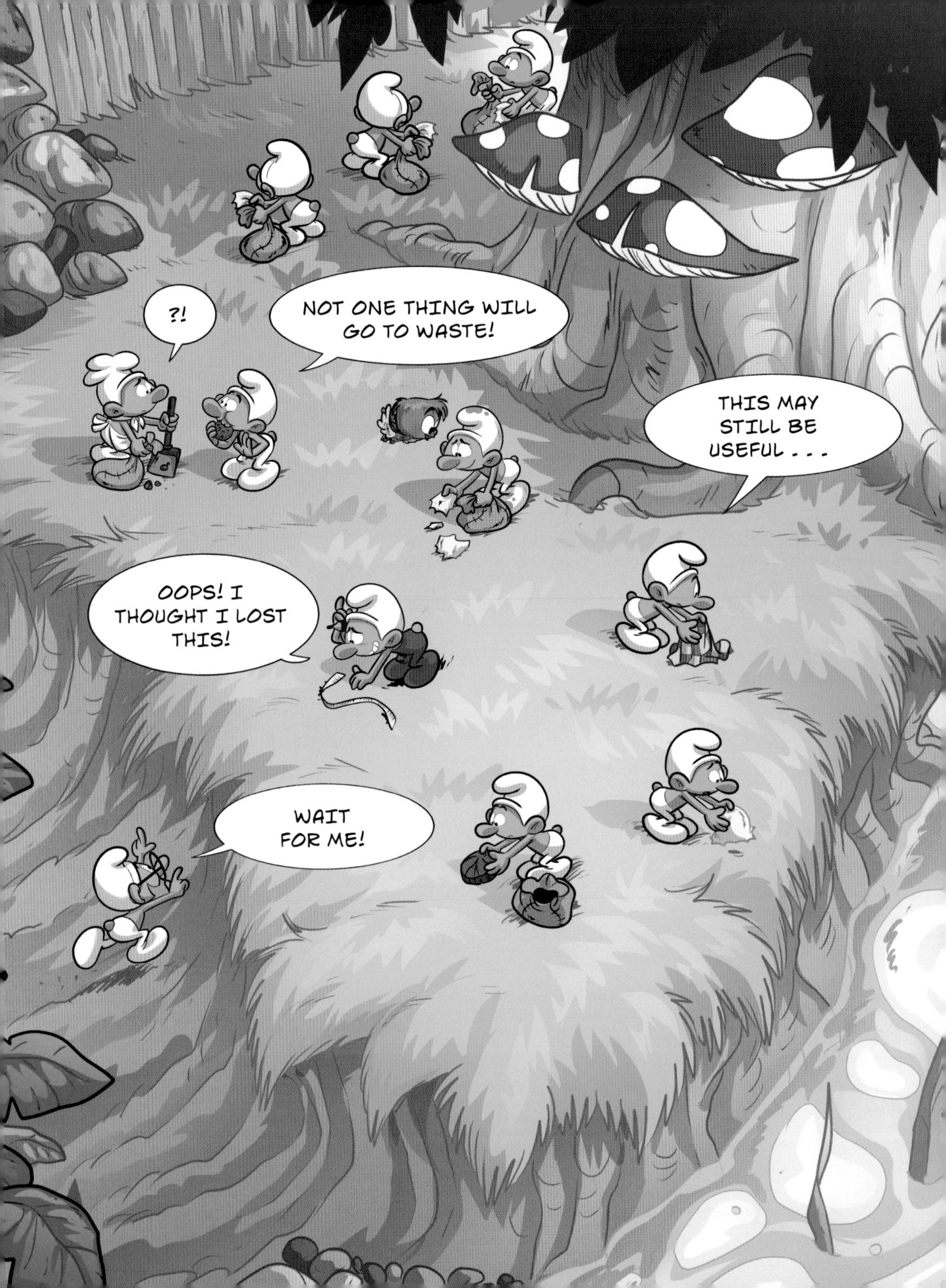
?!
NOT ONE THING WILL GO TO WASTE!
THIS MAY STILL BE USEFUL . . .
OOPS! I THOUGHT I LOST THIS!
WAIT FOR ME!

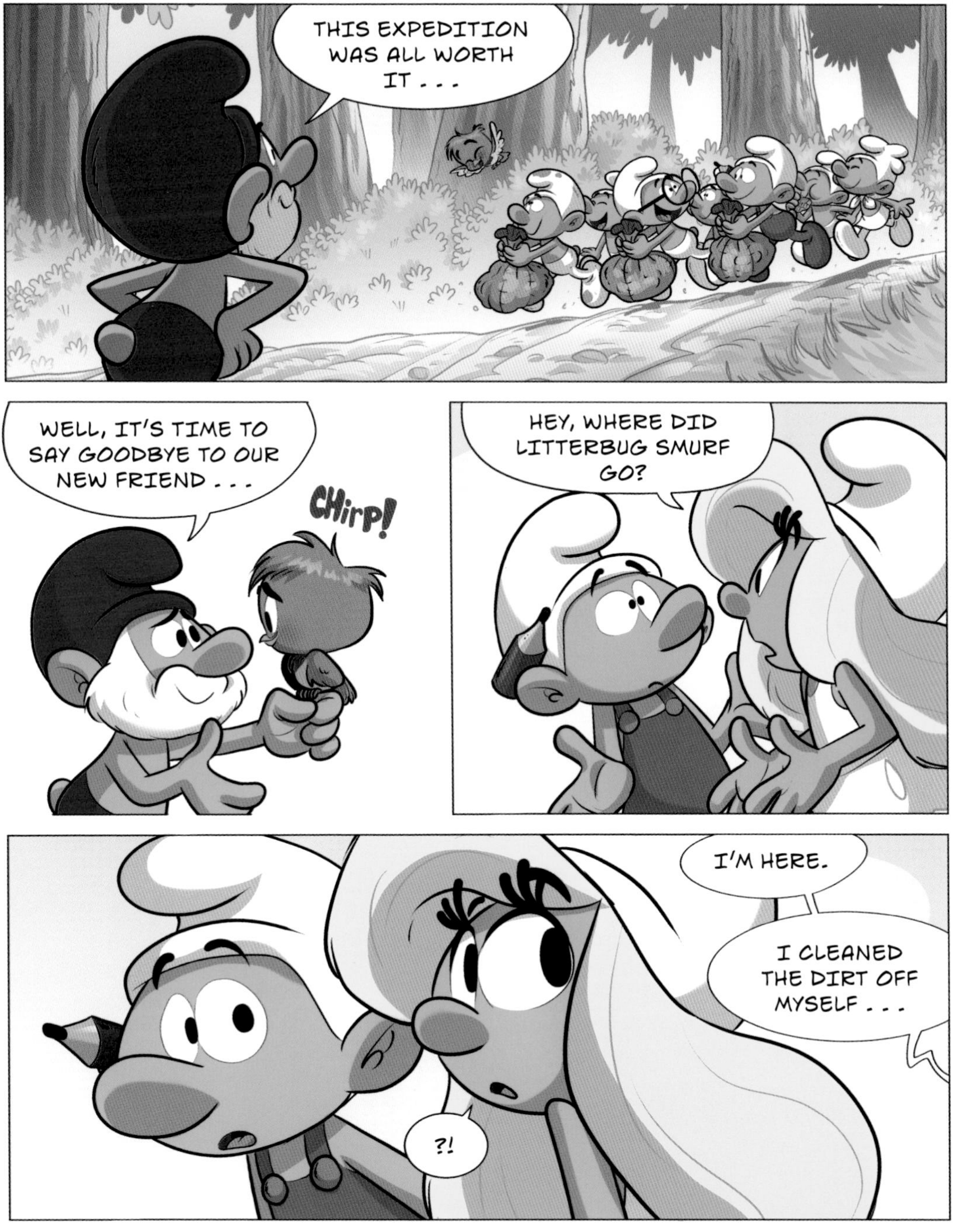

THIS EXPEDITION WAS ALL WORTH IT . . .
WELL, IT'S TIME TO SAY GOODBYE TO OUR NEW FRIEND . . .
CHIRP!
HEY, WHERE DID LITTERBUG SMURF GO?
I'M HERE.
I CLEANED THE DIRT OFF MYSELF . . .
?!

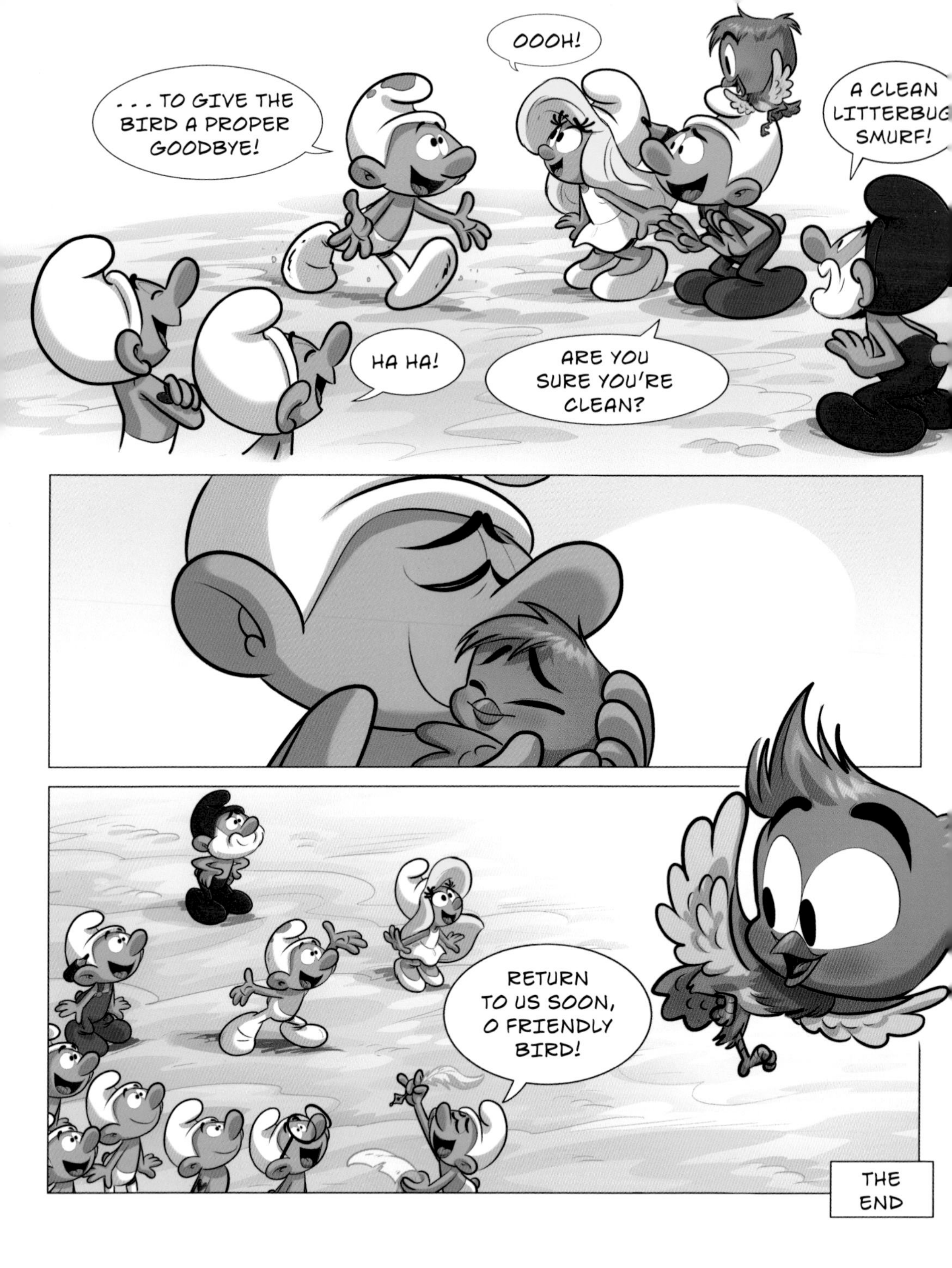
. . . TO GIVE THE BIRD A PROPER GOODBYE!
OOOH!
A CLEAN LITTERBUG SMURF!
HA HA!
ARE YOU SURE YOU'RE CLEAN?
RETURN TO US SOON, O FRIENDLY BIRD!
THE END

THE SMURF THAT LOST A FRIEND

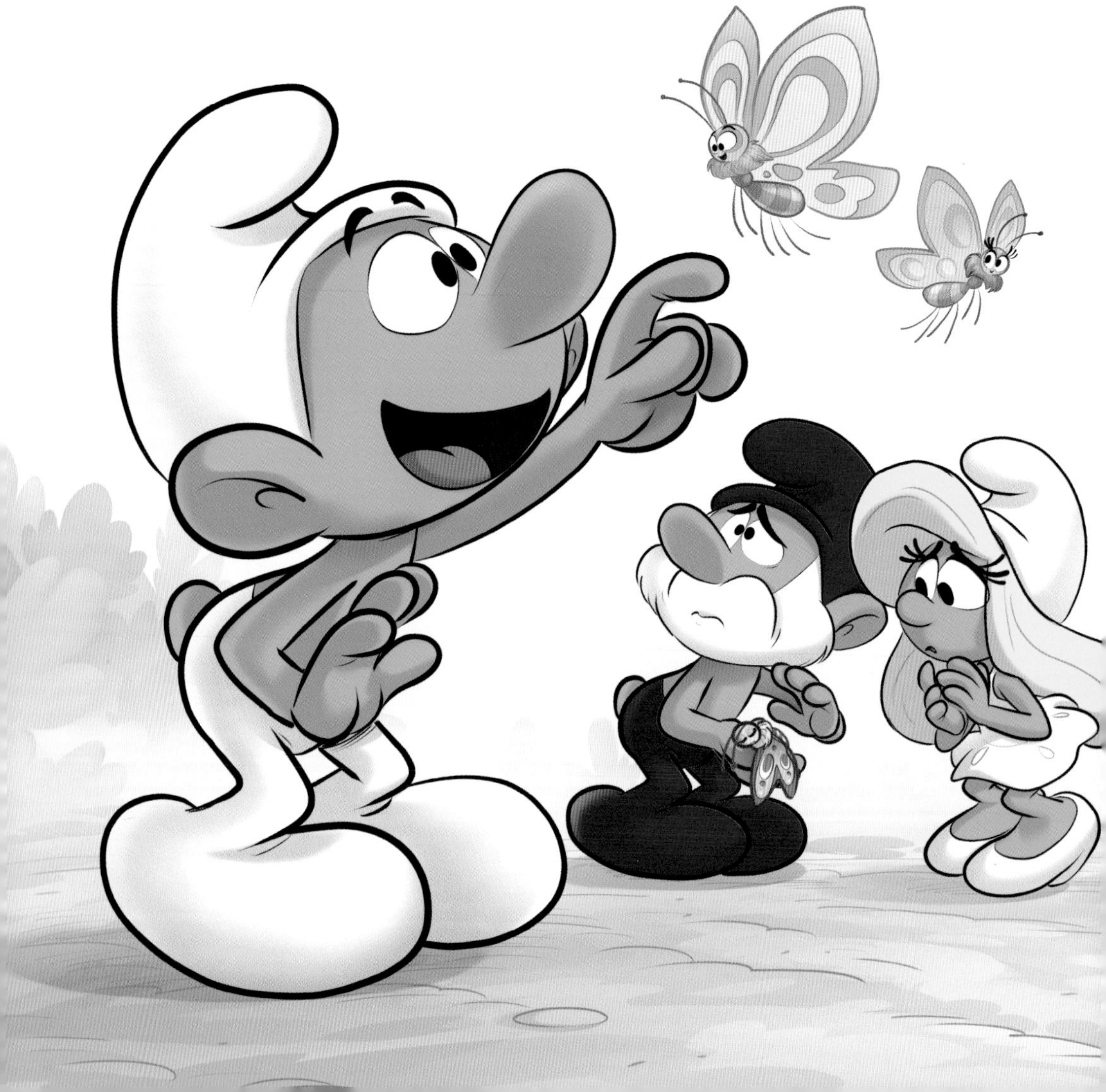

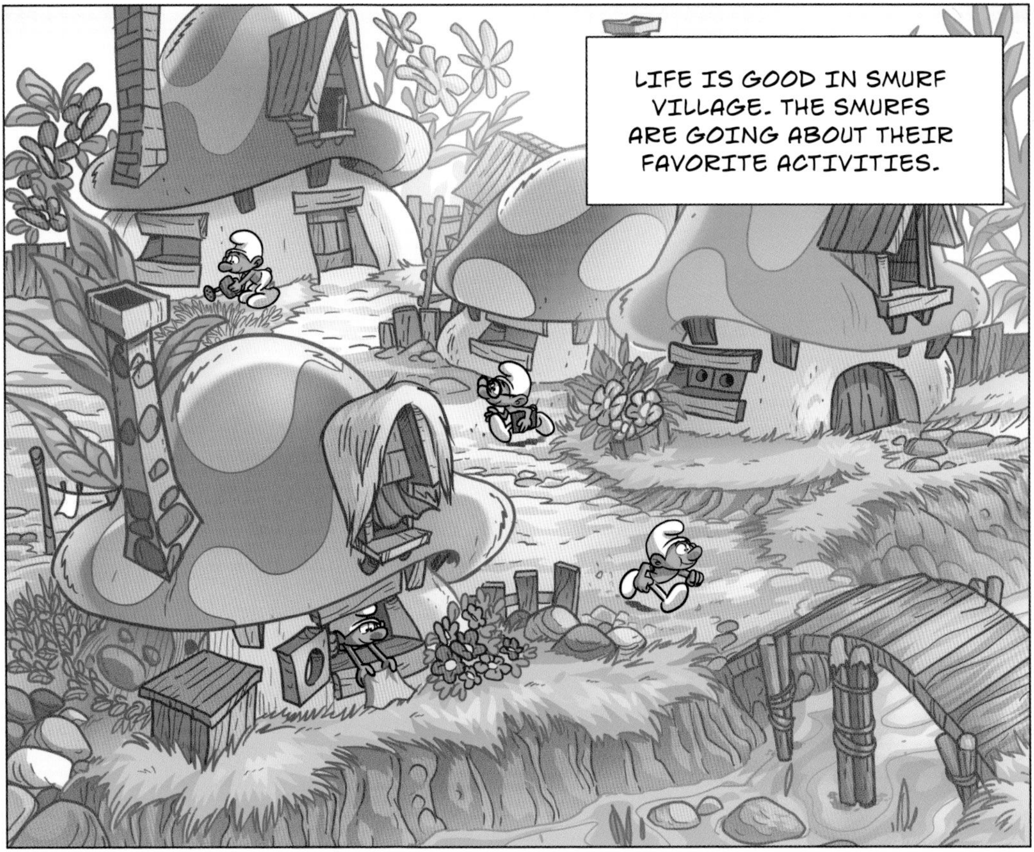
LIFE IS GOOD IN SMURF VILLAGE. THE SMURFS ARE GOING ABOUT THEIR FAVORITE ACTIVITIES.

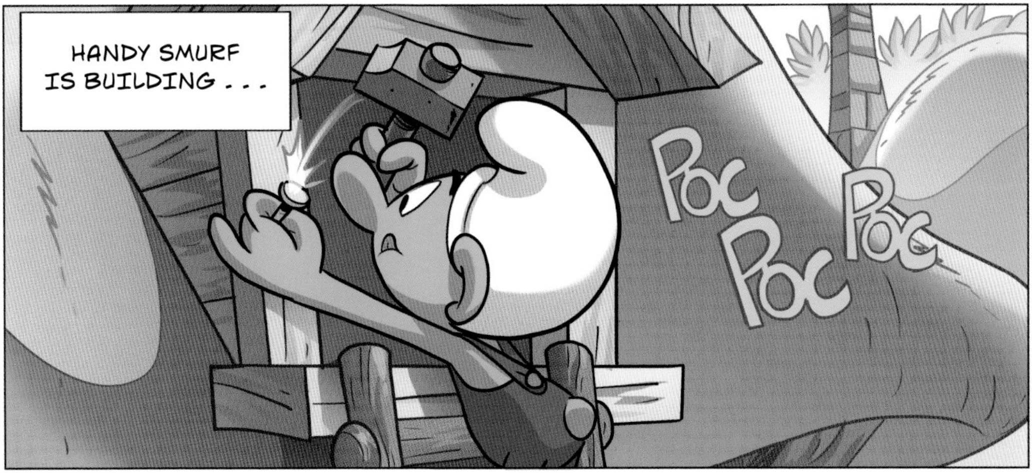
HANDY SMURF IS BUILDING . . .
POC
POC
POC

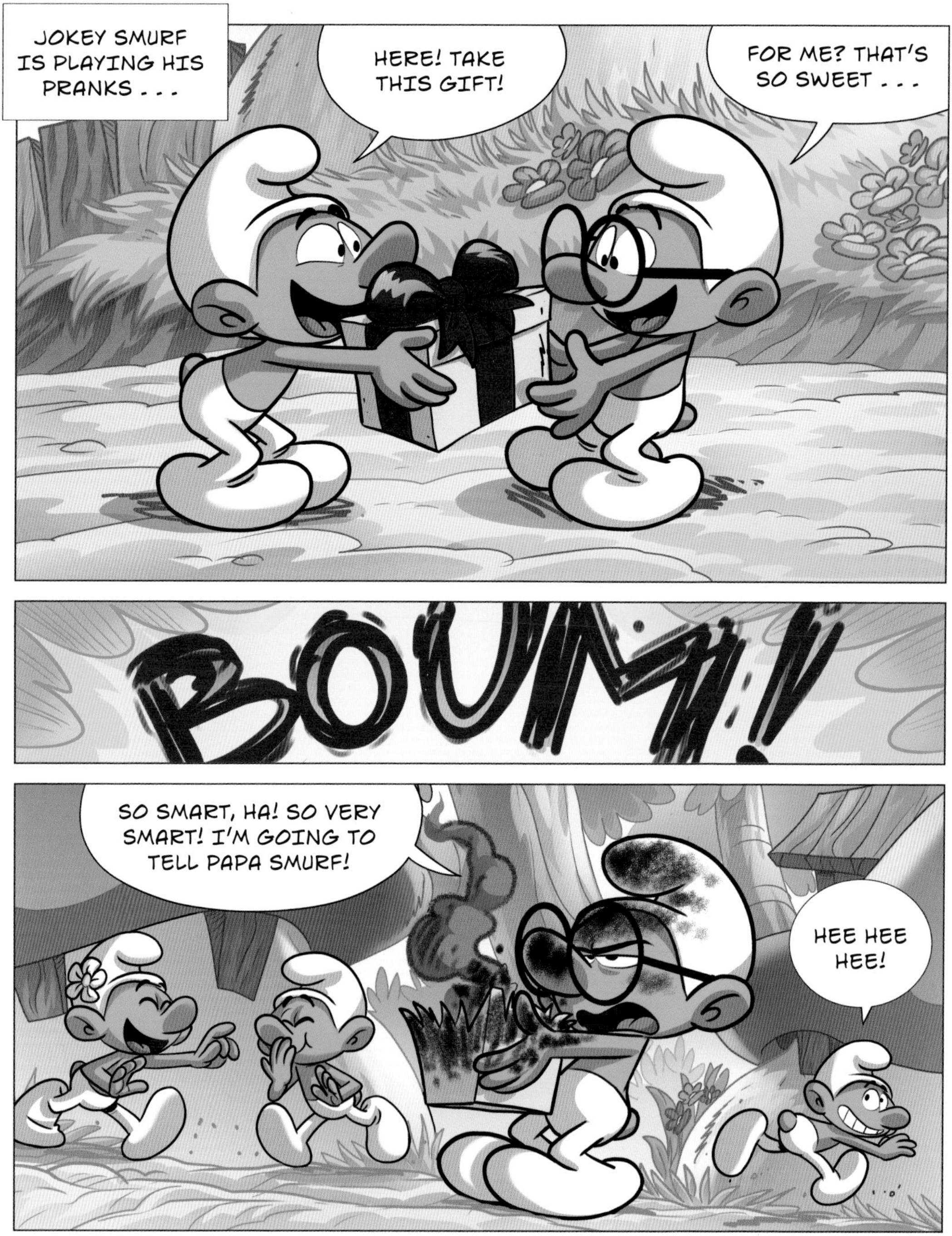
JOKEY SMURF IS PLAYING HIS PRANKS . . .
HERE! TAKE THIS GIFT!
FOR ME? THAT'S SO SWEET . . .
BOUM!
SO SMART, HA! SO VERY SMART! I'M GOING TO TELL PAPA SMURF!
HEE HEE HEE!

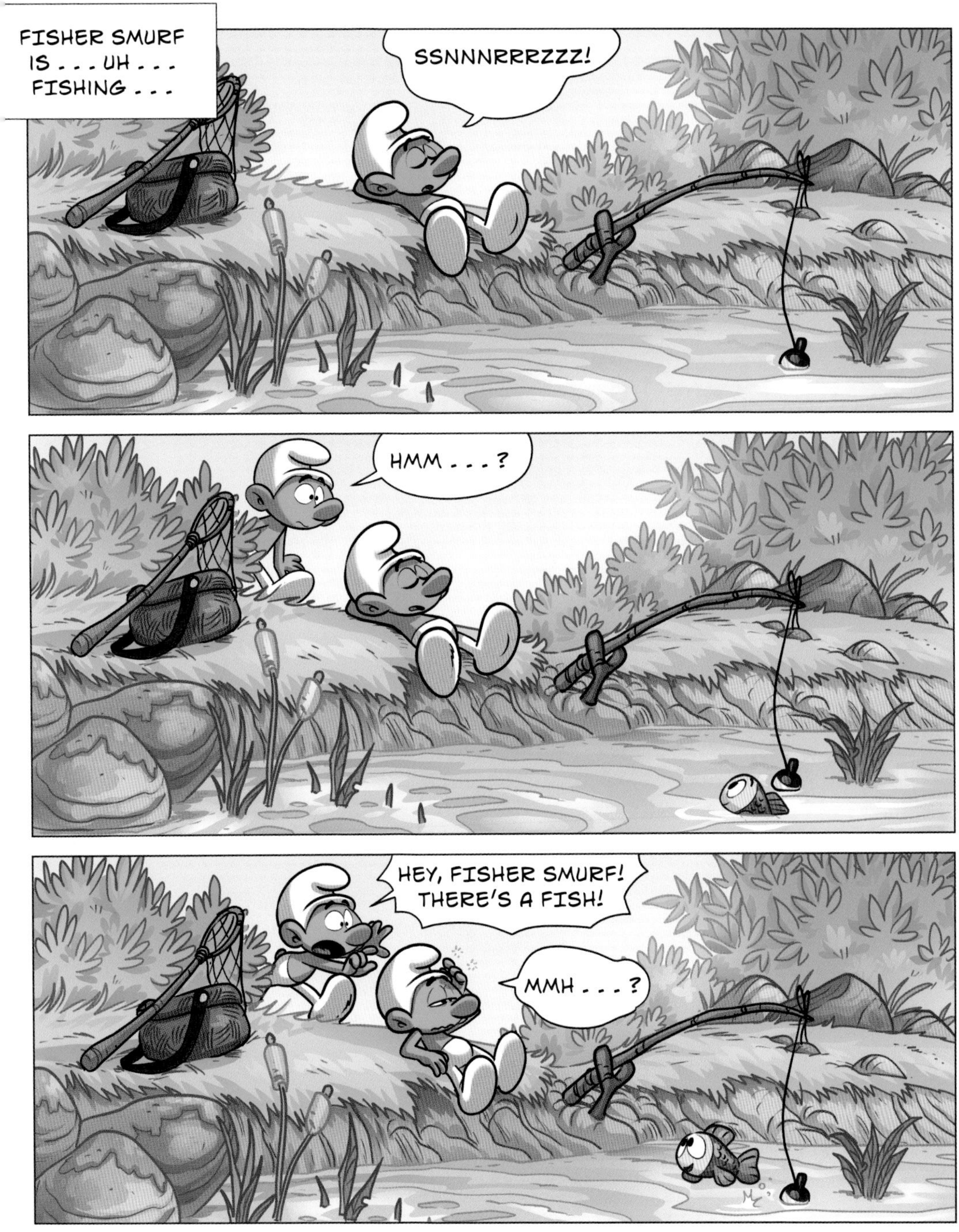
FISHER SMURF IS . . . UH . . . FISHING . . .
SSNNNRRRZZZ!
HMM . . . ?
HEY, FISHER SMURF! THERE'S A FISH!
MMH . . . ?

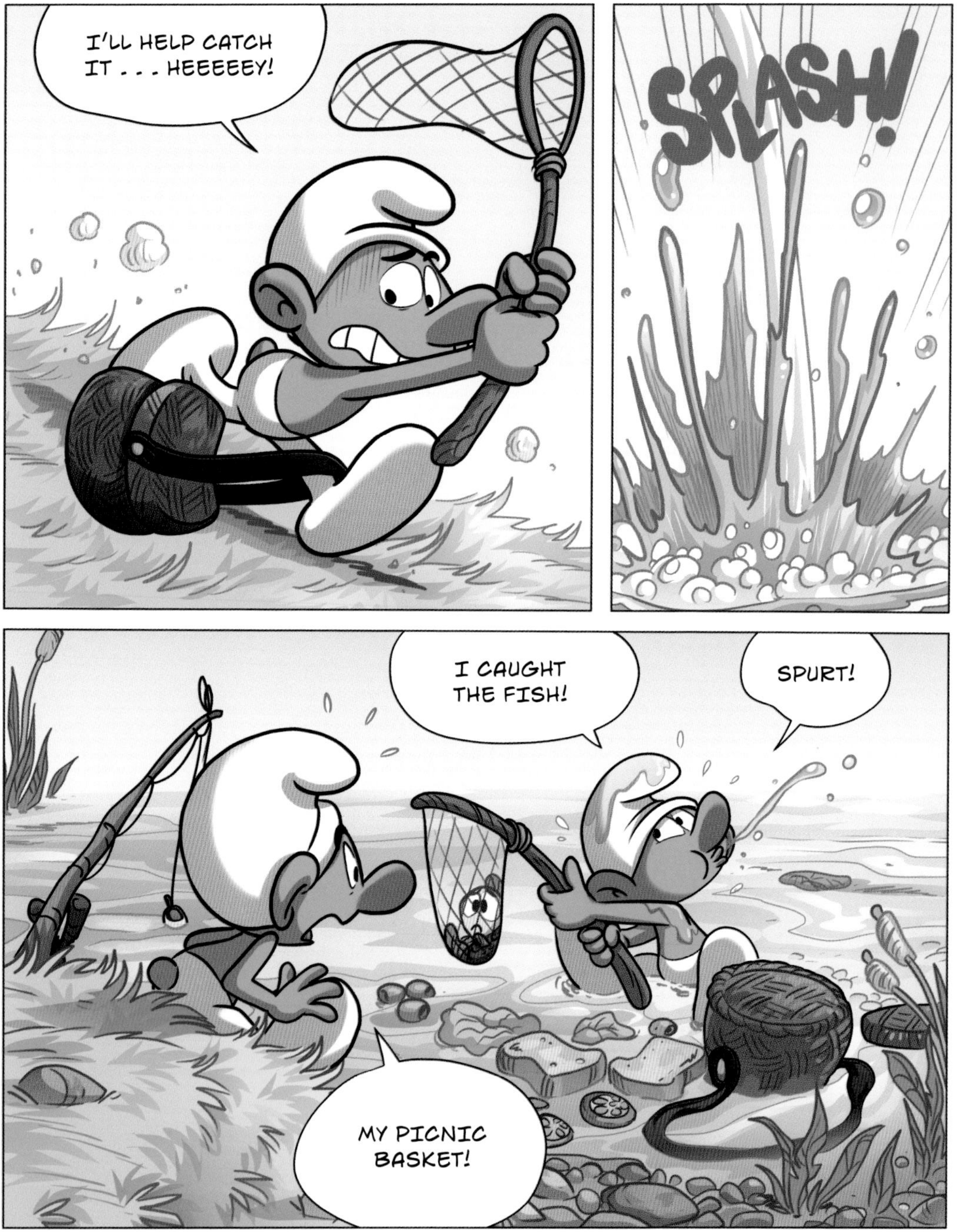
I'LL HELP CATCH IT . . . HEEEEEY!
SPLASH!
I CAUGHT THE FISH!
SPURT!
MY PICNIC BASKET!

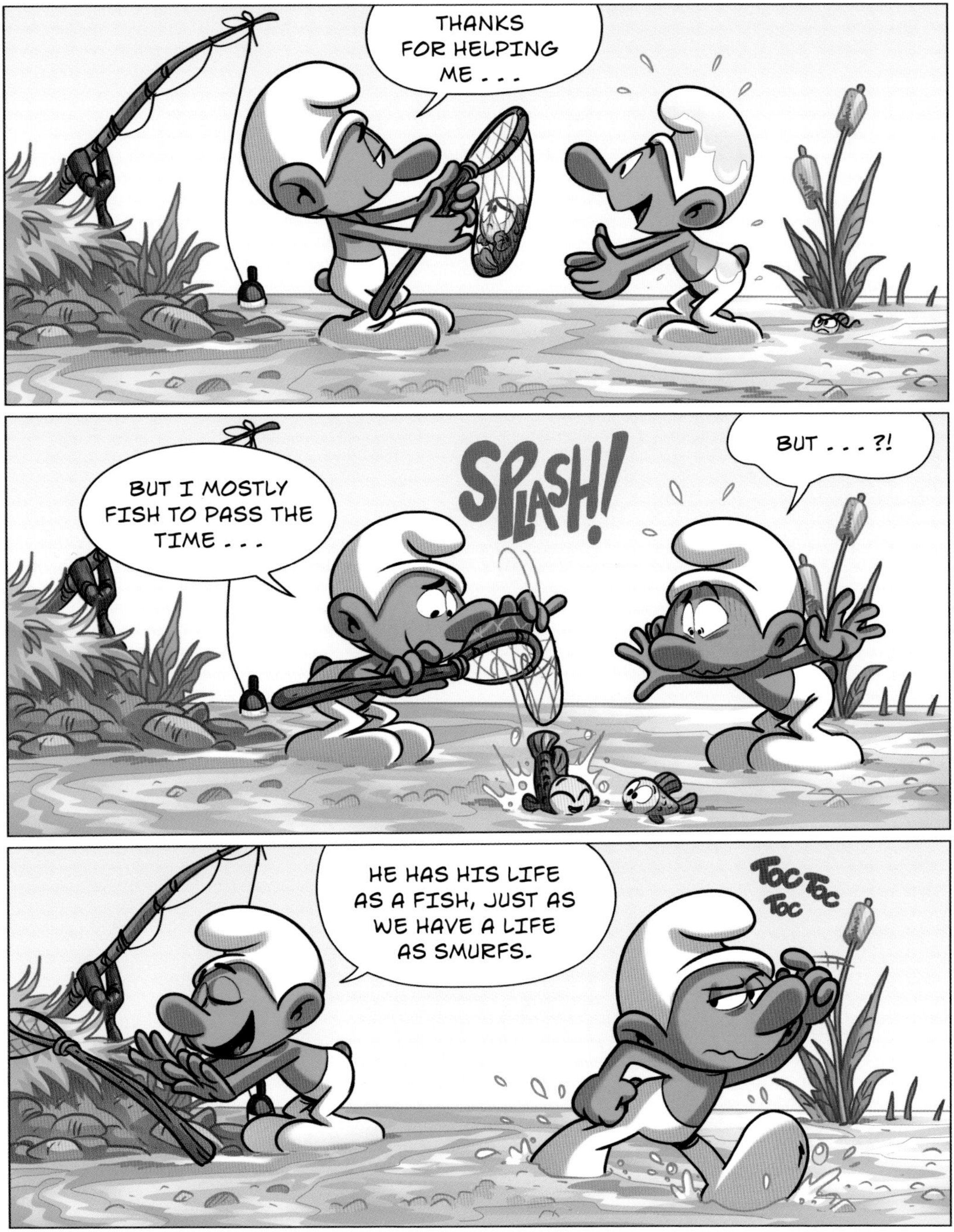
THANKS FOR HELPING ME . . .
BUT I MOSTLY FISH TO PASS THE TIME . . .
SPLASH!
BUT . . . ?!
HE HAS HIS LIFE AS A FISH, JUST AS WE HAVE A LIFE AS SMURFS.
TOC TOC TOC

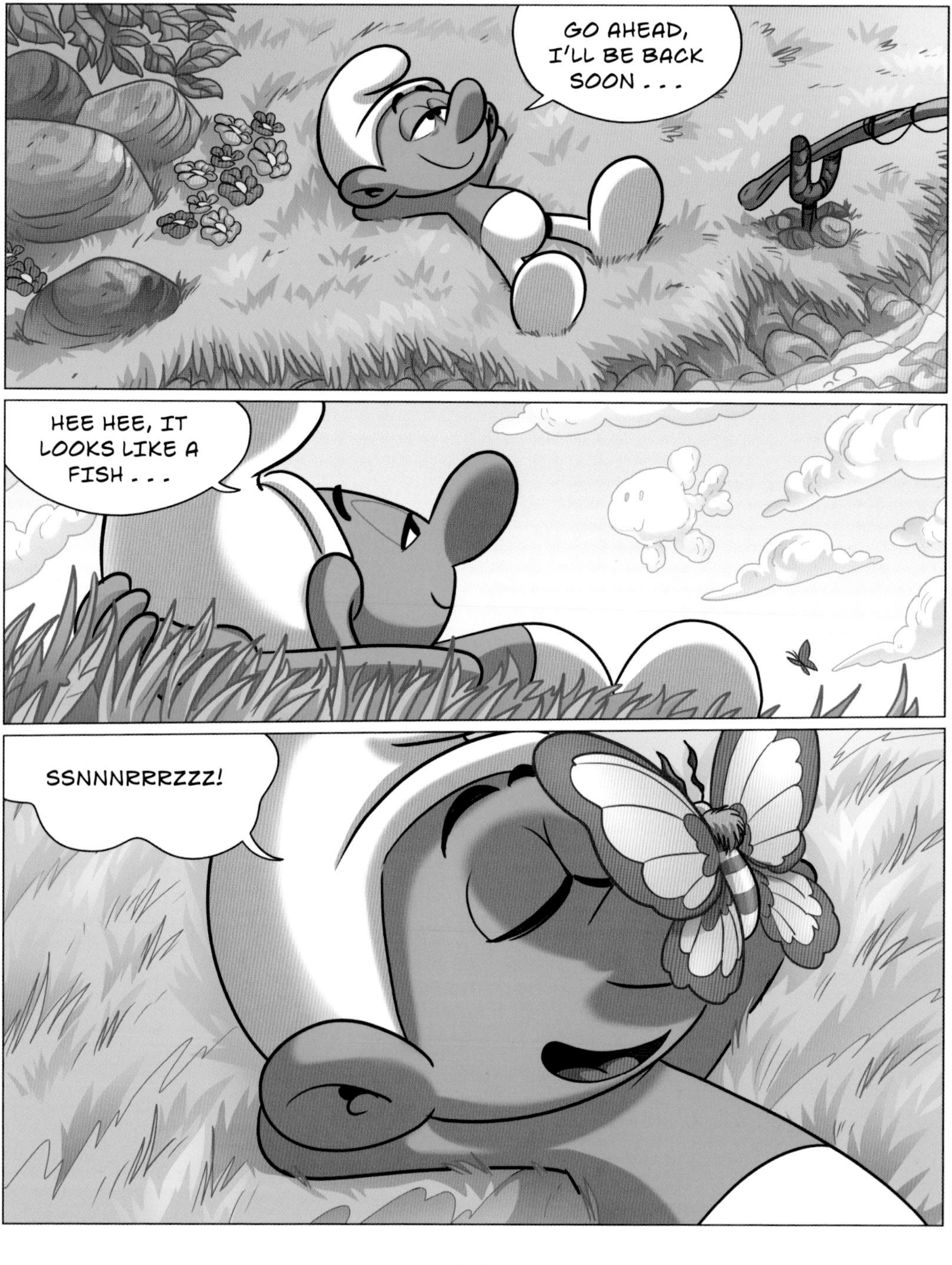

GO AHEAD, I'LL BE BACK SOON . . .
HEE HEE, IT LOOKS LIKE A FISH . . .
SSNNNRRRZZZ!

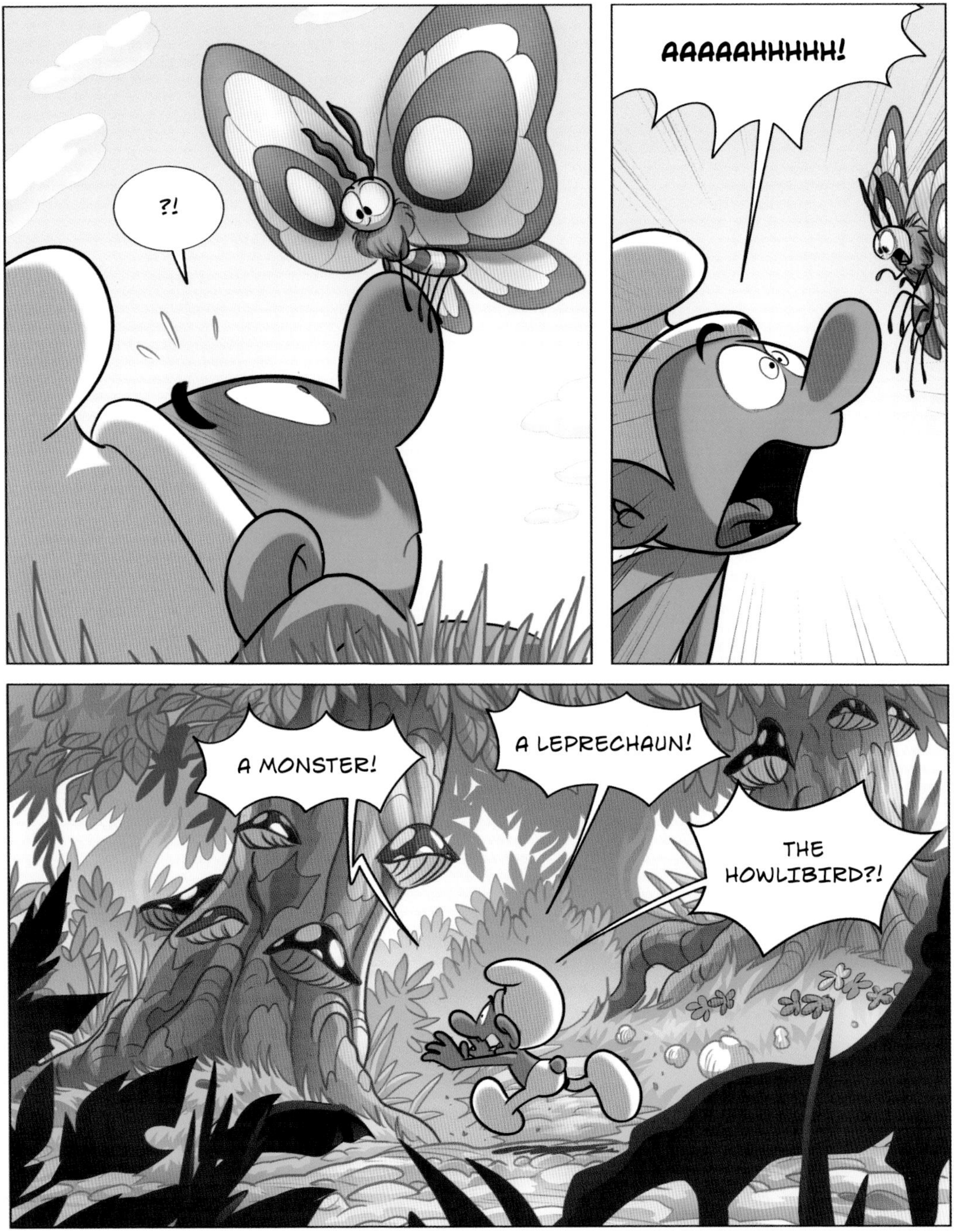
?!
AAAAAHHHHH!
A MONSTER!
A LEPRECHAUN!
THE HOWLIBIRD?!

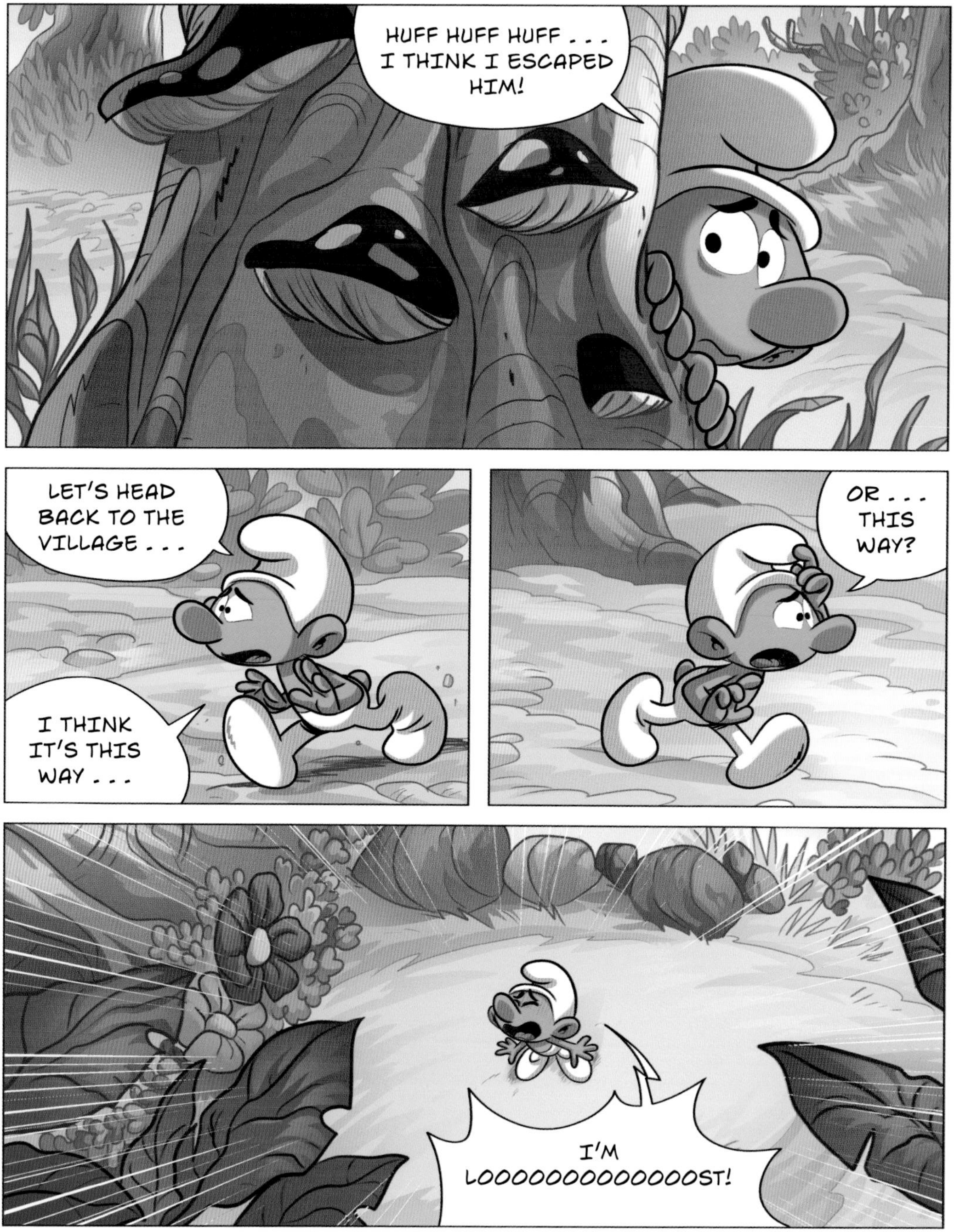
HUFF HUFF HUFF . . .
I THINK I ESCAPED HIM!
LET'S HEAD BACK TO THE VILLAGE . . .
I THINK IT'S THIS WAY . . .
OR . . . THIS WAY?
I'M LOOOOOOOOOOOOOST!

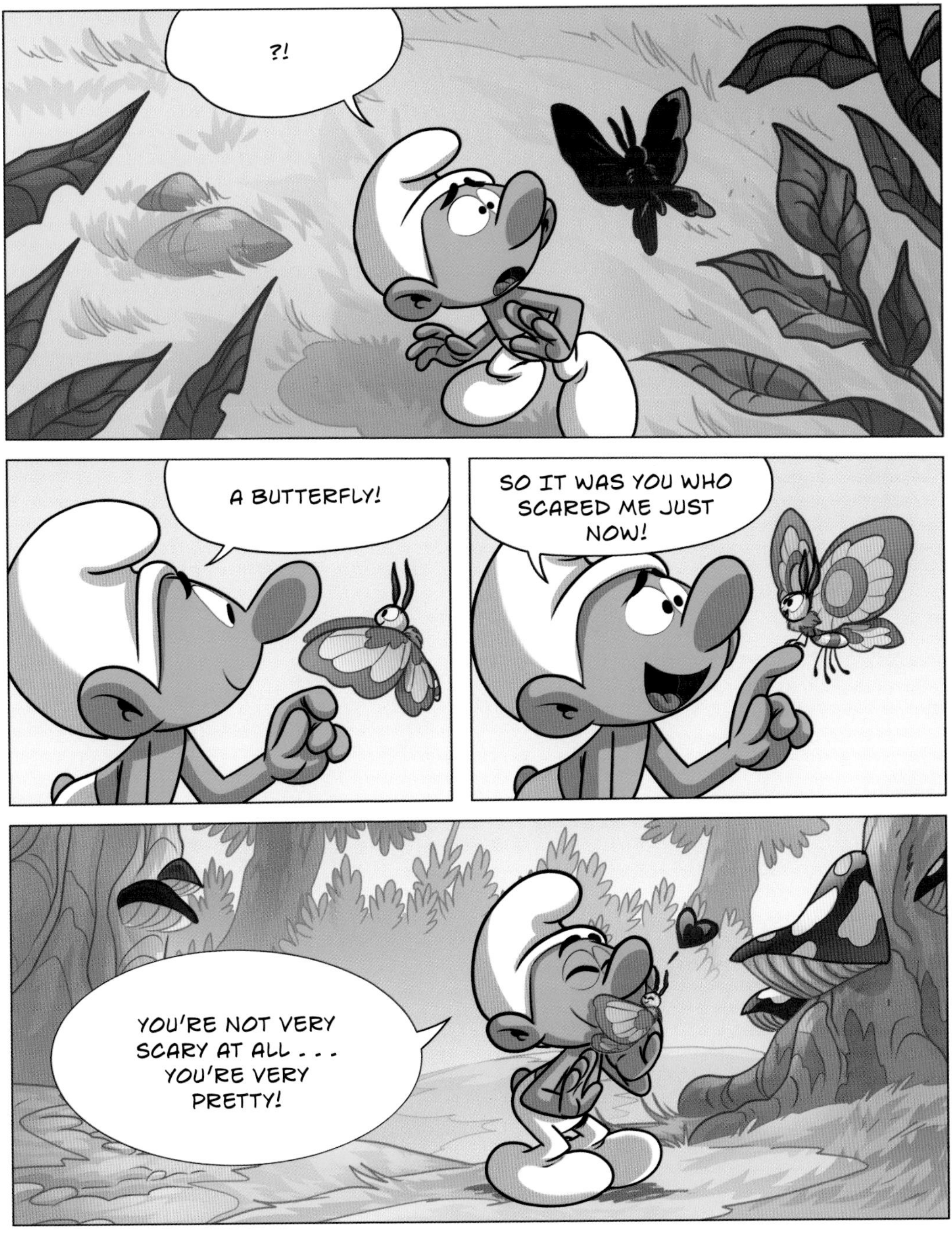
?!
A BUTTERFLY!
SO IT WAS YOU WHO SCARED ME JUST NOW!
YOU'RE NOT VERY SCARY AT ALL . . . YOU'RE VERY PRETTY!

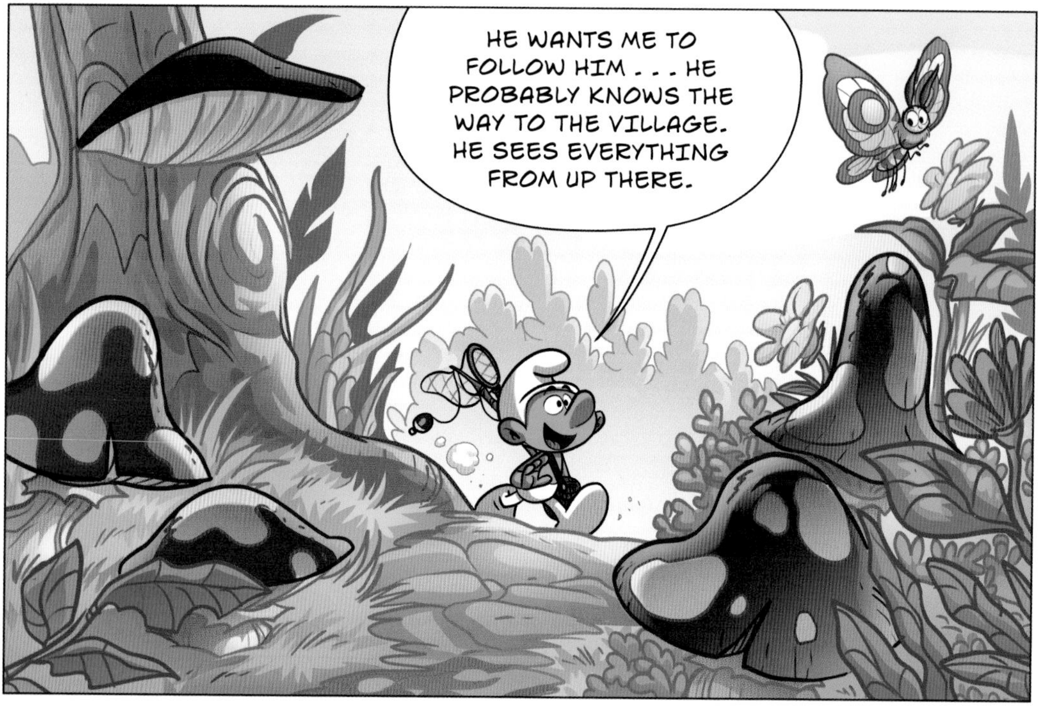
HE WANTS ME TO FOLLOW HIM . . . HE PROBABLY KNOWS THE WAY TO THE VILLAGE. HE SEES EVERYTHING FROM UP THERE.

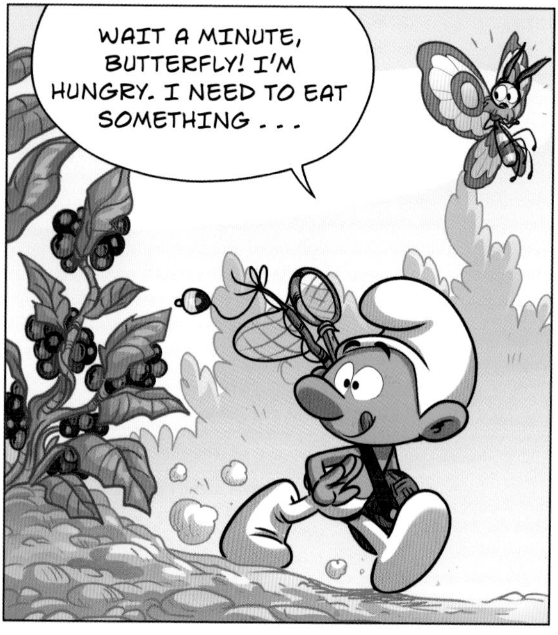
WAIT A MINUTE, BUTTERFLY! I'M HUNGRY. I NEED TO EAT SOMETHING . . .

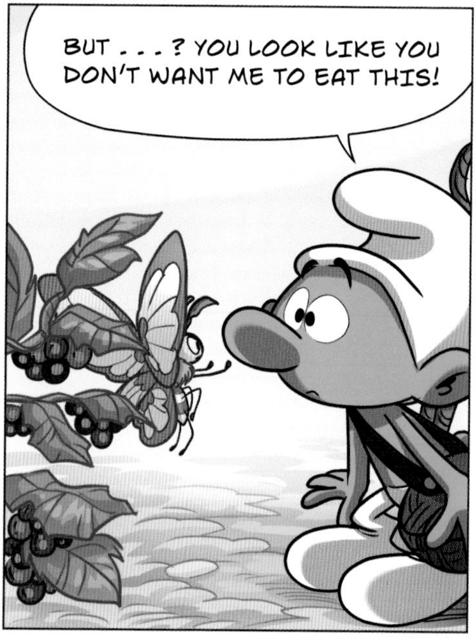
BUT . . . ? YOU LOOK LIKE YOU DON'T WANT ME TO EAT THIS!

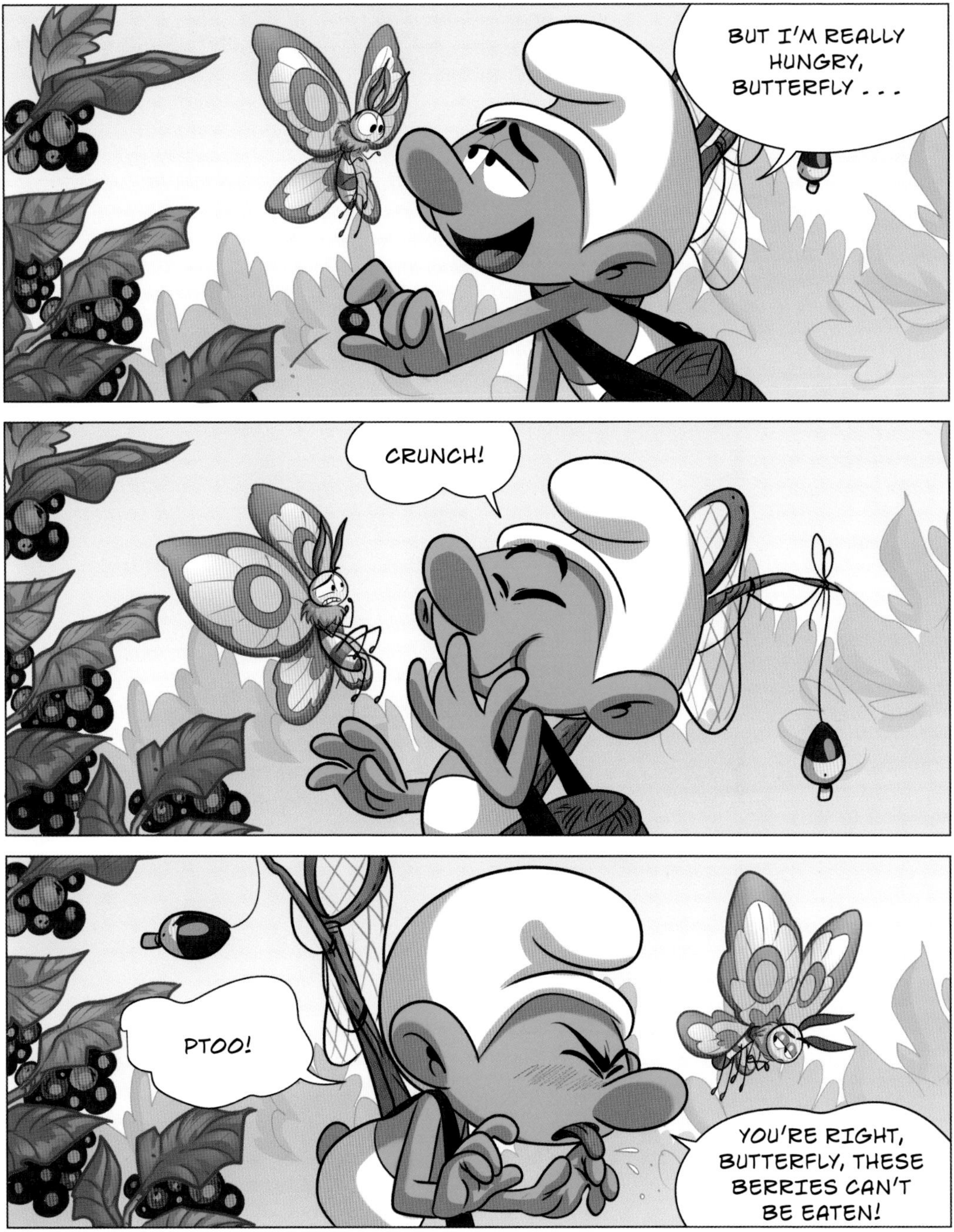
BUT I'M REALLY HUNGRY, BUTTERFLY . . .
CRUNCH!
PTOO!
YOU'RE RIGHT, BUTTERFLY, THESE BERRIES CAN'T BE EATEN!

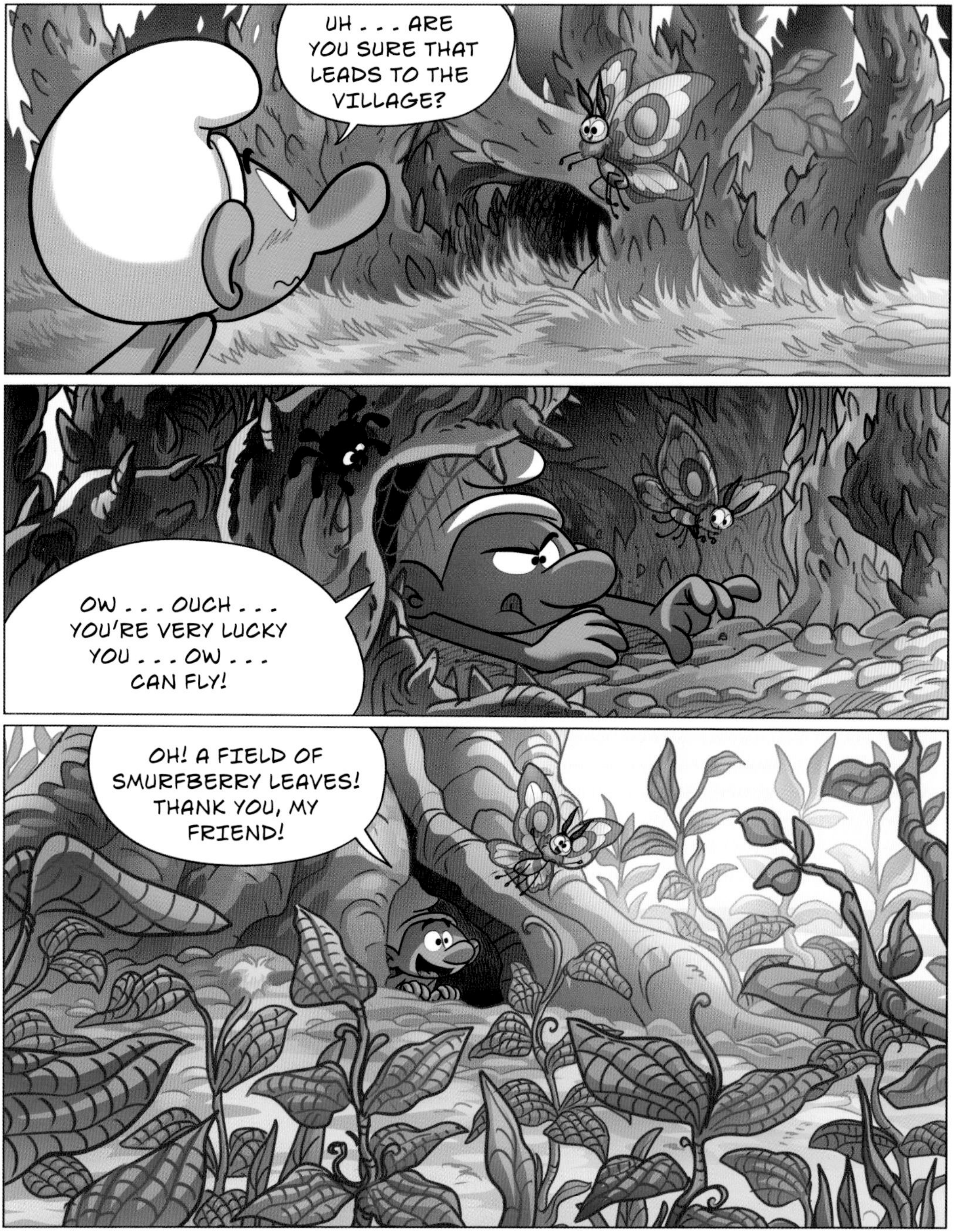
UH . . . ARE YOU SURE THAT LEADS TO THE VILLAGE?
OW . . . OUCH . . . YOU'RE VERY LUCKY YOU . . . OW . . . CAN FLY!
OH! A FIELD OF SMURFBERRY LEAVES! THANK YOU, MY FRIEND!

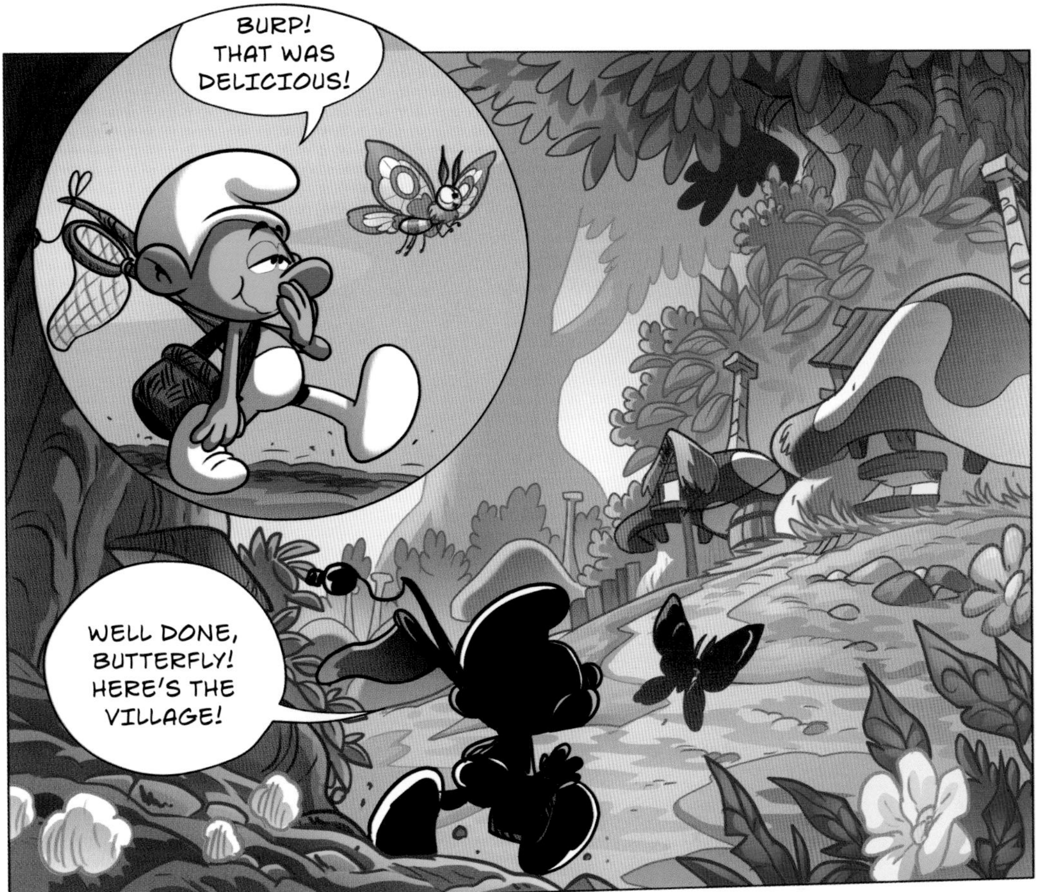
BURP! THAT WAS DELICIOUS!
WELL DONE, BUTTERFLY! HERE'S THE VILLAGE!

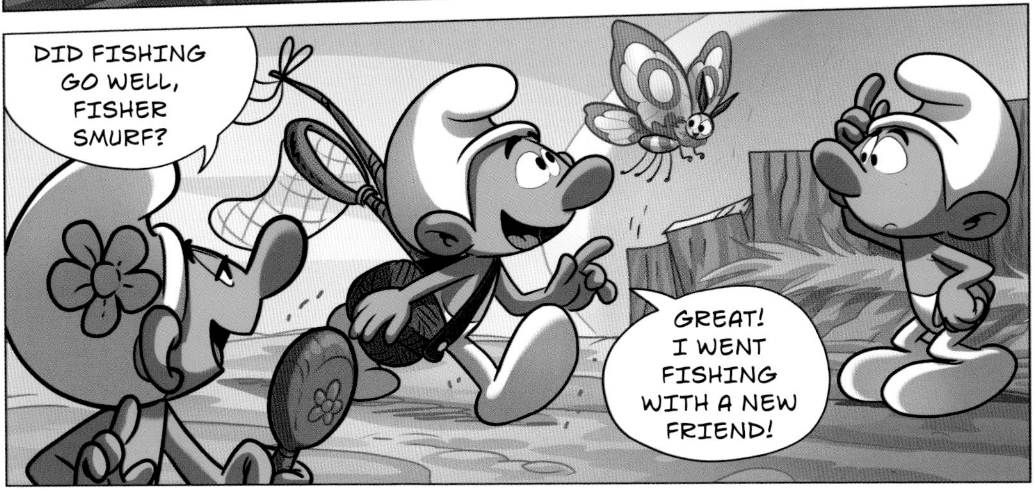
DID FISHING GO WELL, FISHER SMURF?
GREAT! I WENT FISHING WITH A NEW FRIEND!

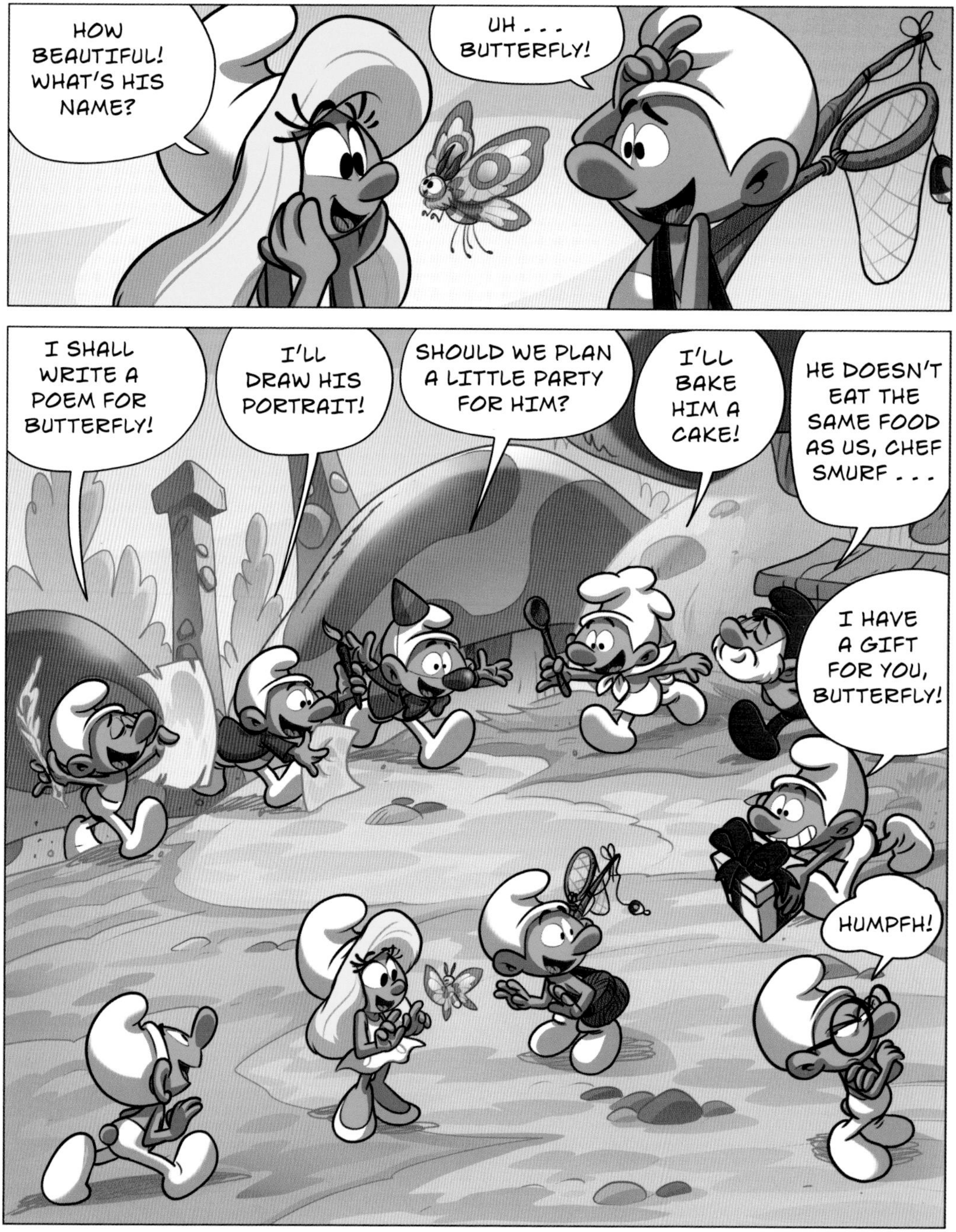
HOW BEAUTIFUL! WHAT'S HIS NAME?
UH . . . BUTTERFLY!
I SHALL WRITE A POEM FOR BUTTERFLY!
I'LL DRAW HIS PORTRAIT!
SHOULD WE PLAN A LITTLE PARTY FOR HIM?
I'LL BAKE HIM A CAKE!
HE DOESN'T EAT THE SAME FOOD AS US, CHEF SMURF . . .
I HAVE A GIFT FOR YOU, BUTTERFLY!
HUMPFH!

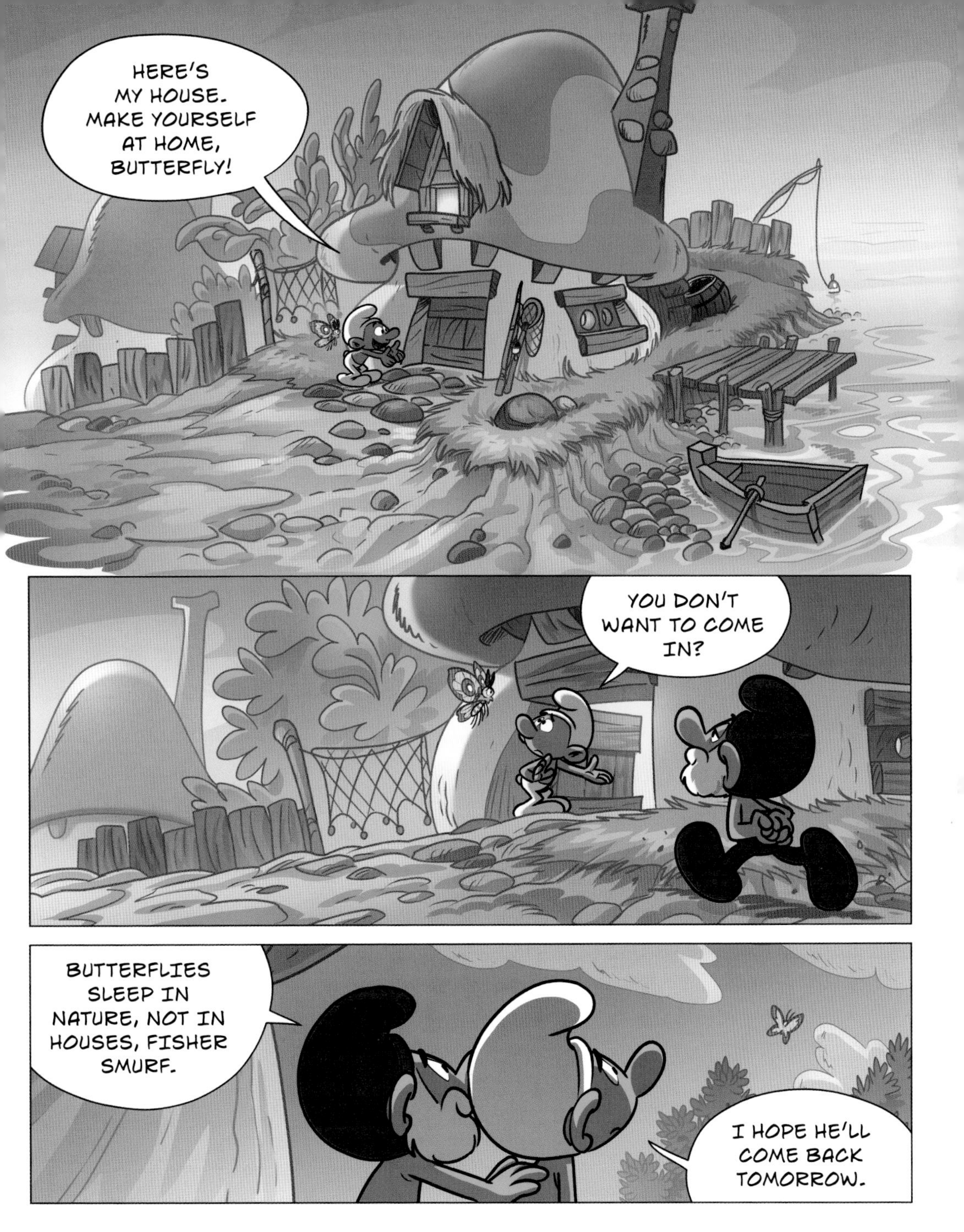
HERE'S MY HOUSE. MAKE YOURSELF AT HOME, BUTTERFLY!
YOU DON'T WANT TO COME IN?
BUTTERFLIES SLEEP IN NATURE, NOT IN HOUSES, FISHER SMURF.
I HOPE HE'LL COME BACK TOMORROW.

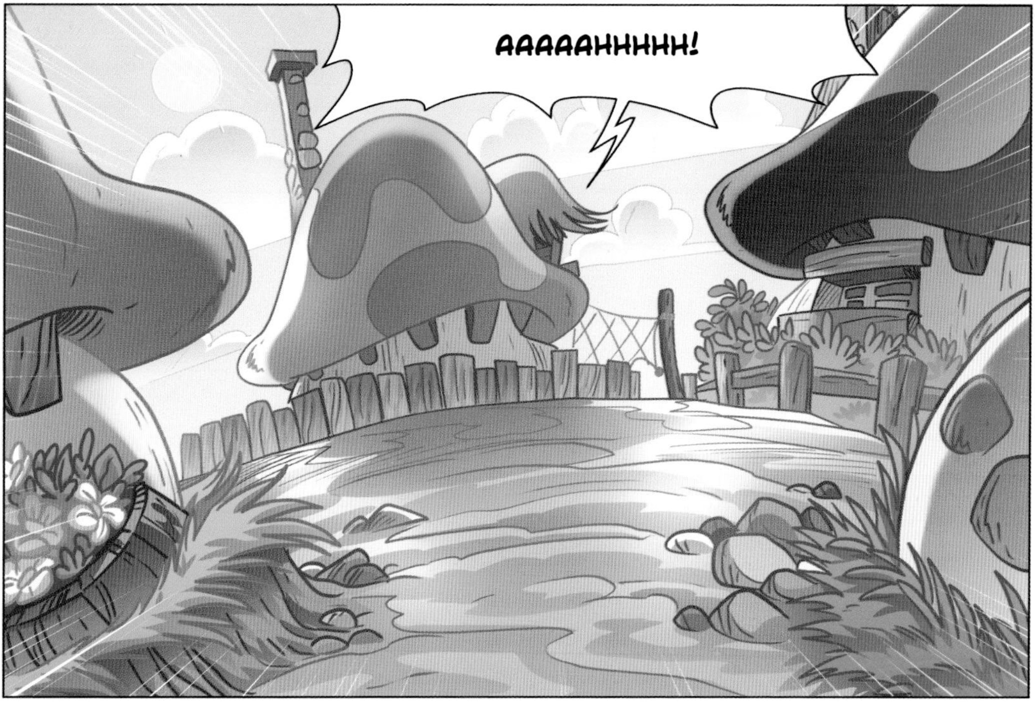
AAAAAHHHHH!

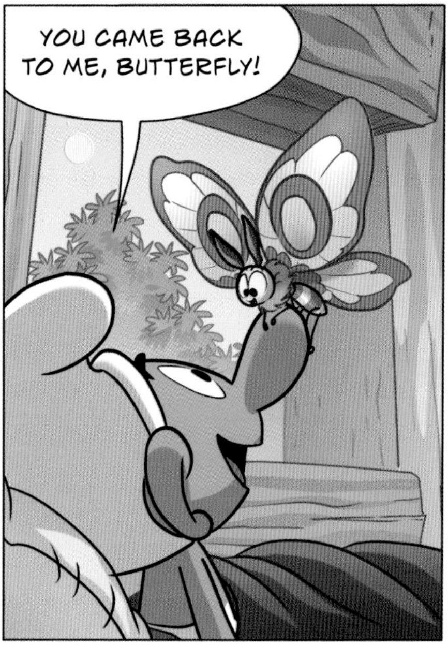
YOU CAME BACK
TO ME, BUTTERFLY!

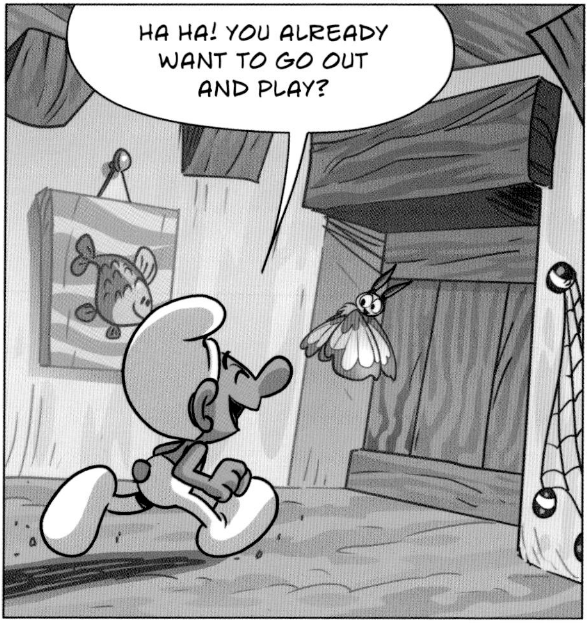
HA HA! YOU ALREADY
WANT TO GO OUT
AND PLAY?

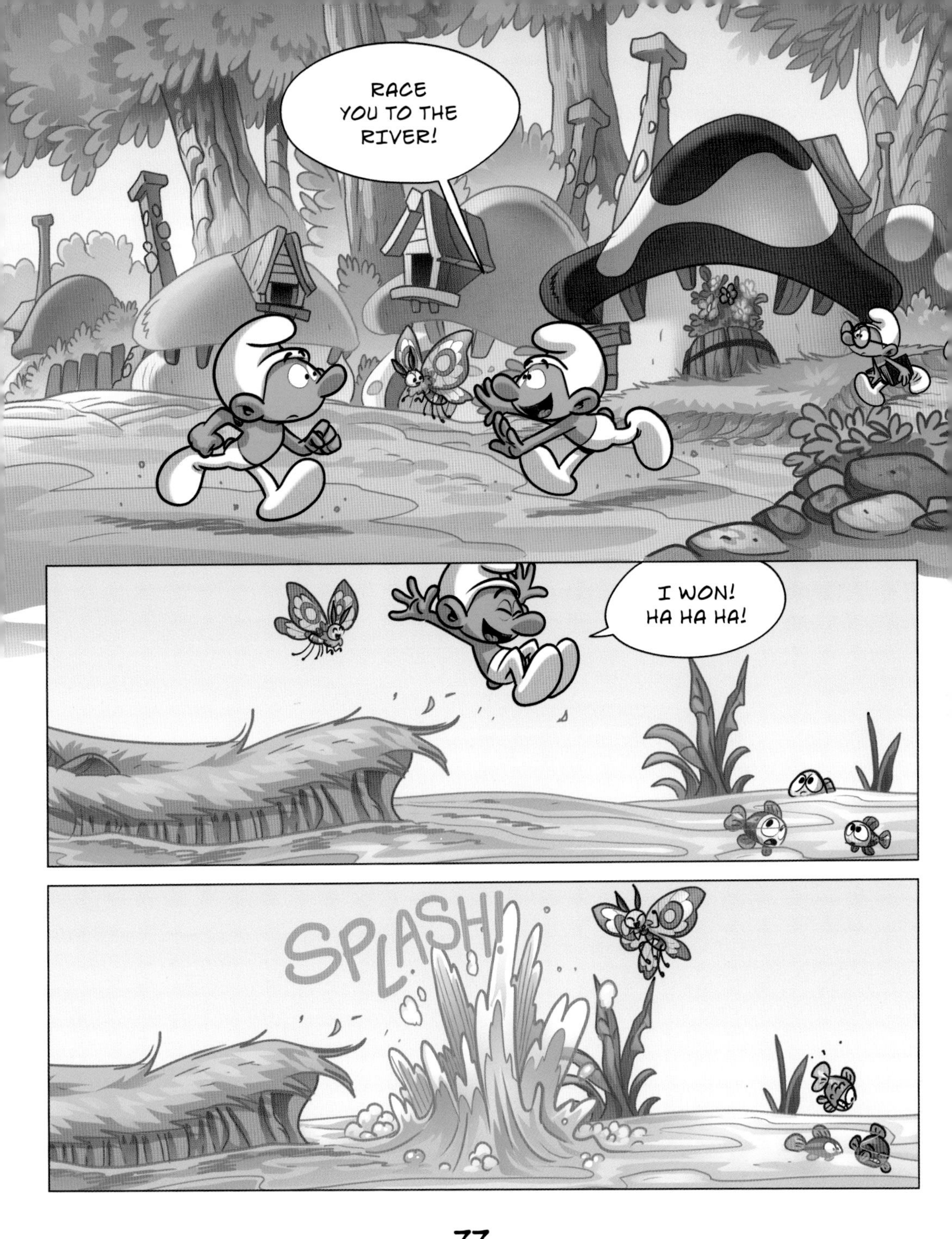
RACE YOU TO THE RIVER!
I WON! HA HA HA!
SPLASH!

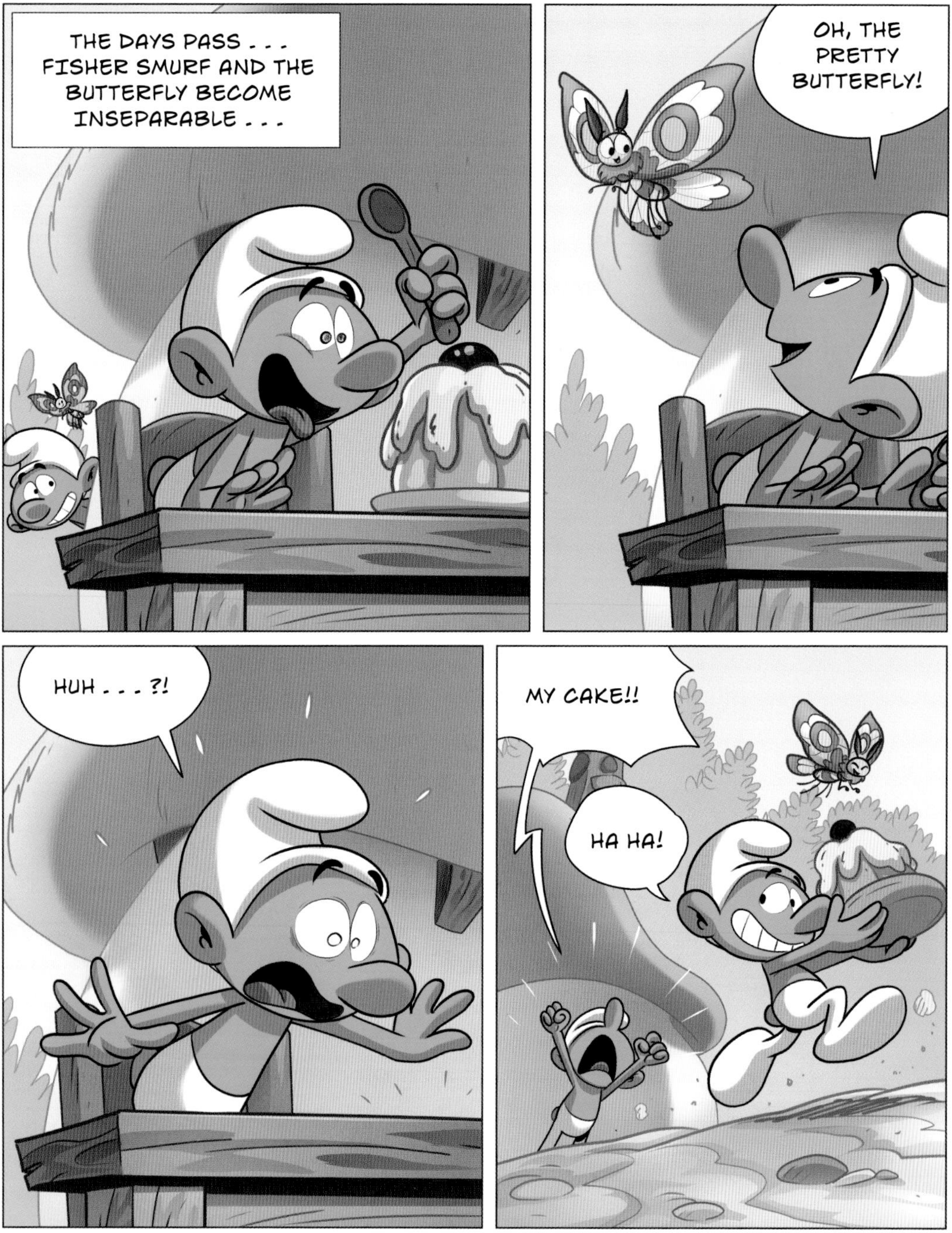
THE DAYS PASS . . . FISHER SMURF AND THE BUTTERFLY BECOME INSEPARABLE . . .
OH, THE PRETTY BUTTERFLY!
HUH . . . ?!
MY CAKE!!
HA HA!

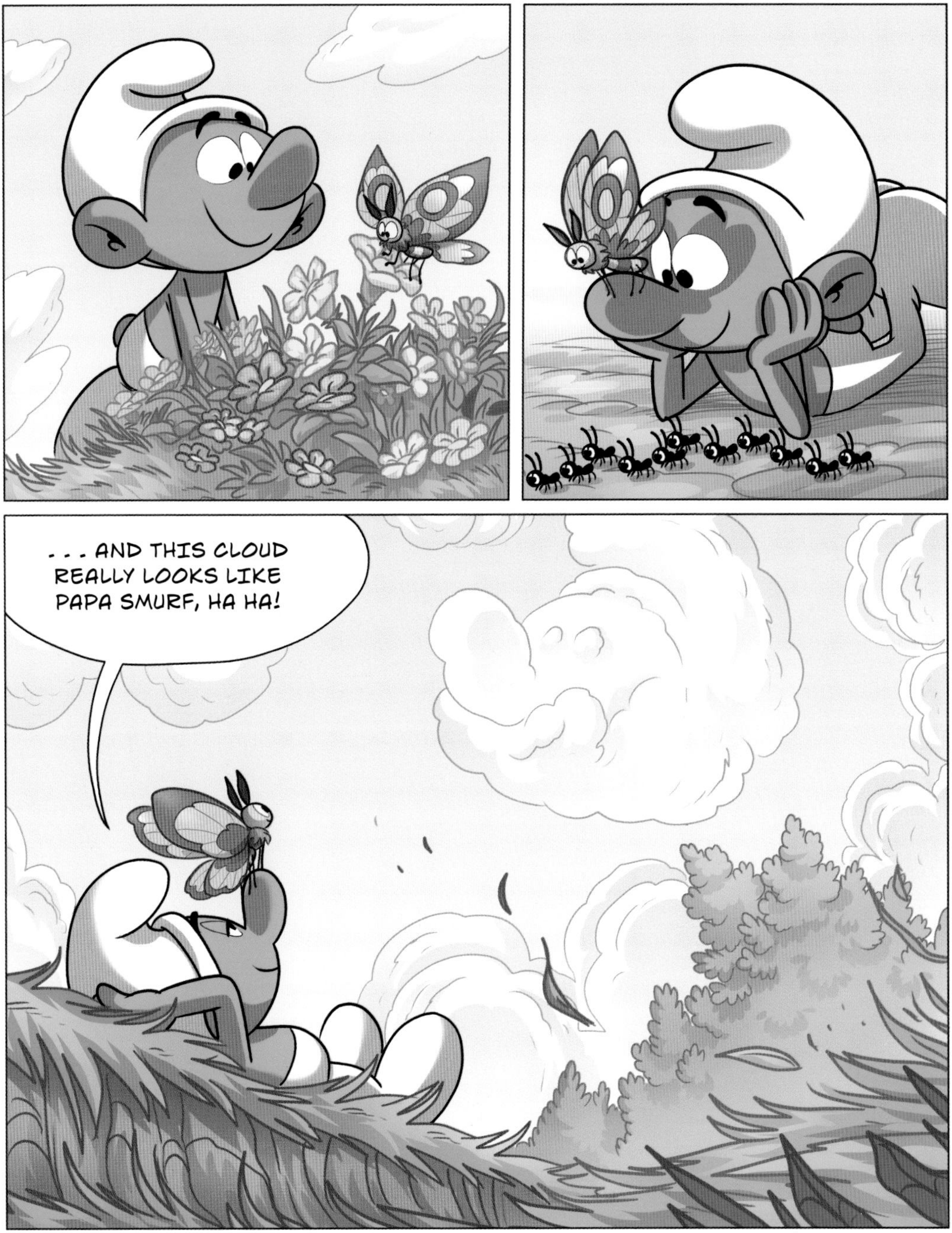
. . . AND THIS CLOUD REALLY LOOKS LIKE PAPA SMURF, HA HA!

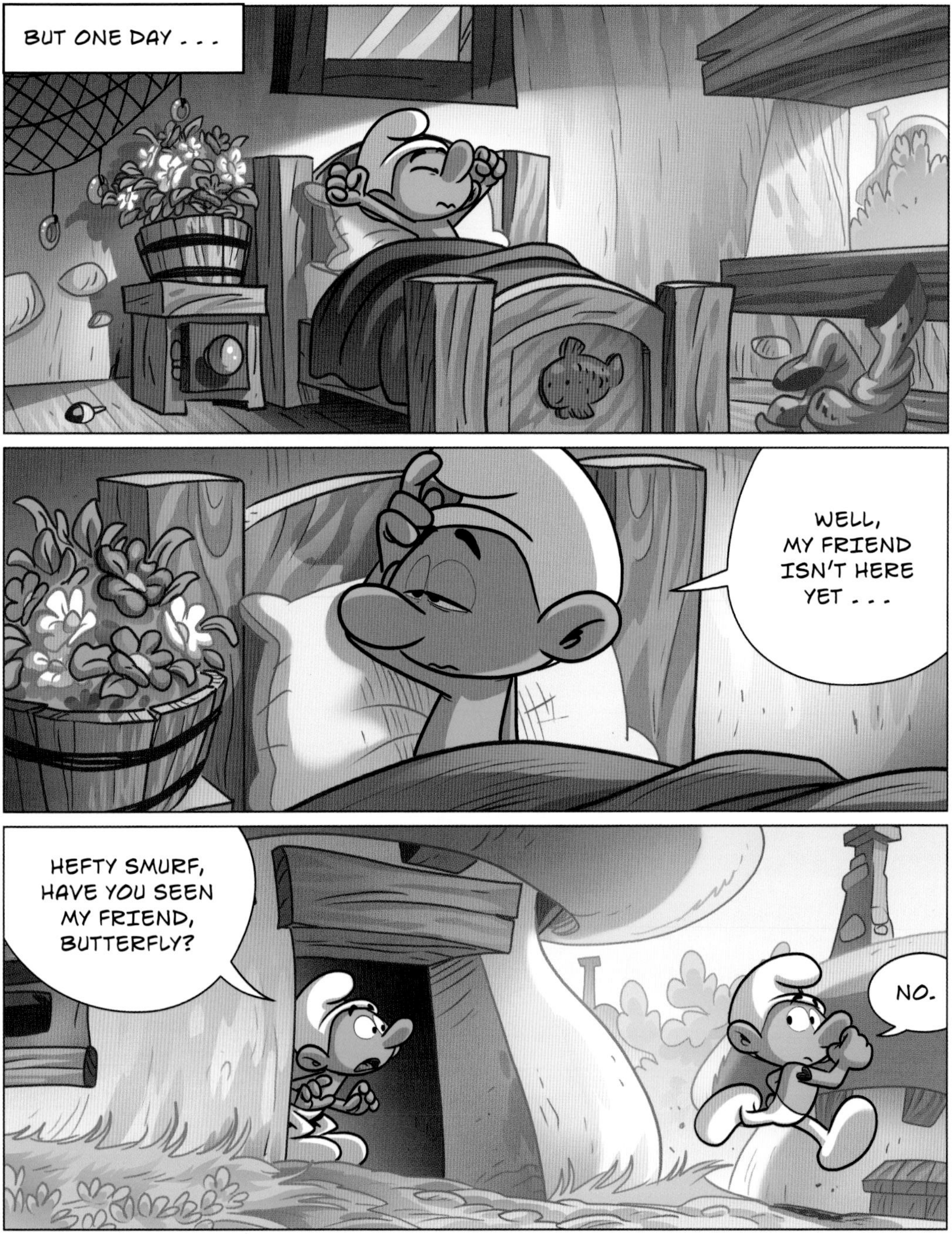
BUT ONE DAY . . .
WELL, MY FRIEND ISN'T HERE YET . . .
HEFTY SMURF, HAVE YOU SEEN MY FRIEND, BUTTERFLY?
NO.

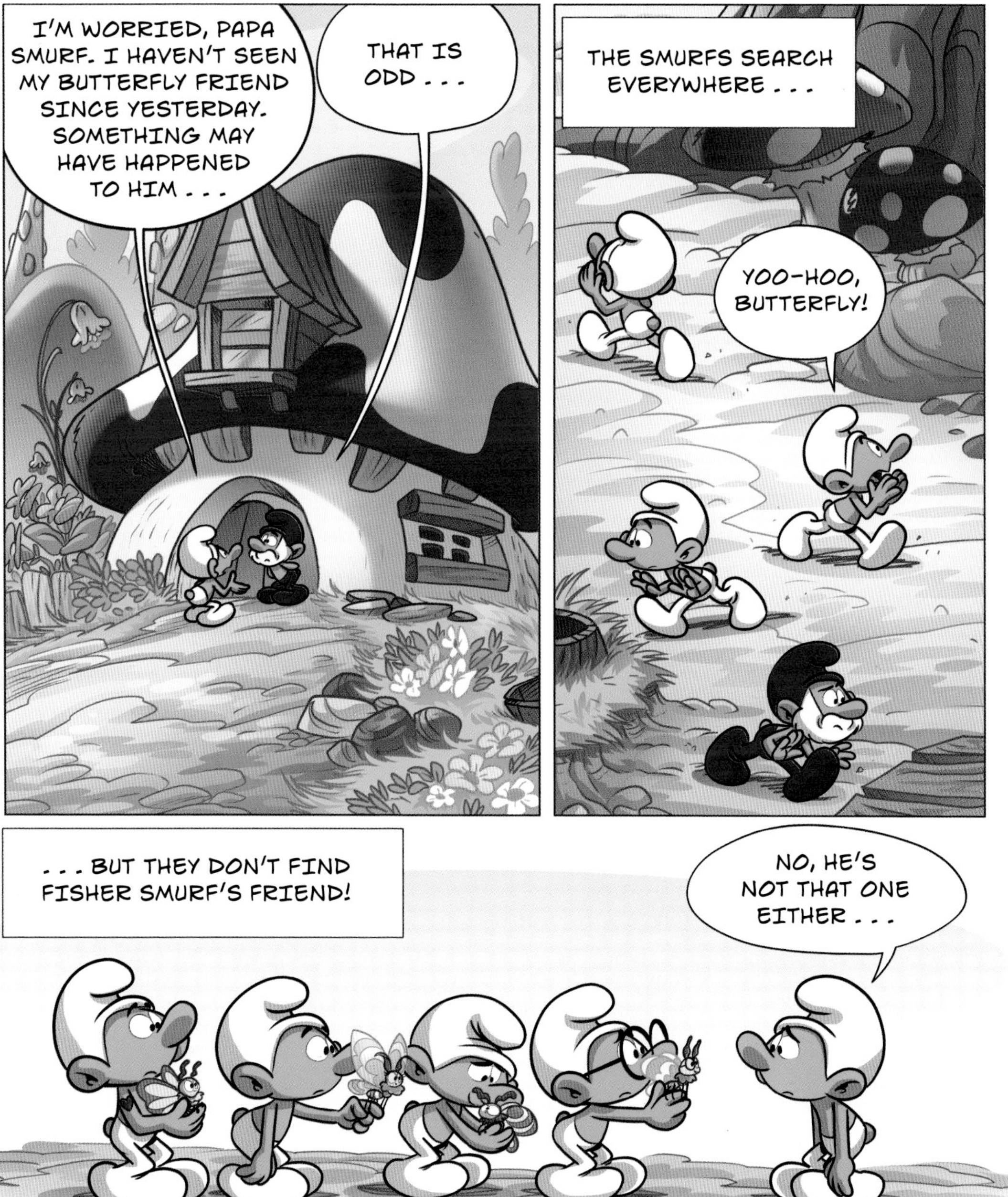
I'M WORRIED, PAPA SMURF. I HAVEN'T SEEN MY BUTTERFLY FRIEND SINCE YESTERDAY. SOMETHING MAY HAVE HAPPENED TO HIM . . .
THAT IS ODD . . .
THE SMURFS SEARCH EVERYWHERE . . .
YOO-HOO, BUTTERFLY!
. . . BUT THEY DON'T FIND FISHER SMURF'S FRIEND!
NO, HE'S NOT THAT ONE EITHER . . .

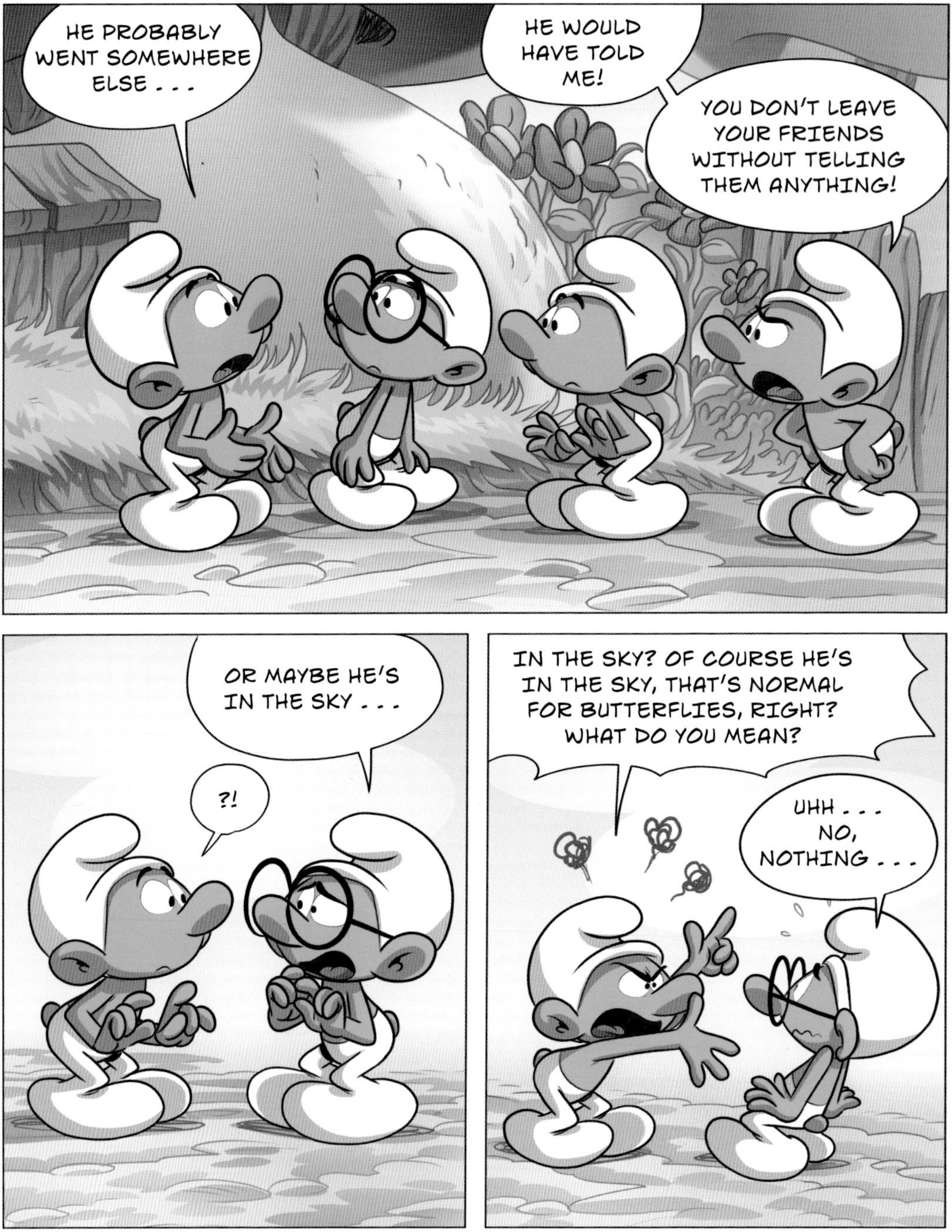
HE PROBABLY WENT SOMEWHERE ELSE . . .
HE WOULD HAVE TOLD ME!
YOU DON'T LEAVE YOUR FRIENDS WITHOUT TELLING THEM ANYTHING!
OR MAYBE HE'S IN THE SKY . . .
?!
IN THE SKY? OF COURSE HE'S IN THE SKY, THAT'S NORMAL FOR BUTTERFLIES, RIGHT? WHAT DO YOU MEAN?
UHH . . . NO, NOTHING . . .

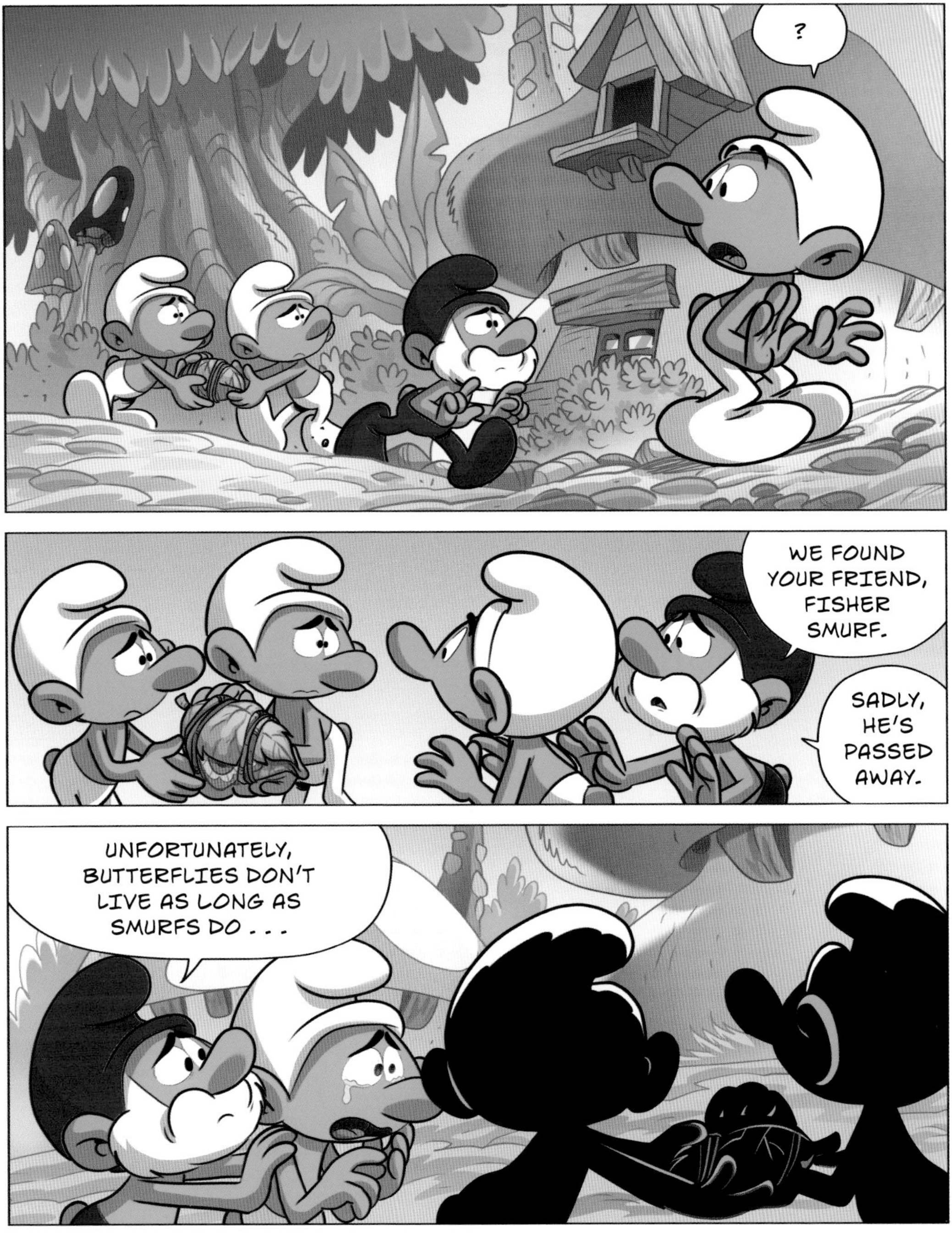
?
WE FOUND YOUR FRIEND, FISHER SMURF.
SADLY, HE'S PASSED AWAY.
UNFORTUNATELY, BUTTERFLIES DON'T LIVE AS LONG AS SMURFS DO . . .

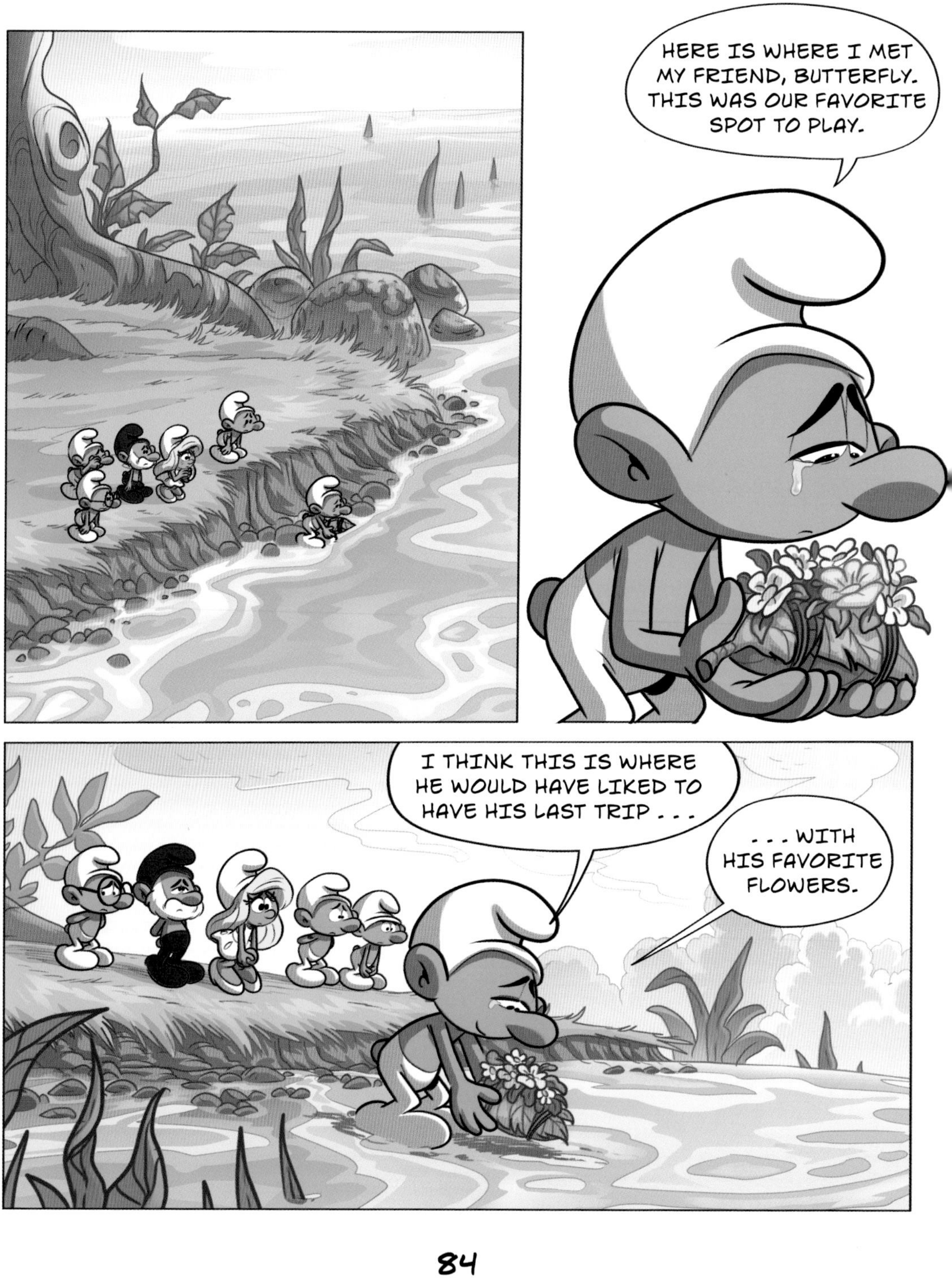
HERE IS WHERE I MET MY FRIEND, BUTTERFLY. THIS WAS OUR FAVORITE SPOT TO PLAY.
I THINK THIS IS WHERE HE WOULD HAVE LIKED TO HAVE HIS LAST TRIP . . .
. . . WITH HIS FAVORITE FLOWERS.

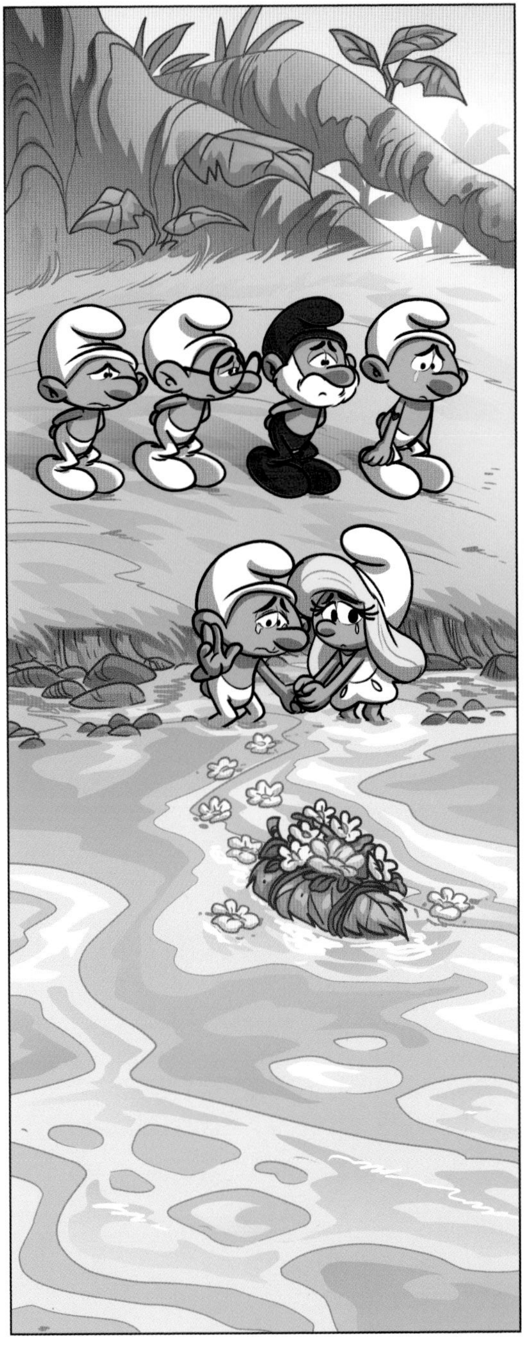

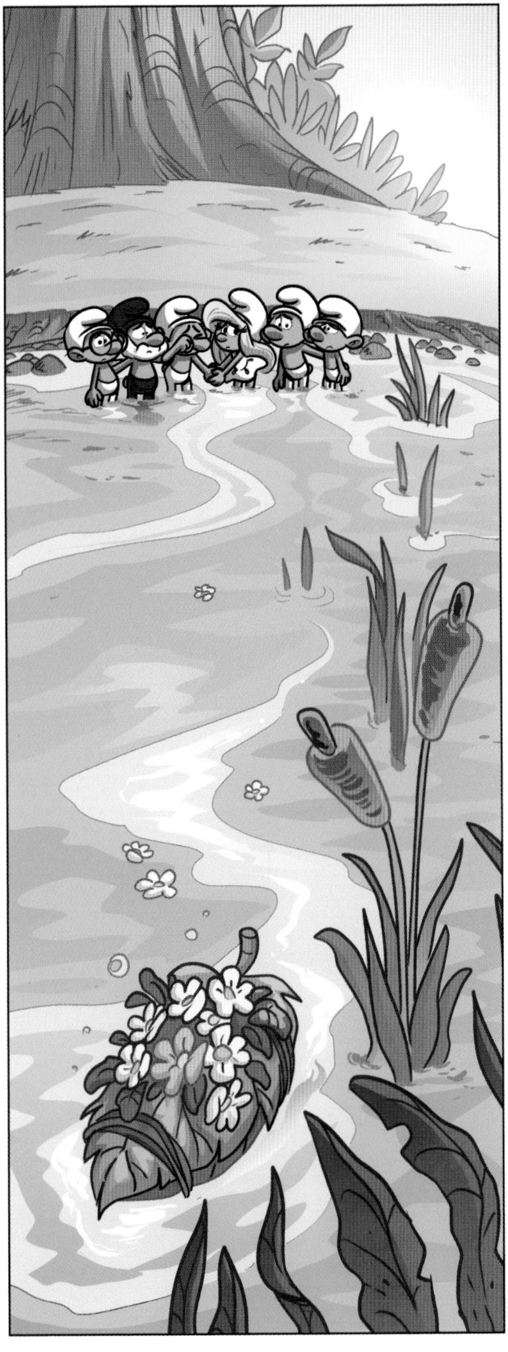

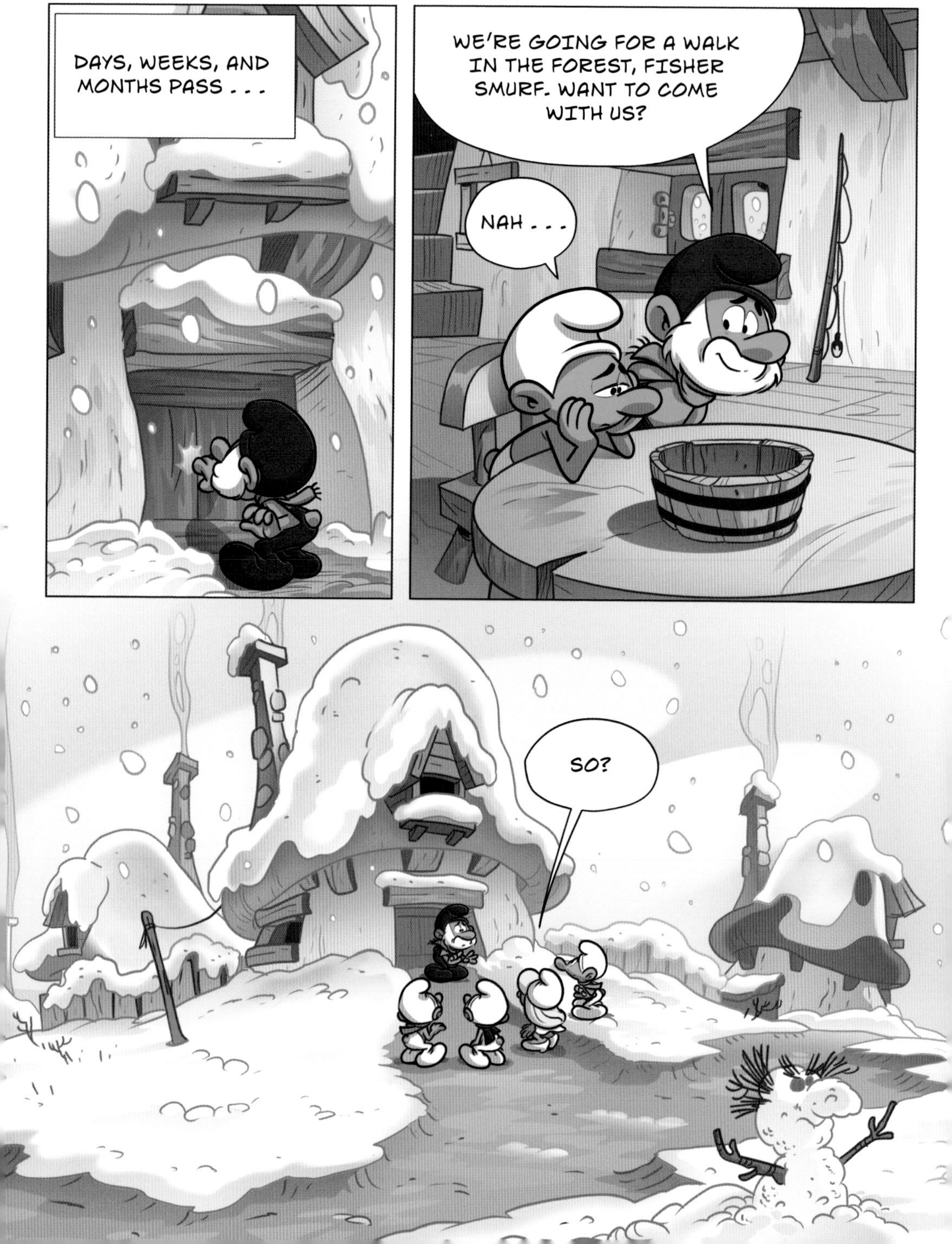
DAYS, WEEKS, AND MONTHS PASS . . .
WE'RE GOING FOR A WALK IN THE FOREST, FISHER SMURF. WANT TO COME WITH US?
NAH . . .
SO?

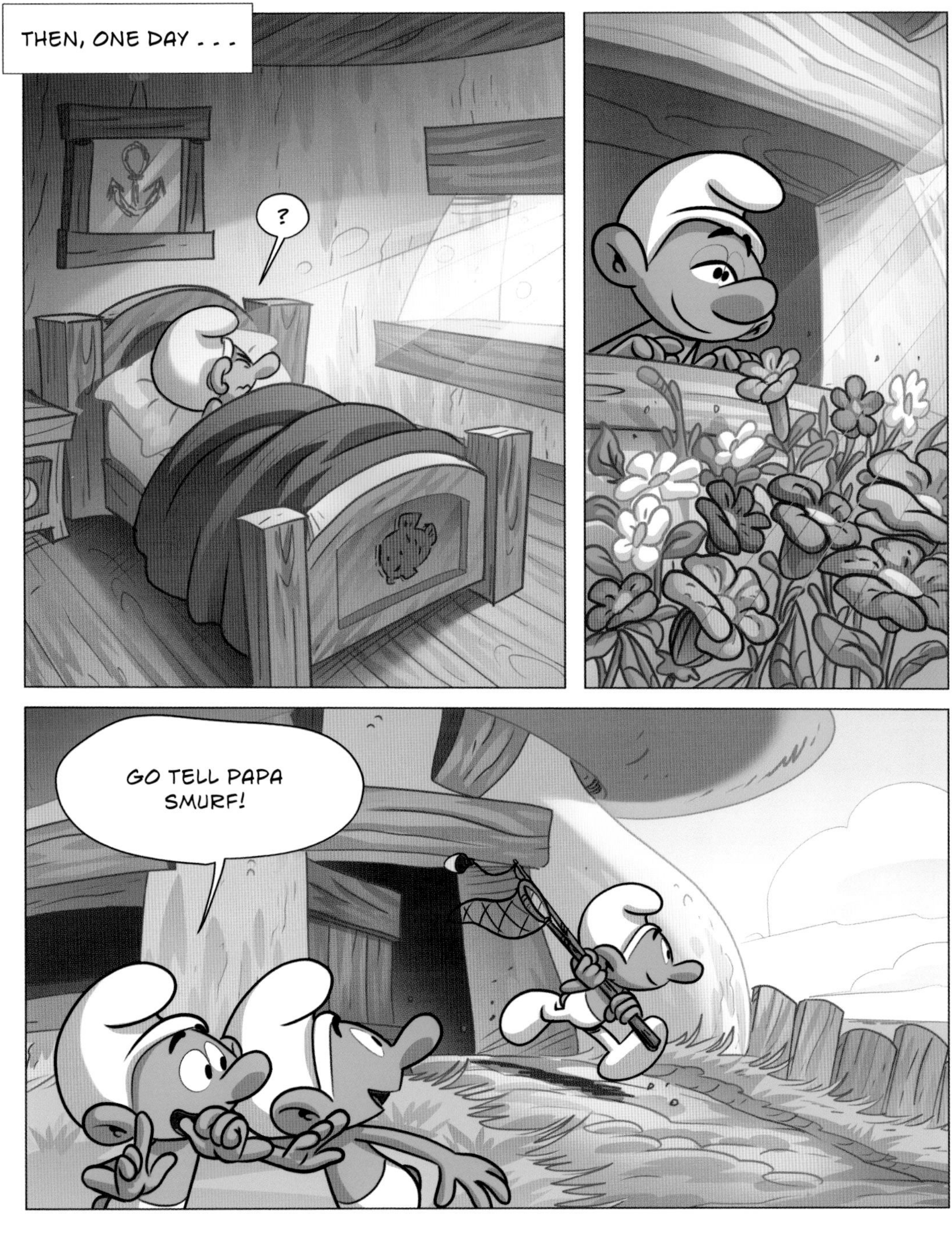
THEN, ONE DAY . . .
?
GO TELL PAPA SMURF!

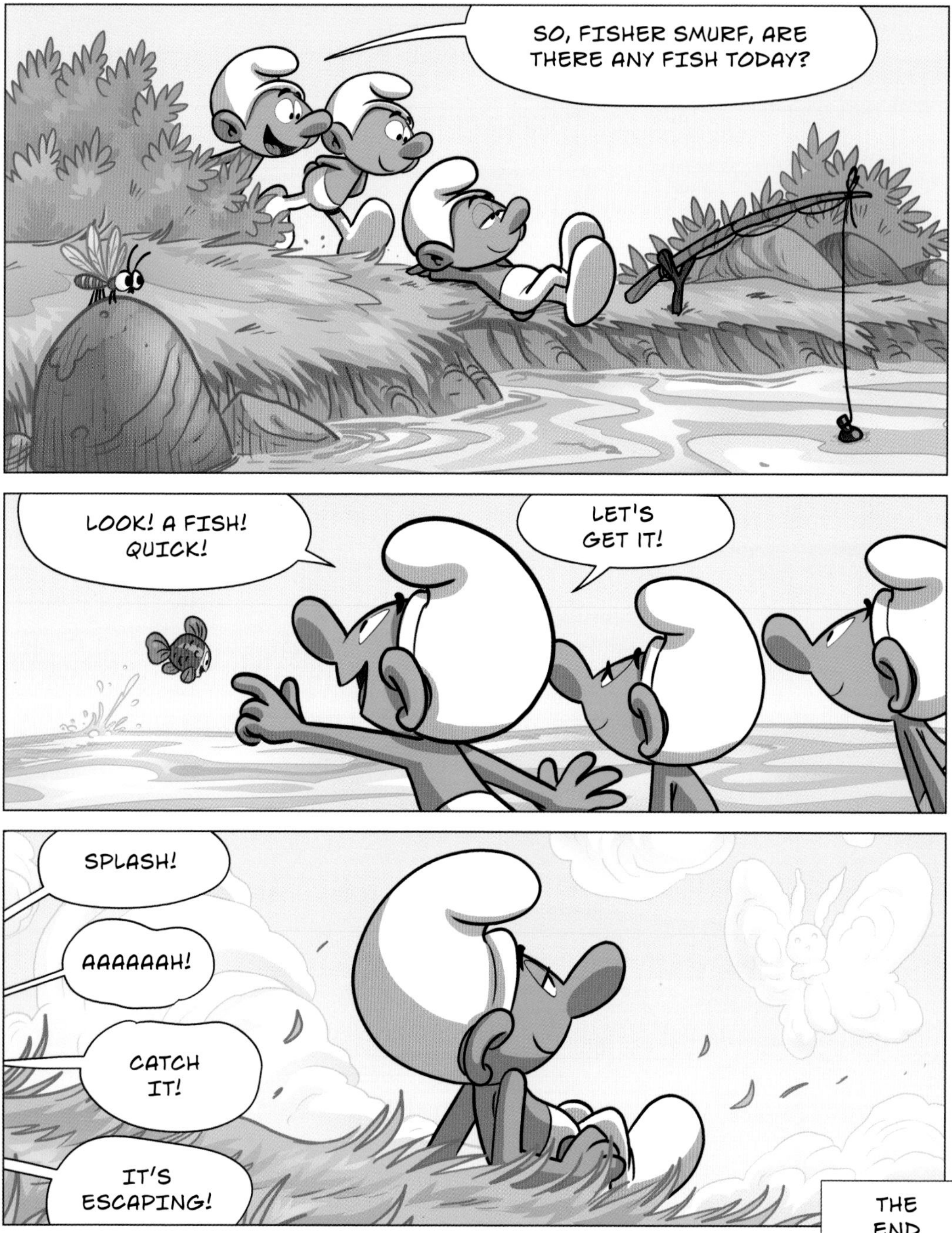
SO, FISHER SMURF, ARE THERE ANY FISH TODAY?
LOOK! A FISH! QUICK!
LET'S GET IT!
SPLASH!
AAAAAAH!
CATCH IT!
IT'S ESCAPING!

THE END

AND YOU, DO YOU EVER FEEL IMPATIENT?

A guide written by Diane Drory

psychologist, psychoanalyst, and specialist in early childhood disorders

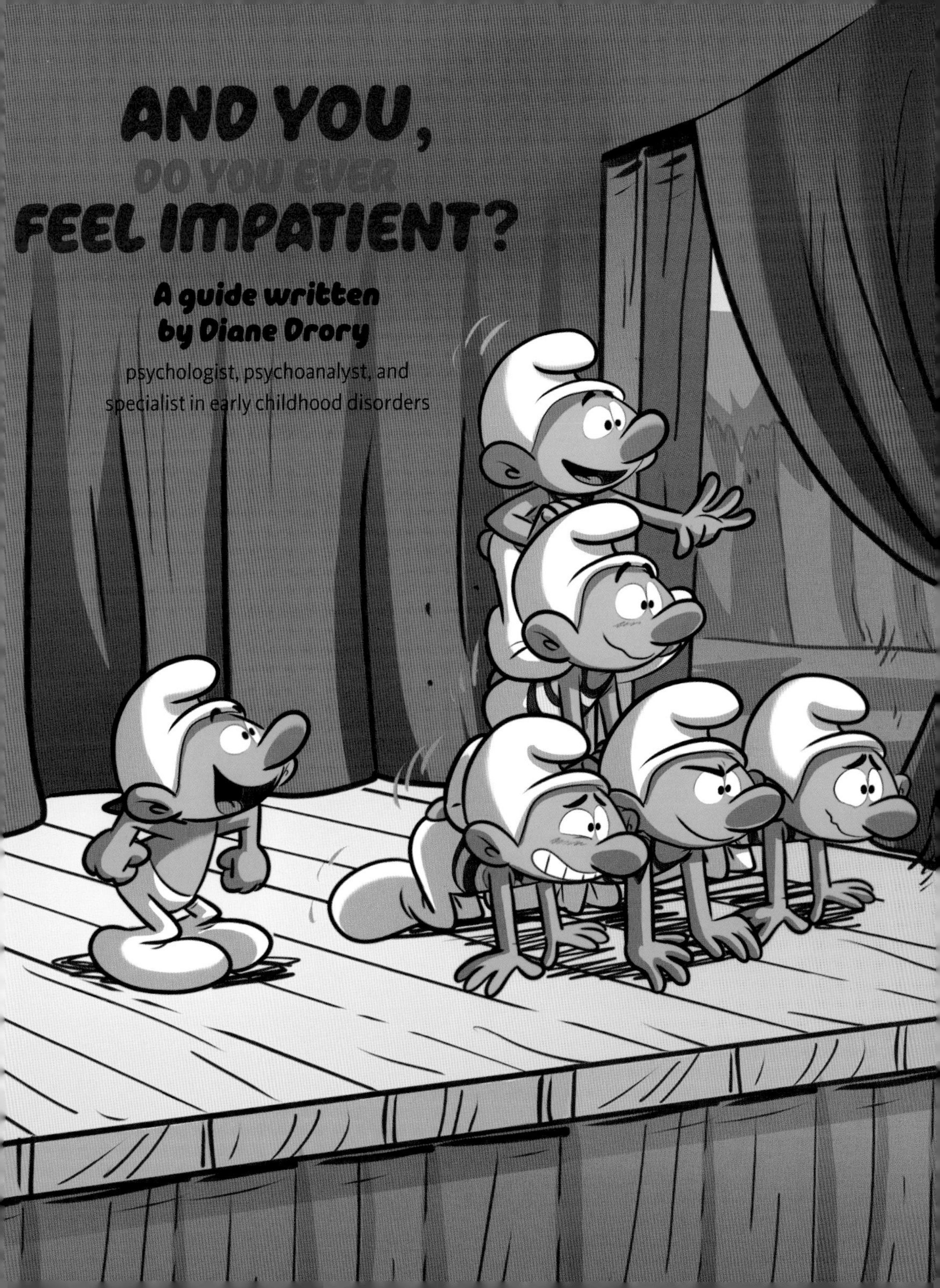

DON'T BE SO IMPATIENT!

You've no doubt heard this phrase before: Rome wasn't built in a day.

To be **impatient** is to not understand why you don't get what you want at the moment you want it.

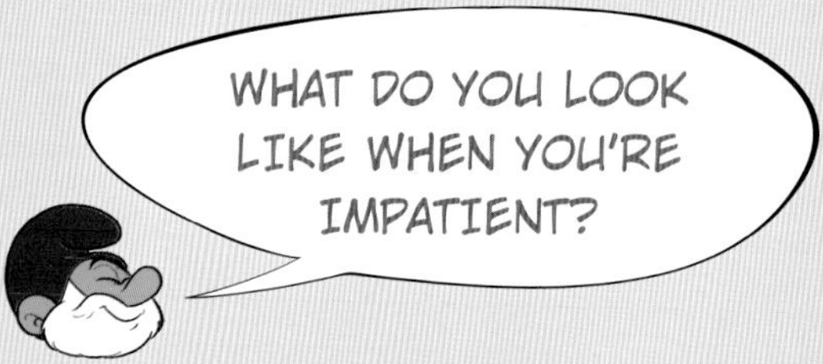
WHAT DO YOU LOOK LIKE WHEN YOU'RE IMPATIENT?

GROWING UP MEANS LEARNING PATIENCE

To grow up is to understand this complicated word: **patience**. Thanks to patience, we learn that we can't always get what we want right away. The ability to wait is a very useful skill!

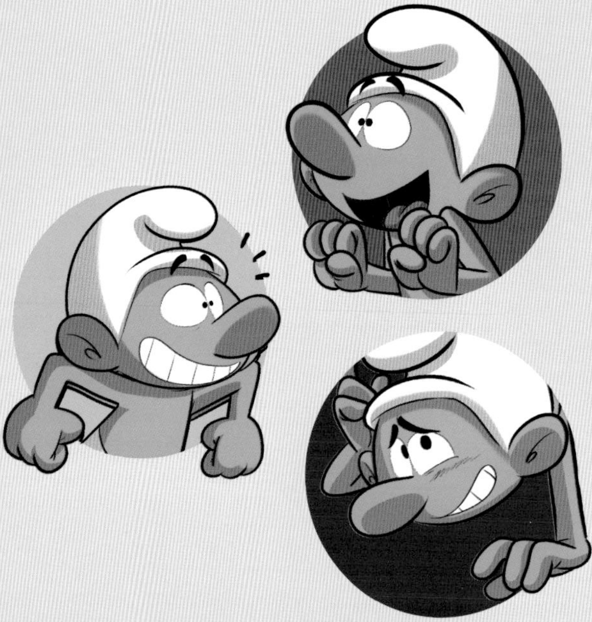

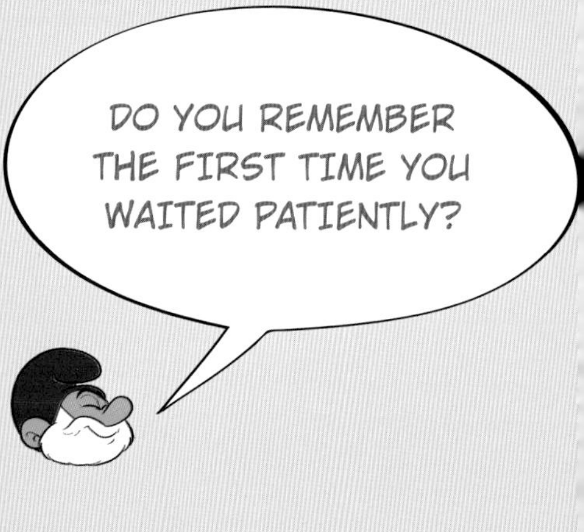
DO YOU REMEMBER THE FIRST TIME YOU WAITED PATIENTLY?

MOST TIMES YOU HAVE TO WAIT

Waiting for your turn in a game, waiting for a meal to be ready, waiting for the bus, waiting to play with someone, waiting in line to pee . . . you wait a lot!

WHEN WAS IT HARDEST FOR YOU TO WAIT?

WE MUST ACCEPT THAT WAITING IS ALL ABOUT TIME.

It's hard to wait, especially when, for a lot of things, we get them right away! For example, if you want to talk to someone you can simply call them on their cell phone. But once we learn that waiting takes time, we can begin to build the foundations of patience.

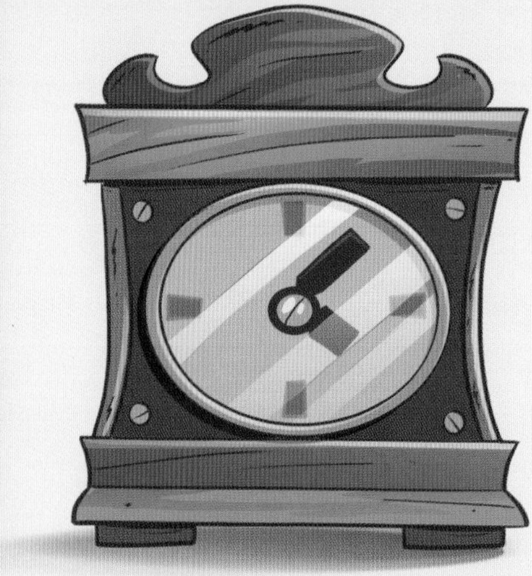

Once you understand it, patience gives us time to **think** and make the best of our talents.

Like you read, it took a lot of time and effort for Impatient Smurf to get better at walking the tightrope. And, in the end, what an exciting walk!

PATIENCE IS TIME'S BEST FRIEND

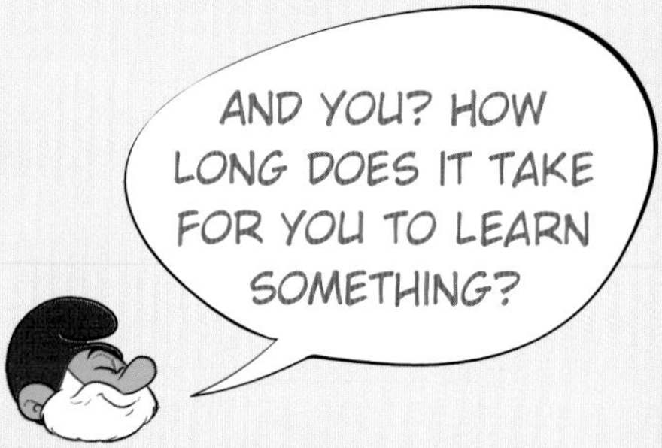
AND YOU? HOW LONG DOES IT TAKE FOR YOU TO LEARN SOMETHING?

Patience requires you to understand **time**, an invisible thing that differentiates between "hurry up" and "wait a minute."

Minutes, hours, and days were invented to help us **understand** the length of time one must wait to get what they want. To build patience, one **must have time**.

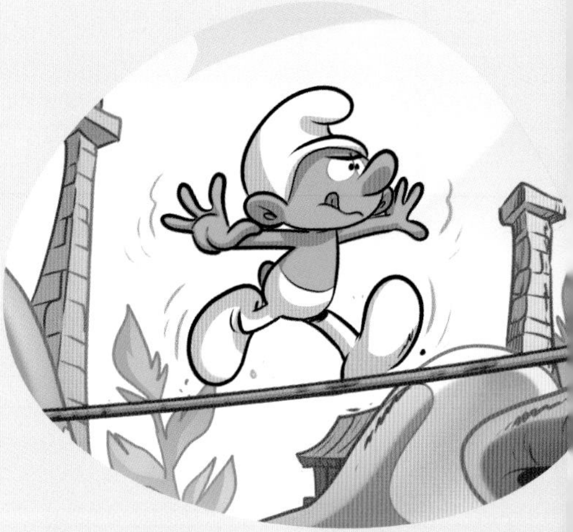

LEARNING PATIENCE TAKES COURAGE

It's very rare to learn how to do something right away. Eating properly, getting dressed alone, and riding a bicycle all take a lot of courage because you have to try, fail, try again, and fail again until you learn how to do it.

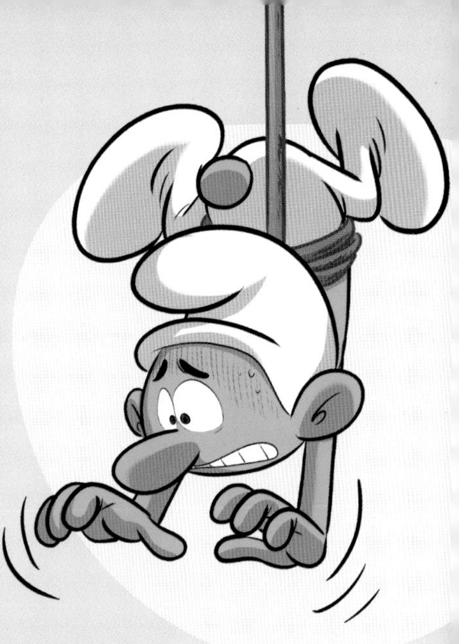

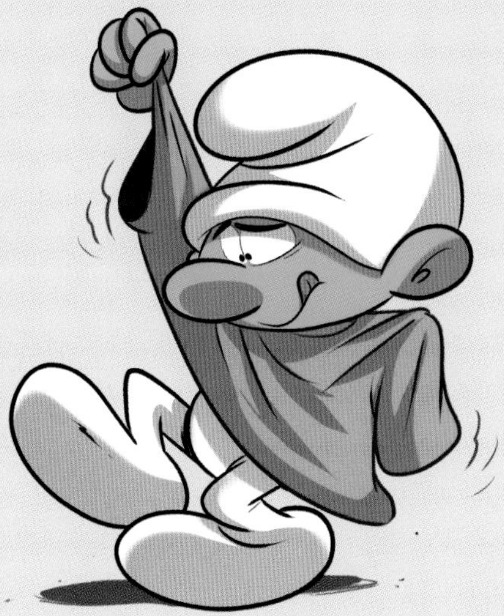

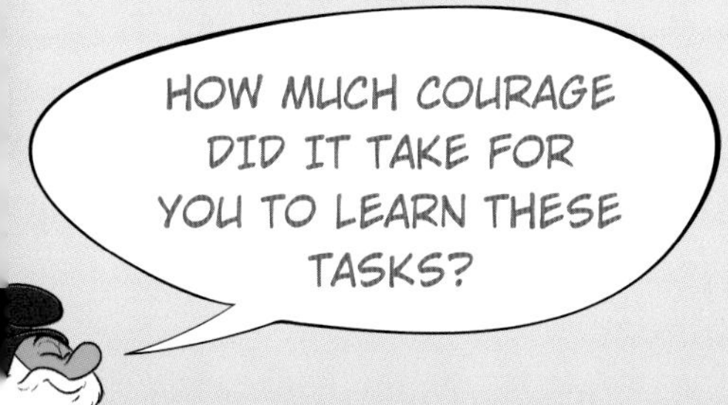
HOW MUCH COURAGE DID IT TAKE FOR YOU TO LEARN THESE TASKS?

PATIENCE REQUIRES PERSEVERANCE

Perseverance means accepting that you may have to repeat steps. Growing up is like a puzzle: You try to place a piece and it may not work, so you try another. It doesn't fit, so you start all over again. Little by little, you learn, and the image begins to take shape.

At first, Impatient Smurf thought it was impossible to walk the tightrope. But with courage and perseverance, he succeeded and learned a task even Hefty Smurf couldn't do!

WHEN THE WAIT BECOMES TOO LONG

When we wait for too long, it can become unbearable. So we get angry, shout, or even cry a lot. This is when we lose patience.

> AND WHEN YOU LOSE PATIENCE, WHAT DO YOU DO?

So many stressful emotions can tire you and those around you. "You ruined everything," say the acrobatic Smurfs.

It's hard to wait because it awakens a fear that we may never get what we want.

Impatient Smurf quickly gave up on the idea of training to climb the pyramid because he thought it was too complicated. In fact, it was his fear of not succeeding the first time that stopped him from practicing.

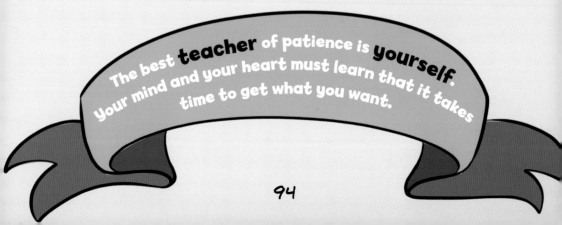

The best teacher of patience is yourself. Your mind and your heart must learn that it takes time to get what you want.

ADVICE FROM PAPA SMURF

Having patience is very helpful. Thanks to it, we worry less when we can't do a task right away.

Patience gives us the strength to succeed at complicated things.

To learn how to measure time and how long it will take to succeed at a task, ask your parents or guardians to show you by using a calendar or a clock.

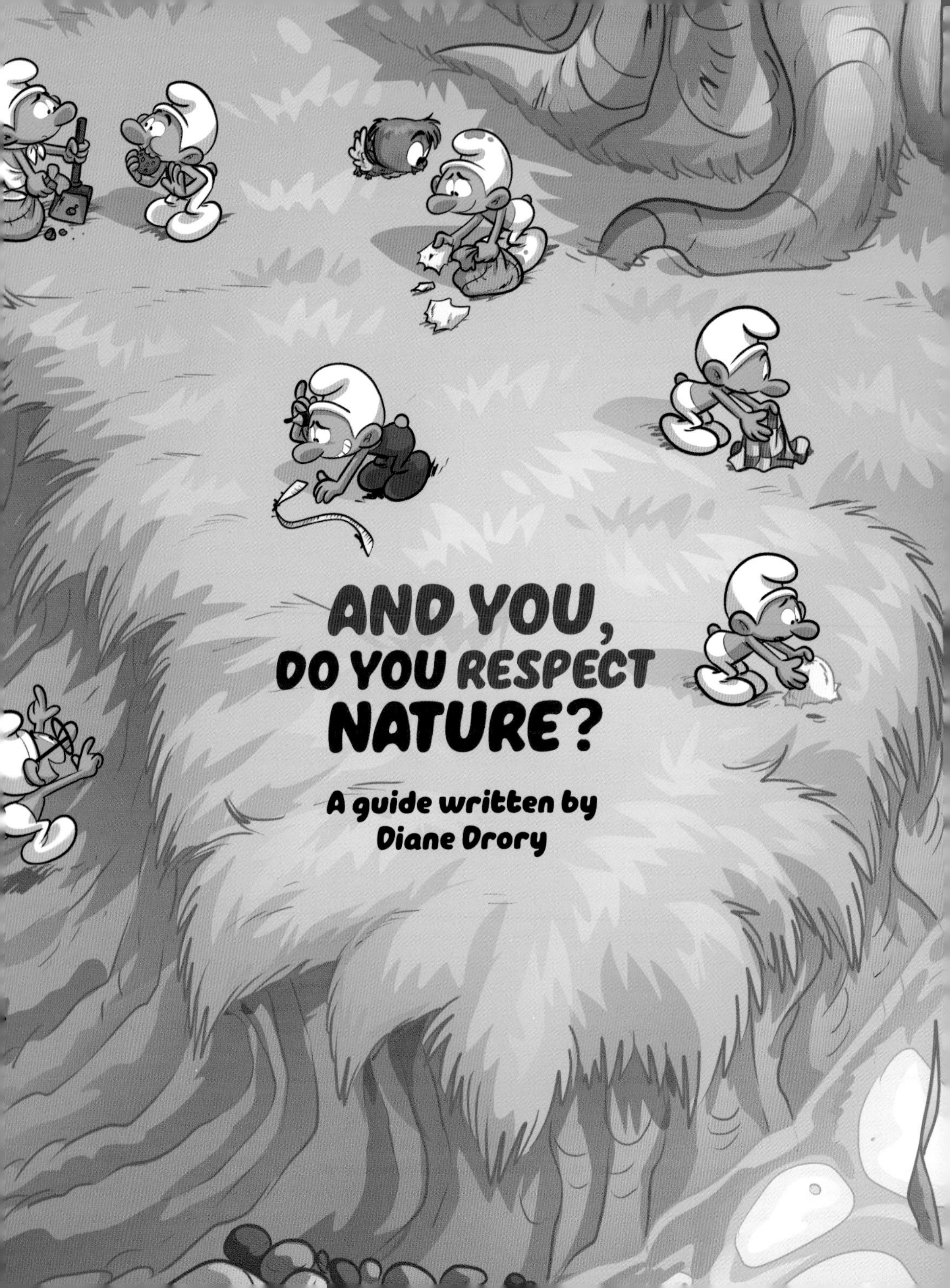

AND YOU, DO YOU RESPECT NATURE?

A guide written by
Diane Drory

WHY SHOULD WE RESPECT NATURE?

Nature is a precious home to humans, plants, and animals alike.

Every living thing, even the smallest plant, has its place in nature. Picking flowers to throw them away, breaking branches, and crushing ants for fun harm the world around you.

Respecting nature means not throwing waste and pollution anywhere. Because of the dangerous actions of those who aren't attentive to nature, many animals get sick or lose their homes.

WHAT IS WASTE?

Waste is what we decide to throw away. Your leftover food, a pizza box, candy wrappers, a broken toy . . . everything you put in the trash is waste.

Did you know that plastic bottles, packaging, and other types of waste are scattered in nature?

POLLUTING: A BAD HABIT?

Polluting is not a bad word, but it is a dirty thing to do! Trash that is not properly thrown away harms our planet.

We pollute the air by burning plastic or rubber, we pollute the ocean by pouring dirty water into it, and we pollute the earth by leaving waste on the ground.

HAVE YOU EVER SEEN WASTE ON THE GROUND?

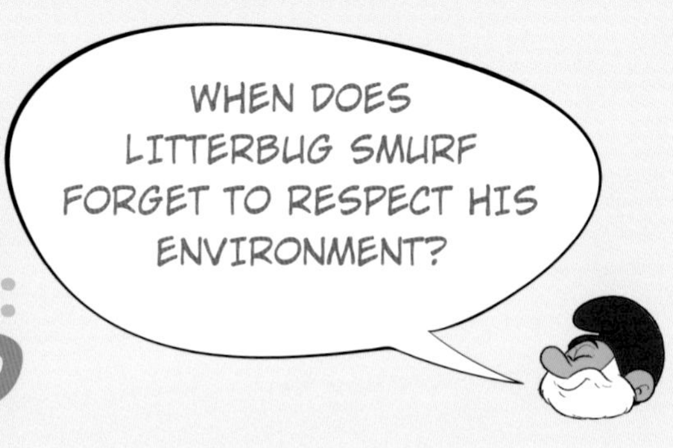
WHEN DOES LITTERBUG SMURF FORGET TO RESPECT HIS ENVIRONMENT?

ENVIRONMENT: A COMPLICATED WORD

The environment is like one big house. It surrounds everything around us: our homes, our cities, and our countries. And just like our house, we need to take care of it—otherwise, it will get dirty! We must protect our environment and keep it clean because the health of the planet depends on it.

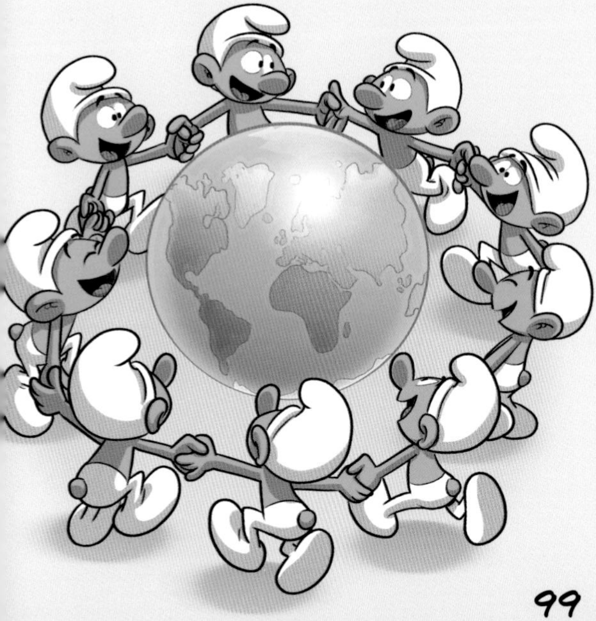

IF YOU WANT TO RESPECT YOUR ENVIRONMENT, BE ATTENTIVE:

Keeping the air clean allows us to breathe properly and without risk. Without clean air, we can get sick.

Don't keep the faucet on for too long. Wasting water is bad for the environment.

Keep the ground waste-free, as we use soil to grow food. The cleanliness of the earth depends on all living beings.

Without everyone's efforts to stop pollution, the earth will heat up too quickly, causing deserts to grow and some animals to disappear forever.

Together, we can reduce pollution!

ANOTHER DIFFICULT WORD: ECOLOGY

Ecology is the study of living things and how they can live comfortably in their environments. Our behavior as humans influences everything on earth. For example, we must protect forests. Without trees, there is less clean air and oxygen in the environment.

DO YOU HAVE ANY OTHER IDEAS ON WHAT YOU CAN DO TO REDUCE POLLUTION?

OTHER WAYS TO PROTECT PLANET EARTH:

Pick up trash and other waste. For example, you can clean up the little pieces of plastic you see on the beach. Or you can help by collecting the candy wrappers other kids drop at school and putting them into the proper garbage bin. All of this will prevent animals from getting hurt.

You can also help encourage recycling. Instead of throwing away your clothes that no longer fit or toys that you no longer like, you can give them to other children!

DO YOU HAVE ANY OTHER IDEAS TO HELP PROTECT THE EARTH?

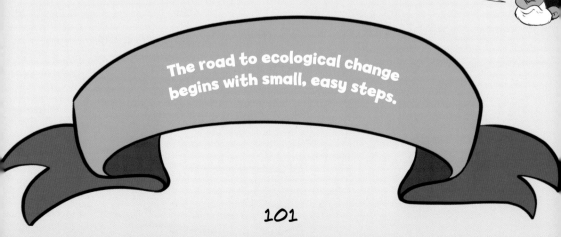

The road to ecological change begins with small, easy steps.

ADVICE FROM PAPA SMURF

Remember:
DON'T WASTE FOOD.

Don't hesitate to collect old toys from your friends, family, and neighbors. Toys that have already been used are just as good as new ones!

Collect seashells, listen to the birds sing, smell flowers . . . enjoy nature! You'll realize how important it is to protect it when you learn to enjoy it.

Talk about ecology and how to take care of the environment with your friends. because with all our efforts, we can save the environment.

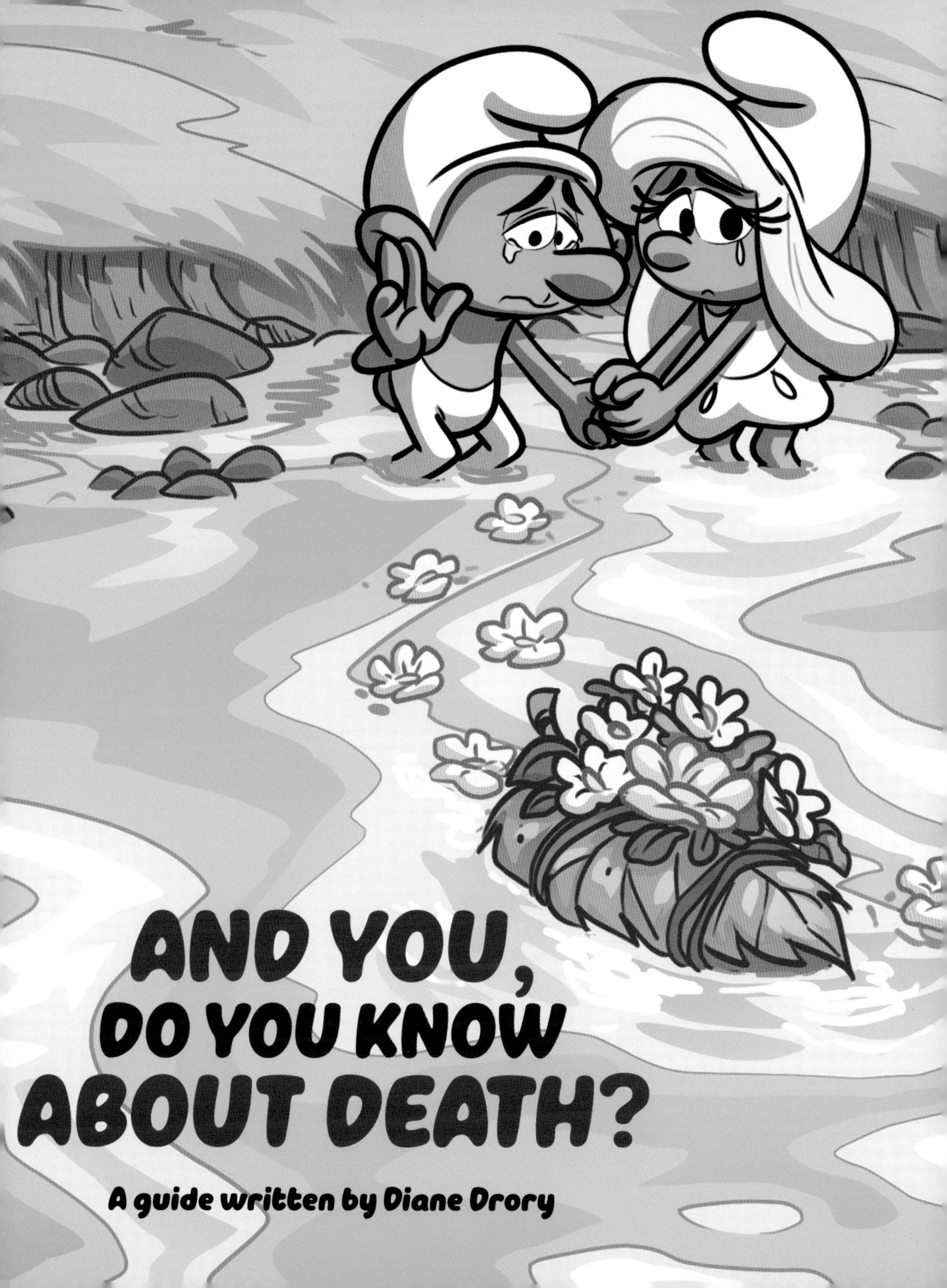

AND YOU, DO YOU KNOW ABOUT DEATH?

A guide written by Diane Drory

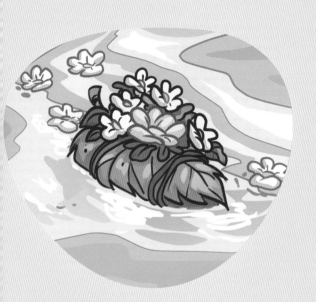

"THEY HAVE PASSED AWAY."

When you hear these words, you may notice grief and stress fill the mood. Some people will become sad or cry. Some people may say, "They're just sleeping." But this isn't entirely correct, as sleeping does not cause death.

Some may say, "They went on a trip." This also isn't entirely correct because when you go on a trip, you come back. Those who die don't come back. You may also hear, "They went away," but then you may ask, "Why won't they come back?"

WHAT DOES IT MEAN TO PASS AWAY?

To pass away means the body has finished living. It no longer moves, no longer breathes, no longer laughs. To pass away means to be at the end of our life. And we can't change that.

WHAT DO THE WORDS "PASS AWAY" REMIND YOU OF?

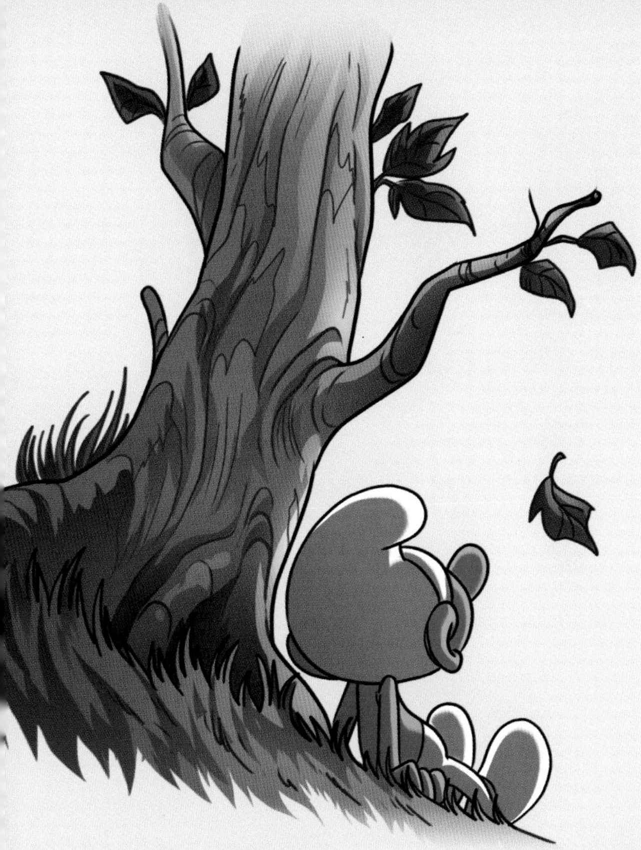

DOES EVERYTHING DIE?

Yes, everything that is alive dies one day. It's how nature works. A leaf on a tree is born. Then it grows up and has fun with the wind and the insects. The one day, it withers and . . . falls from the tree. It has died.

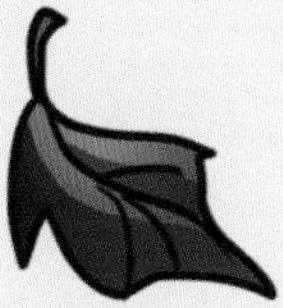

WHEN DOES DEATH END?

Death does not end. When someone dies, they stay this way forever. Their life has left the body and does not return. Even if it makes us very sad or angry.

For someone to be gone forever is very hard to believe and accept. Oftentimes, we want the person who passed away to come back to us.

DO WE KNOW WHEN WE WILL DIE?

No, we don't know. Normally, we die when we're very old. But sometimes, people die from sickness or a serious accident before they become old. This is not the normal way. But when it happens, we must accept it.

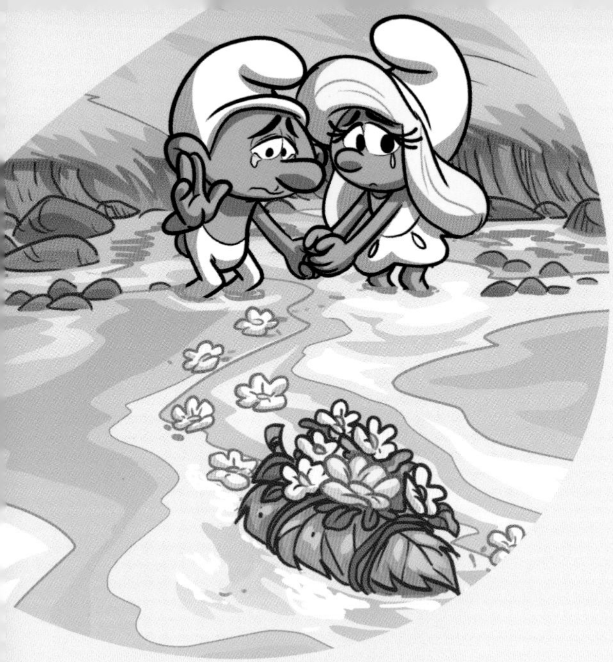

IS DEATH CONTAGIOUS?

No, death is not a sickness.

IS IT BAD TO CRY?

No, it's normal to be sad. It hurts to lose someone you love. It's scary, and your heart becomes very heavy. You may feel abandoned, knowing the person you love is no longer among us.

DOES IT HURT TO DIE?

No, when one is dead, they no longer hurt.

IF WE BECOME VERY ANGRY WITH SOMEONE, WILL THEY DIE?

No, being mad at someone won't harm them. If someone close to you passes away, it is never your fault!

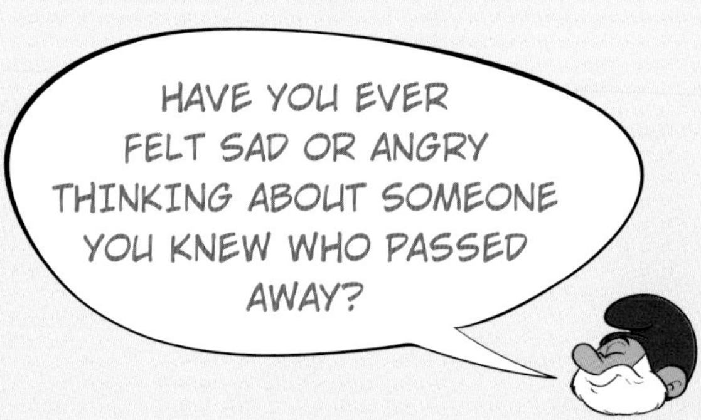
HAVE YOU EVER FELT SAD OR ANGRY THINKING ABOUT SOMEONE YOU KNEW WHO PASSED AWAY?

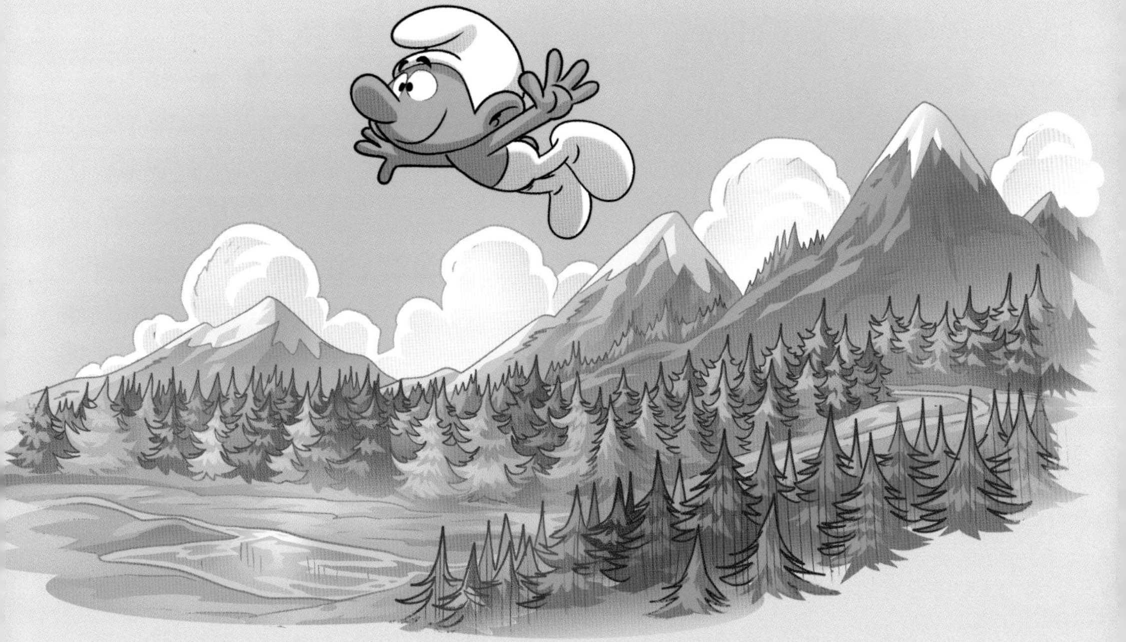

WHERE DO WE GO AFTER DEATH?

That is the biggest mystery! Many people have asked, but no one has answered it yet! Everyone has their own ideas.

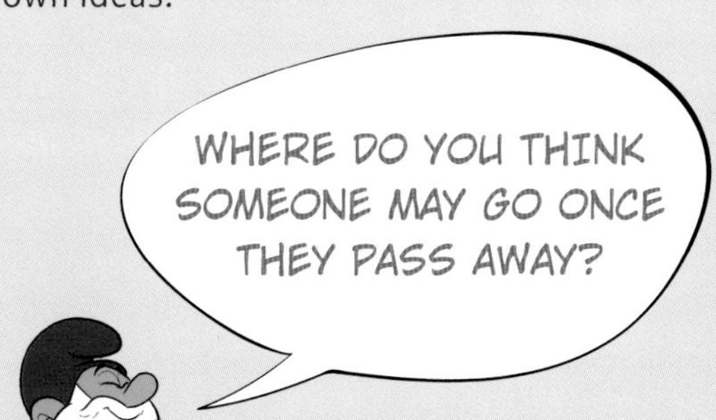
WHERE DO YOU THINK SOMEONE MAY GO ONCE THEY PASS AWAY?

"He lives in the clouds."
"She went to a faraway land."
"They're a star now."
Believing that those who have passed away have become stars is a very nice idea, because you can look at the night sky and feel closer to them. Others believe nothing happens at all, but this is hard to believe.

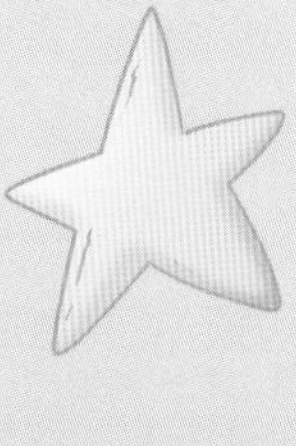

WHEN SOMEONE PASSES AWAY, DO WE FORGET ABOUT THEM?

No! Even if the person who has passed away can no longer remember us, we can remember them. Like in the story, Fisher Smurf will be able to think about his butterfly friend and keep him alive in his heart for the rest of his life.

YOU CAN MAKE SOMEONE'S ABSENCE HURT LESS

By talking about your sadness with others, and by talking about the good memories you shared, the loved one you've lost will continue to exist.

You can also use your thoughts: By thinking of them or looking at photos, you can keep your loved one alive in your heart. You can think of them anytime, when you're awake or sleeping, when it's day or night.

If you've lost someone you loved very much, as long as you talk about and remember them, they will continue to live in your heart. Love never dies.

ADVICE FROM PAPA SMURF

Those who have passed away like to be remembered. If this makes you sad, don't be afraid to cry. Tears help wash away the heaviness in your heart.

Light a candle in memory of your loved one, as it lights up your heart as well.

Even though death separates you from your loved one, the good memories and your love for them keeps you together forever.

It's better to be sad with family and friends than to be sad by yourself.